CW00669700

Praise for M. John Harrison

'The exactness, acute self-consciousness and vigilant self-restraint of Harrison's writing give it piercing authenticity.'
– Ursula K. Le Guin, *The Guardian*

'Stylish, accomplished, evocative short stories, exemplary fictions of unease shot through with poetic insights and most beautifully written.' – Angela Carter

'There are perhaps three or four writers at work today whose new books I seek out with an avidity bordering on fanaticism. M. John Harrison is one of them. His sentences have the power to leave the world about you unsteadied; glowing and perforated in strange ways. He combines sharp clarity of vision with deep compassion of heart; a merciful eagle. Once read, these stories ghost you for days and weeks afterwards.'
– Robert Macfarlane, author of *Landmarks*

'M. John Harrison's slippery, subversive stories mix the eerie and familiar into beguiling, alarming marvels. No one writes quite like him; no one I can think of writes such flawless sentences, or uses them to such disorientating effect.'
– Olivia Laing, author of *The Lonely City*

SETTLING THE WORLD

WORLD

Selected Stories
1970 – 2020

M. JOHN HARRISON

First published in Great Britain in 2020 by Comma Press.
www.commapress.co.uk

'The Causeway' in *New Worlds Quarterly 2* (1971). 'The Machine in Shaft Ten' in *New Worlds Quarterly 3* (as by 'Joyce Churchill', 1972). 'Settling the World' in *The New Improved Sun* (Harper & Row, 1975). 'Running Down' in *New Worlds Quarterly 8* (1975). 'The Incalling' in *The Savoy Book* (1978). 'A Young Man's Journey to Viriconium' in *Interzone* (1985). 'The Gift' in *Other Edens 2* (HarperCollins, 1988). 'I Did It' in *A Book of Two Halves* (Phoenix, 1996). 'Yummie' in *The Weight of Words* (Subterranean Press, 2017). 'Colonising the Future' in *Visions* (2020). 'Science & the Arts' in the *Times Literary Supplement* (2003). 'The Ice Monkey' in *New Terrors 2* (1980). 'The East' in *Interzone* (1996). 'Cicisbeo' was published in the *Independent on Sunday* (2003). 'Doe Lea' was published as a chap book (Nightjar Press, 2019). 'The Crisis' in *You Should Come With Me Now* (Comma Press, 2017). 'Landlocked' in *Seen from Here* (Unstable Object, 2020).

Lines cited, in 'A Young Man's Journey to Viriconium' from R.M Rilke, *The Notebook of Malte Laurids Brigge*, London, Chatto & Windus, 1930, p.49

A CIP catalogue record of this book is available from the British Library.

ISBN: 1912697289
ISBN-13: 978-1-91269-728-1

The publisher gratefully acknowledges assistance from Arts Council England.

Supported using public funding by

**ARTS COUNCIL
ENGLAND**

Printed and bound in England by Clays Ltd, Elcograf S.p.A

Contents

Foreword:
We All Love a Mysterious Country

> *There is something to be told about us for the telling of which we all wait... We listen for our own speaking; and we hear much that seems our speaking, yet makes us strange to ourselves.*
>
> Laura (Riding) Jackson, *The Telling*

IT'S CALLED *SETTLING THE WORLD,* but this being M. John Harrison there is nothing settling about it. In this selection of stories, drawn from a body of work produced over the span of his half a century in writing, there is no sign of a détente, no letting up, no sense of feeling at home in the world at last. Even now, after such an idea has become preposterous, we are still told that stories are necessary fictions, intended to console us with their visions of the world as knowable, the self as more-or-less coherent, with beginnings, middles and endings. If they're the kinds of stories that want the best for us, the argument goes, they might signal to us gently that none of this is actually possible, that these are, after all, only stories. But Harrison came up in a different tradition, as part of that remarkable 1960s generation of literary experimenters, including Ann Quin, B.S. Johnson, Christine Brooke-Rose, Brigid Brophy, J.G. Ballard, Brian Aldiss, Michael Moorcock and others, who turned fiction against itself. Drawing upon the wonkiest fringes of late modernism and the new critical theory emerging from the continent (frequently having already intuited its findings for themselves), they sought to unpick and unmoor the way that the structures of fiction mimic the stories we tell ourselves to try to make sense of the world. He's a fantasy writer, sure, but his work insists the generic distinction is a false one, that dreaming like this is what we all do. He is less interested in building new worlds than in those underlying forces that make us dream of other places and other ways of living. His preoccupation is that endless yearning for things to be other than how they are and what it does to people. As Harrison writes in 'A Young Man's Journey to Viriconium': '[o]n occasion we all want to go there so badly that we will invent a clue.'

Elsewhere, Harrison has remarked that all good stories are about what they do, and there are few writers who fulfil the injunction quite as well as he does. These are stories about people for whom the world has always seemed arbitrary, mysterious and lacking in givenness. They are susceptible, their desire so powerful it appears to be capable of creating (and destroying) worlds. His writing makes us susceptible, too. It seems to beckon us, to emanate from its codex form and set a peculiar cast over the world, to make us apt to fall into his fictions in the same way as his characters fall into their own. Harrison has so much to answer for. For as long as I have been reading his work, I have found myself struck, every now and again, by the uncanny feeling that sometimes we live in the M. John Harrison extended universe, and I'm not the only one. I don't know whether reading him made me like this, or his writing simply gave form to something that was in me already. There will be some minor story, way down in the furthest reaches of the news cycle, that is so outlandishly perplexing, such a peculiar admixture of the banal and the askew, that it seems like he must have had a hand in it. It might be an item about a man who tries to build a 70-foot mineshaft in his back garden, or about a woman who returns to her abandoned flat after some time to find a bag of potatoes she'd left under the sink has colonised her kitchen with creeping rootstalks.

Lately, this feeling has got more acute. As I was writing this introduction, a global pandemic began and there it was: that familiar-unfamiliar sense of our epistemes keeling over, of an endlessly protracted present that runs fast and slow and of a peril that both lies in wait nearby and in some far-off elsewhere. Returning to it some weeks later, at an uncertain ebb in the crisis, there's that recognition again: events simultaneously happening and not-happening, accompanied by the realisation that it will be a long time – if ever – before we can account for whatever this was and is and might mean. This is what Harrison has always been threatening us with: that we would not, after all, get away with something that went wrong long ago. 'There's many a slip 'twixt the cup and the lip' – he alludes to the old proverb twice in the earliest stories collected here. We celebrate writers like him for the accuracy of their visionary powers and yet you sense that, for Harrison, there is no satisfaction in being proved right. I think, perhaps, that none of this is about veracity, I think he's trying to show us something else or, more properly, do something else to us.

*

Harrison is always telling us the same story. It happens like this – although what 'it' might be, precisely, is hard to say. People look up one day and 'all at once' they 'can't make head or tail of anything'. Whether they've eked out their lives lodging in little rented rooms by the glow of one-bar heaters subsisting on tinned soup, or they've done pretty well for themselves, buying wisely in the up-and-coming boroughs of South

London and accumulating a decent set of cast iron saucepans, it's the same. Suddenly nothing makes sense, it's all out of joint, all the familiar meanings have leached away. The string that attaches them to the world has broken or else become a kind of noose. They have arrived at 'some crux only partially visible to the outsider' that renders their lives 'terribly muddled'. They find themselves staring into their own reflections muttering: 'Is this all? Is this all?'

Their suffering might seem like it is prompted by an ordinary, human-sized disaster: the onset of middle age, marital breakdown, bereavement, illness – always a pain of the heart, only sometimes the anatomical one. But the real crisis is more diffuse, slower-moving and far more difficult to locate. They seem to be grieving something. Their lives were not supposed to turn out like this, they were promised something different. Their grief appears to have an historical dimension, to be some private iteration of a broader, collective loss of old certainties and foundational truths: the end of all those twentieth-century dreams of coherence, meaning, continuity, possibility.

His characters belong to a generation taught to want and to dream and then quickly schooled about the foolhardiness of doing either. These are men, generally – of course they are. The women sometimes fare a little better, they can at least try to point to what it is that ails them and sometimes put a name to it, they can make themselves remote and perplexing, they can always keep a bag packed. The men, meanwhile, are filled with what Harrison calls an 'executive misery' that is so encompassing it seems to have its own agency. We mostly do not hear from them first-hand, more often the narrator is their interlocutor, a 'straight' man, drawn to them by good Samaritan fellow-feeling who appears at first to be just about keeping it together but ends up being taken in too. Their charge is 'an abscess of misery and desire so close... it must burst and drench' them.

Perhaps the archetypal Harrison character is the scholarship boy, primed for a life of smoothness and ease – some quiet and handsomely remunerated sinecure at the BBC, or in the higher echelons of the civil service. But the good life never arrived and they never got over it. They're still, like Jones in 'The Ice Monkey', trying to make themselves 'look as much as possible like the ghost of some young Kingsley Amis' because now 'all horizons are remembered ones' and the clothes of 1958 are the only good ones they have. There's a cold, hard class rage seething in these stories that consumes people. Exiled from their origins and yet shattered by what they perceive as their thwarted potential and terrified of their own provincialism, they lurch between self-disgust and competitive one-downmanship. But it's not as if upward mobility solves anything. Harrison furnishes his fictional worlds with a made-up culture all of their own, so it's notable that one of the few real artefacts referenced here is Luis Bunuel's film about a group of wealthy guests unable to leave a lavish dinner party, *The Exterminating Angel* (1962). Becoming bourgeois is just another trap. You can, like Maureen in 'The Ice Monkey', install a new kitchen suite, but the smell of shit will remain. As Harrison has put it so memorably elsewhere: 'Southend will follow you wherever you go'.

Overall, there's the abiding sense of a country, a culture, a way of living that has run itself into the ground, the loss not only of a world but the whole apparatus of understanding it. But, again, that doesn't quite account for it. Harrison is always gesturing at something moving underneath the water. It seems to have to do with language, which is always making the world recede behind it. But it's not that either. In fact, it's not a *loss* at all, it's the opposite: the return of whatever it is that all those dreams were supposed to shield you from. In these moments of sudden shaken aliveness, his characters are maddened by a hieroglyphic sense that everything is trying to tell them something. Everything seems loaded with a secret significance; everything seems apt to sing. It might be a snatch of conversation overheard on the bus. It might be a weird old book, pressed upon them by a stranger. Frequently it intimates itself through smell – a fugitive whiff of a foreign attar or the acrid sweat of a long-abandoned dancehall. Or it might be in the landscape itself, some suggestive arrangement of its contours, or a certain quality of sunlight cast upon it. It fixates them, it feels like someone is taking the piss, taunting them with the remote idea that everything might actually make sense after all.

These bespoke punctums appear to be in this world but not of it – to be the insinuations of a different order of existence entirely:'that glimpse… lobe[s] itself off immediately, becoming its own world'. And this is what obsesses them. They appoint themselves amateur detectives, trying to collect and decipher all those little glitches and losses and holes in the quotidian, convinced that in the way they array themselves can be found the real pattern of life. Thin mysteries open out onto great, hulking metaphysical quagmires. They've caught sight of something, something that's awful, beautiful, perilous, fertile, all at once, roused from their dreaming just long enough to make it out. They are, as Samuel Beckett writes, 'incapable of dealing with the mystery of a strange sky or a strange room, with any circumstance unforeseen in [their] curriculum'.[1] The real, the noumenal, the thing-in-itself, the sublime, the transcendental – whatever you want to call it, reckoning with it draws them into proximity with their own aliveness and they cannot tolerate it at all.

They've got it all wrong, though. Harrison shows us how they've mistaken knowing for *knowing*. By assuming that 'understanding ought to come by epiphany rather than by increments' their enquiry will always be limited. They lurch haphazardly towards quick apprehension and end up with 'instants of self-awareness too confused to be of any use' rather than waiting for those slower, but more profound, realisations with which they might be able to have a proper go at resolving their quandaries about how to live. That Harrison so often makes his characters literary critics, agents, writers or rare book dealers is no coincidence. He's interested in the life of the mind, about what happens when its obscure labours start to fester and mutate, when it goes rogue and grandiose and folds in on itself, fixated on knowing for the sake of the illusion of mastering the world. More than this, they mistake wonders for signs, interpreting these quicksilver moments in the terms of the world they already know. To borrow one of the images in 'A Young Man's Journey to Viriconium': they look out of the plane window at all of that 'immense white space' above the clouds and only recognise 'the vapour trail of another airliner on a parallel course'. As such, their private utopias can only disappoint them, the horizons of their imaginations stretching as far as a blandly pleasant package holiday. Confronted by something they cannot assimilate, something genuinely unknowable that suggests there might well be another way to live, they cannot help themselves but mindlessly smash it to pieces. Or else, they seem to miss it entirely, as if they would rather not know. They are 'brought up short by every smear of melted tar on the road' yet they ignore 'the only real event of the journey'. They do not 'dare examine the thing beneath the tarpaulin'.

It's not that Harrison doesn't want us to dream, it's that he wants us to have better ones. He can be as savage as Muriel Spark about our capacity for self-delusion, but as with her, underneath there's sympathy. By the end of this selection of stories, love is about the only fantasy left unscathed. In 'The Gift', Sophia looks at her lover and sees a face 'incapable of taking shelter... which admits desire but never alleviation'. Within this Harrison might well have found a model for the fantasies we live in and by, as well as the ones we read: not as redemption, or comfort, or resolution, or possession, or seduction, but as an open space for desires to circulate. Not a new world built to contain unaccountable feelings, but a place to try to sit among them. This, in the end, might be the only way that the actual can come to feel less inevitable, our only chance at grace, accidental and fleeting as it is. He seems to be telling us that there is another world, but it's our world and that we will never arrive there need not be a tragedy. Perhaps this is what he means by calling this collection *Settling the World*. I don't always know what he is doing – and mostly I don't really want to – but I think he's using fiction-writing's sleight of hand not to make us believe in a world that does not exist, but to invite us back into our own. For those of us who admit our 'ongoing struggle with the world of appearances'. For the suburban gnostics and domestic occultists and amateur phenomenologists and climbers (real ones and those of us who in other ways long to be more than we are) and apopheniacs and arch confabulators and most of all for those of us who simply dream of calling the office to tell them we will not be coming in that morning, or indeed any other morning. These stories are for us.

Jennifer Hodgson
London, 2020

Note

1. Samuel Beckett, *Proust*, (New York: Grove Press, 1957), p9.

Settling the World

WITH THE DISCOVERY OF God on the far side of the Moon, and the subsequent gigantic and hazardous towing operation that brought Him back to start His reign anew, there began on Earth, as one might assume, a period of far-reaching change. I need not detail, for instance, the numerous climatic and political refinements, the New Medicine or the global basic minimum wage; or those modifications of geography itself which have been of so much benefit. However, despite the immediate, the 'gross' progress, certain human institutions continued for a while to function as they always had. I think particularly of those edifices of a bureaucratic nature, whose very structure militates against devolution.

The Department to which I have given my services for so long was one of these: and so it was in a perfectly normal way that I received the call to visit my chief one Monday morning in the first April since the inception of the New Reign. The memo was issued, passed lethargically through the secretarial system and the typing pool, and reached me by way of my own secretary, Mrs Padgett, who has since retired, I believe to help her mother in a market garden in Surrey. After dealing in a leisurely way with the rest of my post – we were all

1

delightfully relaxed in those first days, settling our shoulders, as it were, into a larger size of coat – I took the lift up to the top of the building where by tradition the chief has his office, to find him in a ruminative mood.

'Look at that, Oxlade,' he invited, gesturing at the panoramic sweep of the city beneath. 'How much *fresher* you must all find it down there, now the hurry has gone. Eh? The air refined, the man refreshed!'

Indeed, as I stared down at the clean and quiet streets, where a brisk wind and bright sunshine filled one with a corresponding inner vitality, I had been thinking the precise same thing. In the parks, hundreds of daffodils were out, the benches were full of elderly citizens taking calm advantage of the new weather, and somewhere a great clock was striking ten in thoughtful, resonant tones. So different from the grey springs of previous years, with their heavy, slanting rains stripping the advertisements from their hoardings to flap dismally in the wind over the downcast heads of the hurrying crowd.

'Even you, sir, must find things changed,' I ventured. 'In the beginning –'

'Ah, Oxlade,' he interrupted, 'there is still so much to be done, and I have little opportunity to leave this wretched office. Events, however slowly, progress; and my time is not my own.' My chief is given to these moments of reserve; perhaps it is his nature – who can tell? – or a nature forced on him by the exigencies of his position. But he allowed it to pass genially enough and turned the talk first to my wife, Mary, and the children – he is always perfectly solicitous – and then to the cultivation of orchids, a hobby of mine. The new climate of Esher is perfect for this purpose and I was able to inform him, with all due modesty, of some truly astonishing results.

After a few minutes we came to the business of the Department. 'Oxlade,' said the chief, 'I would like you to look at some pictures that were brought to me by –' here, he mentioned the name of one of our most trustworthy agents – 'early this morning.'

He darkened the room and on one of the walls there appeared a rectangle of white light, shortly to be filled by a strange series of photographic slides. 'You will observe, Oxlade, that these are still-shots of God's Motorway.' It was, in fact, difficult to make out what they did show; I saw only certain apparently random blocks and slices of light and shadow, and, central to each frame, some blurred image which I could make no sense of; they were of a uniform graininess. 'The quality isn't good, of course: but I have no reason to believe they represent anything other than a sudden intense surge of activity along the whole length of the Motorway.' He paused reflectively and allowed the last picture to remain on the screen for a while (I thought for a moment that I could discern in it some mammoth organic shape) before replacing it with that passive, enduring oblong of white light.

'A perfect whiteness,' he murmured, and we stared at it for some minutes of comfortable silence. Then he said: 'I feel this may be as important as the affair of the atomic trawler, Oxlade.'

A complicated business, with a solution perhaps more metaphysical than actual, which I well-remembered, since it had led to my executive preferment.

'I want you to go down there. Check the information. Look around. Test the air, so to speak. The Motorway must always be of interest to us.'

God's Motorway: a lasting enigma. Certainly, none of us in the Department knew why God had caused His road to be constructed, why He should have need of a link between the lower reaches of the Thames Estuary and a place somewhere in what used to be called the 'Industrial' Midlands; none of the executives, that is – and if my chief knew, he was for some reason of policy or private amusement keeping the knowledge from us. Our curiosity was at that time intense, but necessarily veiled; so I was elated to have an opportunity to catch a glimpse of the great artery. It ran, I knew, a hundred and twenty-five miles inland from the front at Southend; it was by repute twenty lanes and a mile wide; all ordinary traffic was barred from it (indeed, there were no access-points), and it was central to His purpose.

'Go down there tomorrow, Oxlade. Find out who else is there. Come back and tell me.' The shutters slid back, and the chief was gazing once more out of the window. After the projector's harsh white rectangle of light, the sunshine seemed warm and mellow. 'Still so much to be done, Oxlade,' he mused, 'but an inspiring sight, nonetheless. Good luck.'

My chief's orders have been at times difficult of interpretation; but on this occasion, I felt that he had made himself unusually plain.

I reached Southend, by way of Liverpool Street and one of the amazing new trains, at about seven thirty the following morning – to find it full of white gulls, sun, and a curiously invigorating tranquillity. I decided to have a quiet breakfast on the seafront. I have always loved that row of archway cafés on the Shoeburyness Road, each with its strip of carefully tended forecourt crammed with gaudy umbrellas and gaily painted tables, from which you can hear the sailing boats bobbing against the sea-wall on a slight, inviting swell. To choose one to eat in – if mere satisfaction of appetite is your object – is the matter of a moment; to select the *right* one, the one that best suits your mood of the hour, must be a serious business: for you may sit there all morning, captured by the sight of the sea before you.

It was in one of these that I met Estrades, lounging back in his slatted chair with a bottle of mineral water and a long thin cigar.

Under the old order, Estrades had been perhaps my craftiest opponent. All that was dispensed with now, of course: but once, somewhere in Middle Europe, I had had occasion to try and shoot off one of his kneecaps. Only a lucky accident of radio-reception had saved him. We greeted each other now with a cautious pleasure. He was a tall, elegant man given to the most flamboyant of white linen suits and to buttonhole flowers of an extravagant size (although I noticed that today his carnation in no way matched my own home-grown *Palaeonophis*). Some said he was a Ukrainian, others a Kirgizstanian from the western slopes of the Tien Shan; but he had the lazy, undeviating eye for the professional essentials, and the morose, ironic sense of humour of a Polish count. Estrades was certainly not his real name, but it is the only one we have to remember him by.

During my examination of the menu, we exchanged courtesies and anecdotes of mutual friends and enemies. Estrades claimed that he was bored; he had come over, he said, on the strength of a rumour (he would place no greater weight than that on any information from Alexandria), and had been in Southend for some days. 'You must,' he said, 'be interested in the Motorway, Oxlade my friend – no, no, I can see it plainly in the set of your shoulders.' He laughed in a peculiar restrained manner, his thin, scarred face remaining immobile but for a slight drawing back of the lips. 'We are too old to play games. So. Take my advice. I have been here for a week, and have seen nothing in daylight but that which is already known. Go at night, go at night.'

'That which is already known' – how could I admit that I knew so little? I determined immediately to do both, and turned the conversation to another subject.

Later, Estrades leaned back in his chair and yawned. 'Tell me honestly, my friend, what you think of all this.' And he made a gesture which took in the sea, the Shoeburyness Road, the gulls like white confetti at some marriage of water and air. I was puzzled: I thought that it was a remarkably fine sort of day; I thought that I had never eaten such large prawns. He stared at me for a moment, then threw back his head to laugh in earnest. 'As evasive as ever,' he said, wiping his eyes. 'Oxlade, you are either the most stupid or the most careful of men. Look. Nobody is listening except the waitress, and she to her transistor radio. By "this", I mean this whole thing, this –' he paused thoughtfully – 'this paradise for bad poets and old-age pensioners in which we now find ourselves (you and I, who have left toothmarks on the bone in half the gutters of Western Europe!); this Eden in which we exercise ourselves by reading J.B. Priestley in a sunny garden in Kent – or, God forgive us, grow flowers.'

'And yet, Estrades,' I said, a little pointedly, for I suspected that this final lapse of taste had been deliberate, 'you find yourself perfectly in place. I grow orchids, and that is sufficient – in the old days, I asked for nothing more; and you – why, you sit at a café table in Southend, or some estaminet of Antwerp, with perhaps more freedom than before to exercise your wit, your (if I may say so) rather impractical and gauzy cynicism. No-one asks you to write bad poetry – or, indeed, to judge the poetry of others. All of us are satisfied, in our individual ways.'

He nodded slowly. 'It is an argument. It is *the* argument. But it does not impress me. Can one find satisfaction in simply being satisfied? Is it that I am now allowed to be dissatisfied? I have considered it. I chafe.' He gazed out to sea, moved his hands vaguely. Hunger I can't describe illuminated his face for a brief moment. Eventually, he turned back to me, drew on his cigar, examined his graceful, nicotine-stained fingers. 'Satisfaction. Oxlade, I suspect we have been robbed, but I cannot discover how. As you say, each man is content: how then have I been passed over and left to wonder why?'

At that point I said goodbye to him. Like a clever illusionist, he had confused me for perhaps half a minute with his Middle-European angst and his cheap linguistic philosophy. But nothing could mar the eagerness I felt as I strolled along the north bank of the estuary. My very first glimpse of God's Own Road awaited me; the scent of my *Palaeonophis* mingled deliciously with the scent of the sea; and I found it easy to put him out of my mind.

God's Motorway rises out of the water almost exactly opposite the old refineries of the Sheerness promontory. No houses are near it, and here the road to Shoeburyness ends. It emerges along a vast but indistinct causeway, about which the very air seems to hum with agitation: standing there in awe on that pleasant morning, I could see very little of that crucial interface between Road and sea – there, the water boiled and effervesced, and spray hung like some diaphanous shifting curtain, full of the strangest hues. There is no sight more impressive than those twenty lanes of metalled road emerging (as if from some other, longer journey) from the fume to arrow away inland, joyfully precise and resolute.

In a way (though in what a mean way) Estrades was proved right: nothing came up from the water, there was little concrete information to be gained there, and I had to turn elsewhere for something to take back to my chief. Yet I spent all morning watching the ever-changing, spectral colours of that spray and wondering what ecstatic energies had given them birth. Meanwhile, the herring gulls dived and gyred through it, apparently for the mere joy of the sensation, and after passage seemed whiter than before. Had I wings, I would have followed them: how they spun and whirled!

That night, I set out to discover more of the Motorway. It was my intention to strike inland behind the town and meet the road some three miles down its length. The thick sea-fog that hung over the suburbs as I left broke rapidly up into drifting unpredictable banks. I carried a compact but powerful torch, a flask of hot tea. I had provided myself also with a warm coat and field-glasses of a remarkable resolution purchased in Dortmund some years before. In the chilly fields and abandoned housing estates between the north-eastern peripheries of the town and God's Road, I became aware that I was not alone: yet I was sure, too, that none of the stealthy

7

movements in the dark were aimed at myself. 'The Motorway must always be of interest to us,' my chief had said; it must have been of interest to many that night, for a continual procession of agents rustled through the fog toward it.

I became lost (I have never been fond of the night, a serious weakness, perhaps, in a man of my profession, and one that I have often pondered) and consequently my line of travel intersected the Motorway a little sooner than I might have liked: but it did not matter in the end. A tall embankment towered up before me against the strange new constellation which, appearing in the skies about two years before, had heralded the Rediscovery of God; and as I struggled up that enormous earthwork, I could already hear the sound of heavy engines toiling north. The Road had woken up: I took my station close to the chain-link fence, and wiped the condensation from the lenses of my night-glasses.

These now revealed that every one of the lanes was in use; at forty or more points along my field of vision, massive vehicles crawled and groaned northward up the slight gradient. None of them was less than two hundred feet long. The commonest type was composed of a single tractor unit coupled to the front of a great low-loading trailer, although many were built up like trains out of five or six of each component. They were of a uniform matt black colour, studded with large rivets; and while each tractor had what might be described as a cabin, nothing could be seen behind its windows. What sort of motor drives them, I have no idea – they seemed to toil, none moved at more than five or six miles an hour – and yet a sense of enormous power hung like a heat-haze over each carriageway, and the ground trembled beneath my feet.

Shifting fogs made my observations intermittent and superficial, and some actual distortion of the air rendered the carriageways of the far side difficult to see at all. At first, I experienced a sensation similar to that I have already described in connection with the photographs shown me by my chief: while I could now make a little more sense of the general aspects of the picture before me, still the central object of each quick glimpse somehow defied interpretation. The road, I understood; the vehicles, I was able to perceive as such; it was their cargo that remained puzzling. What a strange commerce – what dim and ambiguous shapes in the night.

Suddenly, however, eye and brain seemed to perform the necessary trick of adjustment; I understood the problem to be one of scale; and I was able to see that the objects before me were, in fact, gigantic anthropoid limbs.

Quite close to me in the second or third lane, set upright on its truncated wrist, a human fist moved slowly past, shrouded in tarpaulin. It was clenched, with palm toward me, a left hand perhaps thirty feet high – extended, it would have been twice that from the heel of the palm to the tips of the fingers. The tarpaulin flapped and fluttered round its deep contours: steel cables moored it to the bed of the vehicle. All was for a moment perfectly clear – then a fog bank obscured it forever. For a time, my own excitement betrayed me. I neglected to refocus the glasses, and, desperately scanning the more distant lanes, saw only slow mysterious movements like those of some extinct reptile passing along an overgrown ride in a forest of cycads.

Then a truly enormous forearm slipped by five lanes out, more than a hundred feet long and heavily muscled; and from then on I was witness to an astonishing parade of members – gargantuan calves and thighs, hands and feet, and some shapes difficult to interpret that I took to be more private, possibly internal, organs; a parade accompanied by the groan and throb of God's Engines, by the shuddering of the earth, and, above all, that sense of vast energies almost accidentally dissipated into the air.

Toward dawn, the traffic became sporadic. One last limb crept past, supported by trestles and requiring two trailers to accommodate its length; the fog reasserted its grip; all movement ceased.

Stiffly, I rose from the crouch into which I had fallen, my knees aching and reluctant, my hands numb and cold. Minute beads of moisture clung to everything: my coat, the binoculars, the chain-link fence. My ears felt uncomfortable in the silence, as if some pressure on the inner passages had suddenly been relieved. For a minute or two I flapped my arms against my sides in an attempt to restore some warmth and vitality; but it was in a stupor of weariness that I stumbled away.

I stood for a moment at the foot of the embankment. Silence was no longer absolute – all about me were mysterious shiftings as other observers shrugged, yawned, put up their instruments and prepared to leave the Motorway. Dawn now illuminated the fog, filling it with a diffuse internal glow which in no way aided the eye. Two or three men passed me within touching-distance, conversing in low tones – they were quite invisible. Then, faint and thin, a cry of despair reached me through that drifting, luminous mist; running footsteps thudded along the top of the embankment, moving south. 'Stop him!' someone shouted, then added something made unintelligible by excitement.

I turned to look back. Estrades was suddenly standing beside me, the mist seeming to give him up without sound. A fur-lined leather jacket, the patched and oil-stained relic of some European aerial war, bulked out his slim figure. He was breathing heavily. He stared at me for a second or two, as if he hardly recognised me, then called urgently to someone invisible in the mist, 'He's yours, Eisenburg – about a hundred feet ahead of you, now!' A shot rang out. The running man blundered on.

'For God's sake,' said Estrades disgustedly. He took his cigar out of his mouth and frowned at it. 'Never trust a bloody Kurd.' Then, in a different tone, 'Think about what you've seen, Oxlade,' he advised me quietly. 'Esher is no longer yours. How will you ever feel safe again?' He considered this statement; nodded; pulled a small revolver from the pocket of his flying jacket. 'Must I do it all myself?' he demanded of the man Eisenburg. 'It's all up if he gets away!' And he vanished once more into the mist, casting wolfishly about him as he went. Later, two more shots startled the bright air. I waited, but Estrades did not return. I made my way back across the damp fields, wondering if the poor wretch on the embankment knew who was pursuing him. It was a dreary trudge.

Somewhat later in the morning I considered my position carefully. I had made progress of a kind which may be summed up in the following problem. At a maximum observed speed of six miles an hour, it would be quite impossible for God's Vehicles to complete their entire journey in one night; and yet by day the Motorway lay silent, abandoned to the wind and sunshine along its whole length; where, then, did the traffic go? A fascinating and significant anomaly – but had I any assurance that it was not already known to my chief? Estrades was aware of it; there may have been others. It would be injudicious, I realised, to commit myself too early to one point of view and return to London with what would certainly be regarded as an incomplete report. It was safe to assume that my chief had some other interest – one that had appeared up until now to be peripheral.

Again, I thought of Estrades.

That saturnine expatriate, survivor of a thousand and one labyrinthine excursions beneath the political crust, liked to present his motives in terms of simple curiosity (and indeed there lay concealed behind his objectionable languor not only the keen and feral energy I had seen released that morning in the Essex mist but also, as I had discovered to my cost on more than one previous occasion, a mind subtle, relentless and unassuaged) – but only some specific object could have drawn him from his retirement among the bleached river terraces of North Africa to kill by pistol on a cold morning in England. What tenuous thread had he followed through the brothels of

Marseilles, the grey boulevards of Brussels, to Southend-on-Sea?

All the rest of the morning I sought him out along the crowded sea-wall, submerging myself in that fierce and unrestricted tide of bare red forearms and light opera, with its odours of fried fish, lavender and bottled stout. I knew he would be waiting for me. At noon, a light uncustomary drizzle began to fall from a sky filled alternately with gunmetal cloud and weak sunshine. The esplanade was all of a sudden bleak and empty. In the shadow of the pier I sat on a stone, gazing up at the salt-caked fretwork of struts and warped boards that support the thumping slot machines and shooting galleries. Shouting children hung over the white railings high above. When I looked toward the mercuric thread of the surf, Estrades stood at the end of the avenue of corroded iron supports, motionless and shining in a single watery ray of sun.

The rain died off as we walked toward one another. I wish sometimes that I had walked away instead. Up above, the planking thumped and rattled. By the time we met, the front was thick with people again, issuing, with no more than a single shiver to dispel the chilly interruption of their day, from the cafés and shop doorways that had sheltered them.

'I've been watching the faces on the beach,' said Estrades, 'hoping to recognise the old familiar ones. You remember, Oxlade? They were grey, as if moulded out of a flesh like soft wax, grey with insecurity and lost sleep, wincing from short tense encounters on windy street corners. (Can you remember even those corners, Oxlade, from the comfy recesses of your new dream?) They were sick but real. They were our faces.' He shook his head. 'There must be fifty men out on that embankment every night. Many of them I must have known before. I look for them on the beach every day, but if they are there, they are burnt red like renders on holiday, they wear open-necked shirts and rolled sleeves. Like you, Oxlade, they have relaxed.'

He sighed, indicated the promenade crowds. 'And there,' he said, 'you look for spirit. You watch them, you hear the noise and expect to find some visible motive for this happy, happy seething.' He shrugged. 'Ha. Their eyes are pale and blind. They have been robbed. They perform by rote, like some kind of animal.'

'If that is true, Estrades – and I suspect it isn't – then it may simply be what they prefer. And look at the children. They seem happy enough. You can't deny that they seem happy enough, and aware of it.'

He looked instead at the shingle, and hacked with his elegant heel at a hank of bright green seaweed. He bent down quickly and prised something loose from it with his long, strong fingers. 'Children ask less. Are they to remain children all their lives?' He flicked his fingers distastefully to remove a bit of seaweed, then held up an old threepenny piece, still somehow bright and untarnished. God knows how long it had rolled about the foreshore. 'Even here there is spirit,' he said gnomically, and flipped it away – it sped out of the shadow of the pier, glittered briefly in the exhausted light and vanished.

'Up there on the promenade is a festival of mediocrity, a feast of tolerance, an emptiness filled with wheelchair entertainers –' For a moment he watched them pass. 'You don't want to know,' he asked distantly, 'who was killed this morning by the Motorway?' I must have revealed my tension in some way, for he turned back with a triumphant grin. 'Oh, the Department is so careful with its executives. I killed your back-up operator. He sent a radio message, "All goes smoothly," then I killed him before he could transmit again. Will you tell them?'

'I have never,' I said carefully, 'been informed that back-up operators are in use. You may have killed an innocent man.'

'Then you are remarkably ill-informed. And no man on that embankment this morning was entirely innocent.' When my face remained blank, he laughed uproariously. 'Oxlade!

Oxlade!' he gasped. 'If you could see yourself!' He recovered his composure. 'Oh, how sick I am of all this faith,' he muttered bitterly. I had, perhaps, succeeded in making him feel uncomfortable.

'Why did you kill him?'

He smiled off at something in the distance. The sun had come out fully; on the pier, a small orchestra had begun to play selections from Gilbert & Sullivan.

'I intend to put an end to this half-wit's Utopia,' he said quietly. 'I want you with me, if only as a representative of your organisation; but I can allow no more reports until the thing is done. Your shadow was an embarrassment.' He studied me intently. 'What do you say, Oxlade old friend? Set against one another, we were always wasted.' And before I could make the obvious answer, 'Why, if you come you may even be able to stop me doing it! What a coup! And all else failing, you will enter the most astonishing report on the episode. It will mean another promotion. More orchids will bloom in the quiet backwaters of Esher.'

'Come where?' I asked.

'The Midlands,' he said, 'by way of the Road of God.'

I started to walk away.

'What you are intending to do is more hopeless than blasphemous.'

He allowed me to leave the shadow of the pier before calling, 'I will have you killed before you can reach a telephone, Oxlade.' I looked up and down the front. Eisenburg the Kurd stood negligently at the foot of the seawall. He grinned and lit a cigarette, staring at me over his cupped hands. Fifteen yards separated us. 'I can't take the risk,' said Estrades. I believed him.

'You are an evil man, Estrades,' I told him. 'The rest of us have forgotten how.'

He laughed.

'That is what is wrong with you,' he said.

Up above him children flocked into the shooting galleries.

Their cries drowned the noise of the orchestra.

That was how I entered into my unwilling association with Estrades the anarchist and became a party to the plot against God. Why that madman really wanted me with him, I don't know. Murder would have been so much easier. I believe now that it merely gratified his vanity to have a captive observer. He was an enormously vain man. At any rate, I could do nothing about it; and all that afternoon and part of the evening I watched passively as he prepared his ground in a series of visits to what were presumably 'safe' houses scattered across Southend.

It was at one of these that Eisenburg took charge of the mysterious three-foot packing case upon which they had placed their hopes. It must have weighed half a hundredweight, if not more, but he carried it – together with a pair of long-handled bolt cutters with which they intended to breach the fence at the top of the embankment – under one arm as if it were empty. I grew to loathe that crate (although I had no idea at that time of what it contained – had I done so I might have taken my chances with him in one of the more crowded streets behind the esplanade) and he knew it. Whenever Estrades's attention was occupied elsewhere, Eisenburg would catch my eye and go through a long, complicated dumb-show of insinuation, tapping the thing significantly, making motions as if to open it, grinning ferociously all the time, so that his scar made ghastly furrows in his forehead. He never let it out of his sight, and he never tired of taunting me.

Meanwhile, Estrades, his pristine suit and carnation exchanged once more for flying jacket and revolver, had become tense and excited, given to romantic gestures which constantly reaffirmed the emotional instability of his character. 'So!' he exclaimed, as we made our way across the sodden fields behind the town. 'Here we go! Everything staked on one throw! Three men against God!' Even the sunset seemed alarmed at this vast, childish vanity: the sky was one great inverted bowl of cloud, tilted up a little on the horizon over Shoeburyness to show a thin strip of blood-coloured light. 'Oxlade, you think it can't be done. Pah. It can! We'll liberate Esher; and if the orchids are a little smaller next year, a little less gaudy – well, they will be your orchids, at least!'

'You aren't uneducated, Estrades. You must know it's been tried before.'

'Not by a *man*, Oxlade.' He nudged his accomplice. 'Not by a man, eh Eisenburg?' And they winked excruciatingly at one another like boys about to raid an orchard.

Up on the embankment we waited for the last shreds of light to be dispersed. A thin cold wind sprang up and hissed across the fields; for a moment, hung there between night and day, all seemed a grey and empty waste, an end to independent struggle under aimless airs – had God, I wondered, already lifted the protection of the New Reign from us three? Estrades shivered and zipped his jacket up. As darkness fell and the sound of God's Engines came throbbing up from the south, Eisenburg got to work with his bolt cutters. The chain link proved tougher than expected; the Kurd grunted and swore, Estrades fumed impatiently about; reluctantly each strand of wire curled back on itself like burnt hair. By the time the first vehicle had crawled into view, we had our breach, although it was small and mean.

Estrades then replaced Eisenburg at the wire and remained crouched in the gap for perhaps half an hour, frequently consulting his watch. His face had become drawn and uncommunicative, as if he realised for the first or possibly the last time what his own actions meant. Did he see in the slow, enigmatic shapes crawling up the incline his own final annihilation, the Hand irrevocably withdrawn? The ground shuddered, the air above the road shimmered and reverberated with awful energies. Suddenly he seemed to gather himself. He showed me a hunted, almost panic-stricken face and shouted, 'Now or never, Oxlade! If you want to live, run!'

And he squirmed through the breach.

I remember so little. For a second or two, I know, I watched as he sprinted for his life, a tiny, energetic mote weaving and dodging under the threat of those huge wheels; then I felt a tremendous blow between the shoulder blades and turned to find Eisenburg sweating and grinning at me in the gloom. 'You next,' he said, and gave me another push. We fled like insects across the broad back of the Road, the Kurd shoving me on in front of him; the wind eddying round those massive machines whipped at our clothing; black dizzy expanses of riveted steel towered above us. When I stumbled he dragged me upright, raging incoherently.

Out in the third lane, Estrades, by dint it seemed of sheer hysterical strength, had gained the bed of an immense trailer. Eight feet above me, white faced and peering, he extended a hand to haul me up. Eisenburg tossed us the crate and the bolt cutters, but at his first attempt to board the vehicle, missed his stride. His jump took him six inches below Estrades's straining hand. For a full half-minute he had to run along behind the vehicle gathering his courage for a second try, his face a perfect mask of fear.

Panic and fear – all that remains to me of the journey.

How long we clung freezing and immobile to the back of that machine, I can't tell. Blue waxy light pervaded all that space which might be described as 'the Road', and time moved unreasonably along its warped perspectives. Estrades's watch had been damaged in his scramble up the side of the vehicle. A regular modulation of the cyanic light suggested we might have been aboard the thing for days. What we saw of the Motorway's environs we saw transfigured, blurred, and it gave us no help or comfort. (The Road has, I suspect, little 'real' existence in this way. On my eventual return to the World I confirmed that three days had passed since our breaching of the fence. But I place no significance on such crude measurements. They are at best only a device for the description of the human *Umwelt*. We travelled in the *Umwelt* of God, which, to my admittedly limited knowledge, no theologian has yet undertaken to define.)

To begin with, Estrades was determined to make some sort of study of the vehicle which we had infested like morose and frightened lice – even, I think, to gain access to the tractor cab and 'commandeer' it; but this came to nothing. We shared the trailer with something unimaginable and shrouded. We were from the start too awed, too precarious. We sat apart, drew our knees up to our chins, and stared silently before us. Eisenburg did once take a turn round the trailer, out of bravado or to ease some cramp of the joints, but even he didn't dare examine the thing beneath the tarpaulin, and Estrades soon called him back. He seemed glad enough to obey.

It was a wonder, finally, that any of us retained energy enough to make decisions, even to move (although move we did, and soon enough). The tarpaulin cracked and flapped dismally, like a tent pitched in a dark valley. Belts of fog came and went, to leave beads of condensation on the black metal; sudden winds chilled us to the bone. Our vehicle never left its precise position in the order of the convoy. We were stiff and tired and hungry, our ears were battered and stupefied by the constant beat of God's Engines. In that dreary blue suspension, we felt like the ghosts of the newly dead – who, filled with horror, stare numbly at one another in continual discovery of their irreversible state. Later, Estrades took to brooding for long periods over the crate, hoping perhaps to find his salvation there.

At last, Time, in an understandable human sense, was returned to us; the light ceased its steady fluctuation; ahead, the perspectives of the Road shifted and straightened, enabling us once more to estimate speed and distance; and for the first time the adjoining landscape became clearly visible to us. We found ourselves moving slowly across a great arid peneplain touched here and there by sourceless orange highlights and shadows of the profoundest purple. The earth was cracked and bare, like mudsoil on some abandoned African plateau. Nothing moved beyond the fence.

You will say, and quite reasonably, that there is no such view to be found in the British Isles. I can only agree. This was nothing to us. On the horizon had appeared the tall and awful shape of God.

Eisenburg bent his head and whimpered suddenly. Estrades stared astounded. 'Christ, Oxlade!' he shouted, and lapsed immediately into some Magyar dialect I couldn't follow. He produced his revolver and for some reason began to wave it excitedly in my direction. Eisenburg, meanwhile, wept, choked, and tried to kneel; Estrades saw this action from the corner of his eye, and went at him like a snake. 'None of that!' he hissed. 'Get the bloody box open, Eisenburg! We've got Him!' But his eyes were captured by that unbearable Enigma or apparition and when the Kurd failed to obey he didn't seem to notice.

How can I describe Him?

He crouches there in my memory as He will crouch forever. He is in part profile, silhouetted against the sky. Ten square miles of earth lie between His six splayed legs. Rainbows of iridescence play across His vast black carapace. If He should ever spread the wings beneath those shimmering elytra! One compound eye a hundred yards across gazes fixedly into realms that we may never see. A mile in the air, gales thunder impotently round His stiff antennae and motionless, extended jaws. In the shadow of His long abdomen, the giant factories seem like toys, and it is as if He had brought with Him from the hidden obverse of the Moon an airlessness that makes the sky a harder, brighter place. We see that where His legs touch the earth, deep saucer shaped depressions have formed. From each of these, huge fissures radiate. Can the World bear His weight without a groan?

19

What has He taken away from us, what has He come to give us in return? Estrades claimed to know – but Estrades had long been destroyed by his own despair. Staring speechlessly up at that gargantuan entomic form, *Lucanus cervus* omnipotent, I knew there must be more. If I am no longer sure of that, it is because I am no longer sure of anything.

Eisenburg gaped, vomited. He wiped his mouth with the back of his hand and began to laugh. 'It's a fucking beetle!' he shrieked. 'It's only a bloody beetle!' Estrades winced, stared at his own feet for a moment; then he started to laugh, too. They embraced, sobbing, rocking to and fro in a sort of clumsy dance. 'Quick!' cried the Kurd, disengaging himself. 'Quick!' He grabbed the bolt-cutters and used them to lever off the lid of the crate. Grey-faced and shaking, the two of them knelt over its contents and began to make feverish adjustments to a nest of coloured wire and electrical components. In their haste, they fought briefly over the only tool they had, a small screwdriver. Eisenburg won.

Estrades glanced over his shoulder and shuddered. 'It's about five miles,' he said. 'Set it for that.'

He felt my gaze on him. 'Freedom, Oxlade,' he murmured. 'Freedom.' A fit of shivering got hold of him. Up ahead, that enormous shape was coming closer and closer.

'An hour and twenty minutes,' he told Eisenburg, 'to be on the safe side. We can't be certain what happens once it gets there.'

'You can't mean to carry on with this!' I found myself shouting. I can't express the panic that had come over all of us. It was almost physiological, some old fear etched into the cells of the nervous system. 'Estrades! Not so close to Him–!' I clutched his shoulders. His trembling communicated itself to me, and for a second we clung to one another, unable to speak. Estrades made noises. I tore myself away. 'What's *in* that crate, man? What are you going to do?' Slowly, the trembling died away. Estrades drew along, shuddering breath; his face writhed, he lifted the pistol. Then he laughed bitterly and turned his back.

'Ask what all this is for,' he suggested quietly, 'instead.' And he gestured at the Motorway, at the impossible landscape and the factories in the Shadow.

'Ask what this thing intends to do with *us*, why it has turned us into tourists and parsons and performers of simpering amateur dramatics in a world we no longer control. Ask –' But he began to tremble again, and couldn't go on. He clenched his fists against the onset of the fit. Eisenburg, dropping the screwdriver, looked up in horror, his jaw muscles quivering uncontrollably. Racked and quaking, I thought, 'It will get worse as we go closer; He cannot allow us any closer.' I was terrified in case I should see those gigantic mandibles *move*. Estrades clutched at his gun with both hands, as if it offered anchorage. 'I have ten pounds of plutonium in that box –' each word forced out between clenched teeth – 'Eisenburg built the trigger. Twenty men died stealing the stuff, a hundred more are committed in Europe alone. I shall go...on... whatever happens...'

He groaned, and gave himself up to shivering.

I don't know quite what I intended to do. When I saw them both overcome, I threw myself at the bomb – I thought that if I could heave it over the side it would be broken, or at least irrecoverable. But they were on me in an instant, clubbing madly at my head and groin. Estrades's revolver went off with an enormous bang. Something smashed into my lower legs. The Kurd roared, dropped his body squarely across mine and probed with stiffened fingers for the arteries in my neck. We flopped about like fish in the bottom of a rowing boat, panting and groaning. Then I discovered the discarded bolt cutters under my hand and beat him repeatedly under the ear with them until he rolled away from me and stopped moving.

Scrambling to my feet, I discovered Estrades kneeling about two feet away. 'For Christ's sake Oxlade,' he pleaded, 'it's

21

the *world!*' The pistol was pointing directly at my belly, but he was shivering so hard he couldn't pull the trigger. I opened his head up with the bolt-cutters. He knelt there, covered in blood and said, 'You shouldn't have done this.' Then he went down like a dead man.

I took a step toward the bomb; my left leg folded up under me; and, clutching helplessly at the empty air, I fell into the Road – where I lay on my back for a moment unable to move, watching the vehicle draw inexorably away from me. Hot and stinking of rubber, huge wheels ground past me through a fog of pain and nausea. About a minute later, the figure of Estrades reappeared on the trailer, looking small and desperately unsteady. His shoulders were a mantle of blood. He staggered about for a time, waving the revolver. A couple of rounds splattered into the metalling beside me; then he turned away and emptied the weapon defiantly into the air toward God.

That was the last I saw of him.

The rest is nothing. I turned my back on it all and ran, despite the hole Estrades had put in the muscle of my calf (I still limp a little, although not now as proudly as I did in the weeks of my convalescence). 'God,' I remember praying, 'let me get away before it goes off!' So close, it might even be that He heard me. I don't recall what I offered Him in exchange. Several times, I made some feeble attempt to cut my way through the fence; but I never managed to break more than a strand or two of wire before panic overtook me and I began to run again, timing my prayers to the sound of my own ragged breath. I was painfully conscious of the Mystery looming immobile and abiding behind me; but I never looked back.

Eventually, I fell down exhausted. There, where the Motorway ran through a cutting with broad, gently-sloping sides of soft red earth, I scraped a shallow hole. Into this I thrust my face; I clasped my hands behind my neck; and in that submissive position waited for Estrades's madness to find me out. A long time later, I passed out. Perhaps they had built the thing badly, or failed to complete the fusing sequence – perhaps I had, after all, killed them both. At any rate, the bomb never went off.

I suspect it never would have. I realise now that it was a failure of Faith to believe even for a second that they could have succeeded; and I suspect that a dozen bombs would have made no difference to Him – I imagine Him spreading His great transparent wings to the blast, like a housefly in the sun.

The driver of a quite ordinary lorry, I am told, found me stumbling along the verge of the A5 somewhere near Brownhills. How I got there, I am at a loss to explain. Presumably I succeeded at last in breaching the fence. God rises majestically above the suburbs of Birmingham and Wolverhampton, where His factories are: but He seems smaller than He does in that other place, that Simultaneous or Alternative Midlands which can only be seen from the other side of the chain link; and people live at ease within the sight of Him.

What a pure pleasure the convalescent experiences when he is at last released from his prison of a bed! The sheets, chains and fetters of his sapling vitality, become mere sheets once more; his dull fellow-patients, now that he must leave them, seem the most interesting of human beings; and the view from his window, that sad fishbowl stage for his obsessive fantasies of recovery, peopled by actors whose motives he can only invent, becomes the World again, and he its newest participant. And what a world! – What rediscoveries, what heartfelt reconsiderations! It was with just this profound sense of being made anew that, a little after a month after my adventures in the Realm of God, I made my way home from the offices of the Department.

I had been released from hospital that morning; my preliminary report was made – though there remained necessary some sharpening of its edges, the sketch, so to speak, was completed; and before me stretched the most poignant of May afternoons. I dawdled down Baker Street, and paused for a while to admire the flowerbeds by the Clarence Gate. Regent's Park was full of cool laconic breezes, but beneath them there moved a heaviness, a languor, a promise of the Summer to be. In my absence, cherry blossom had sprung in every corner, the waterfowl had put on a fresh, dapper plumage and were waddling importantly about in the white sunlight that scoured the newly painted boards of the boat-house.

Calm and happy, I let the faint cries of some large animal draw me across the jetty footbridge toward the distant Zoological Gardens. The wind brought me declamatory voices and the laughter of children – at the Open Air Theatre, they were presenting *A Midsummer Night's Dream*; and as I crossed the wide spaces north of the lake, the glowing phrases of my lunchtime interview with the chief mingled inextricably with strains of a Flanders & Swann medley issuing from the new bandstand: 'A most genuine contribution – A hundred others rounded up in Europe alone; in Africa we move with speed and caution – We were of course well aware of Estrades and his cynical conspiracy – Nothing less than a victory, a triumph for decency and common sense – Certain promotion.' Old men were flying their kites from the benches by the pagoda – white and ecstatic as the gulls above God's Causeway, they danced and bobbed in tribute to the dashing air!

Since childhood the elegant cages, the precise spaces, the immense colour and vitality of the zoo have been a passion with me. Where else can be seen such relentless grace, such refined energy as we see in the leopard? – Or such mysterious moonlit depths as those of the Small Mammal House? What a cacophony of wisdom the lories and macaws generate, what a deep spring of humour lies beneath the elephant's hide! That afternoon, I was remade; Mary and the children, I thought, would hardly begrudge me an hour: so I took it with the gibbons and the mountain sheep, and with the tiger who so reminded me of Estrades – pacing, hungry, so economical and feral that I caught myself trying to attract his eye…

That was surely enough; the polar bear like a fixated ballet dancer run to fat, the sharp ammoniacal smell of the rhino, the flocking children, that sense of peaceful yet animal activity, these were surely enough: I shouldn't have gone to the Insect House.

I don't believe it was a beetle of any kind, much less *Lucanus cervus,* that captured my attention – rather it was something grey and leafish, looking absurdly like a woman in muslin rags. It was resting on a twig, almost invisible and quite immobile, and perhaps this very quality of stillness – this perfectly alien perception of the passage of time – was sufficient; as I stared into the hot yellow recesses of the vivarium, I remembered the Mystery that lies at the end of God's Motorway, and I thought: What possible emotion could this thing have in common with us? I recalled the twisted perspectives and quaking blue light of the *Umwelt* of God, the factories in the Shadow, Estrades's final bitter suggestion – 'Ask what this thing intends to do with *us*, in a world we no longer control.'

In what continuum or sphere of reality would we find that nightmarish Simultaneous Midlands, with its pocked dreary landscape and vast presiding deity, if we once thought to look? Why is God building an enormous human body while we build bandstands? What does He want with us?

As I re-read what I have written here I can see the progression of my loss mirrored in the very words I have used; Estrades began it, perhaps, on the seafront at Southend – but that was only a moment's uncertainty, whereas now… Since the revelation in the Insect House, where the only sound is a shuffle of feet as visitors file past the specimens like communicants, I have been unable to recapture my sense of wonder. My attention wanders from *Palaeonophis*; I grow bored and restless at rehearsals of the Esher Light Operatic Society; I chafe.

And I confess that it frightens me now to visit that penthouse office where my chief crouches high above the neat, the eternally bright and windy streets of the city, whispering 'Still so much to do, Oxlade,' as he grooms with quick strokes of his forelegs his feathery antennae, or flexes the horny wing-cases which, closed, look so much like an iridescent tail coat – or in the gloom fixes his enigmatic compound eyes on that white, perfect rectangle of light cast by the slide projector, engaging in some renewal of the senses, some exploration of a consciousness I will never appreciate. I am his deputy now, and have risen as far as a man can rise. I look out over the pensioners in the trim parks below, and I should be proud.

What did Estrades know? He was an old man. He retired, he took himself off to North Africa and a study of Byzantine military history long before the Rediscovery. He had never stood above the streets of some familiar city, faced with one of the small energetic replicas of Him that fill every responsible office in the World. He had no chance.

Why has God come to us in this way? We were so eager to accept Him.

1975

The Gift

1: The Rainbow Shuts Its Gate Against You

IF YOU PROBE IN the ashes, they say, you will never learn anything about the fire; its meaning has passed on.

There are as many as seventeen good hotels in the city. On the 'entresol' floor of one of them, the Central, a woman lounges in the tropical heat of her single room, drinking rum. The TV is on, the sound turned down. It's eleven o'clock at night. Downstairs, the railway station from which the Central takes its name is almost deserted. When a train arrives, the air is filled for a few minutes with shouts, laughter, people calling to one another in the crush, and the concourse sounds like a zoo or an asylum. As if to soothe the inmates the concourse muzak will suddenly play a schmalzy, faraway version of 'Rhapsody in Blue'. To this the woman in room 236 listens only briefly, tilting her head at an intent angle as though she is trying to catch some tune underneath the music, before she shrugs and turns away from the window.

"'Black Heart Rum",' she reads aloud from the bottle in her hand. "'The Heart of Darkness".' She laughs and adds, "'All the sweet lacunae of the Caribbean Sea – "'

Now it is the television that captures her attention, and she turns up the sound just in time to hear '– unease in the minds of ladies. Considerable unease in the minds of ladies.' But this sentence, read out in a bright yet concerned voice, is the end of the item, and the scene changes abruptly to some grainy night footage of lorries being manoeuvred in and out of a shed. 'Real unease in the minds of some ladies,' she thinks, sitting on the bed with her shoes off and allowing her arm to rest briefly along the padded headboard. In this position she is revealed as a tall woman whose clothes – a black two-piece suit with lightly padded shoulders, a striped grey and black blouse of some glazed material – scarcely hide a kind of untidy sexuality, a gawky and almost absent-minded sleepiness of the limbs.

Her eyes are blue, a little watery and indirect. Her age is hard to tell.

Wherever you are at night in the city you can always see, beyond the roof of the next building, the faint glow of the floodlights of some monument. This is less a light than a sort of luminescence of the air itself, soft and tremulous, as if it is full of mist or water. Out of it rises a Victorian minaret, which you cannot quite see; the crenellations of a castle, which you can; or a flagpole. The parks are full of statuary.

The woman in room 236 remembers how, at the end of a holiday in Europe, she flew back into the city onboard a jet: first passing over the great cool neon signs hanging in the air at its outskirts – *TEXACO, MOWLEM, ALFA-LAVAL* – the Internationals signalling steady as beacons into the night – then entering that soft meniscus of light, that city of floodlit monuments as far as the eye can see. Her loneliness, she felt at the time, was complete.

Now, with the room darkened and the television turned off, she lies back on the bed and allows this faint illumination to fall on her from the open window. Turning restlessly one way and then the other, as if she were trying to sleep in her clothes, on the undisturbed counterpane in the trembling light, she stares up at the ceiling. At first her hands are quite still at her sides. Soon though they draw themselves up along her thighs, flat, palm down, pulling the hem of the skirt up with them. They are tender but nearly impersonal. With the skirt bundled awkwardly around her waist, and her silk knickers rolled down round her ankles, she seems to be offering her sex not so much to her own hands as to the room, the city, anything as long as it is beyond herself. 'Oh,' she says quietly after a minute or two, 'it's so beautiful!' But then a train clatters into Central Station, and the Muzak plays 'Rhapsody in Blue', and she gets up from the bed in despair or rage and switches on the fluorescent lamp above the make-up mirror.

Her name is Sophia. She was disfigured at birth by a mark like a splash – as if, her parents said, someone threw red ink in her face the very day she was born – down the right side of the nose, all round the eye on that side, and across the right cheek. Splatters and dots radiate from the raw-looking central stain like the headlands and islands of some heavily fjorded coast.

2: Narcissus Fires

At this time of night Peter Ebert can usually be found at the Doric Restaurant, which is not far away across the city at the corner of Acol Street.

The Doric is often crowded with young men like himself. Hands thrust into the pockets of their baggy black trousers, they wait for a table, gazing at the bottles above the bar with the musing expression you give to art, while the pictures – gigantic loving pencil sketches of a link of dockyard chain, which looks pumped-up and organic and about to explode, like a black pudding or a huge turd – go unnoticed on the walls. Bottles are a feature of the decor: spirit bottles in optics over the bar, green ends of wine bottles goggling into the room from racks, empty bottles stuck with cheap white candles to light the long oilcloth-covered tables. At the height of the evening, waitresses are running in and out distractedly, the room becomes suffocatingly hot, the air stuffed to bursting with the smell of choux pastry with ham and cheese in a gooseberry sauce, the walls yellow with cigarette smoke.

'After all,' someone shouts across the racket, 'it's no good cutting the Speak Your Weight machine out of your will because you don't like everything it says about you!'

'I know.'

At Peter Ebert's table a girl passes her finger through the candle flame, an expression on her face of distant enquiry, as if objectivity were not so much an act as a very faint emotion: one so removed from humanity – or at least everyday humanity – as to be hardly detectable in oneself without special training; yet an emotion nonetheless. Ebert stares at her.

This morning someone gave him a book.

It was such a curious transaction – hermetic, contingent, having its own rules, like a bubble of meaning in the ordinary events of life – that even now he feels tempted to tell someone, 'I bet this has never happened to you. At the station this morning' – Ebert means not Central but the city's less important station, Eastern, popularly known as Regent's – 'a man I had never seen before came up and offered me a book.'

Between the end of Regent's platform 4 and the mouth of the tunnel which takes the line out of the city centre, there is a deep walled cutting. On a wet day rain blows about in this space; as it circulates there, the light striking into it from the street above the station makes it seem distinct and photographic, as romantic as rain falling in a new Russian film. Watching from the dim, sheltered platform, you have the impression of an illuminated curtain, out of which noses every so often the yellow front of a train, streaked with oil, shiny with water, and bringing with it a cold stream of air. People waiting near the edge of the platform step back momentarily to let the carriage doors swing open; passengers alight and rush away.

Making room like this with all the others, Peter Ebert found himself staring at someone's face. It was quite close to his: one of those old or ill-looking faces at whose salient points small tight lumps of muscle seem to have gathered, as if the flesh had retreated there to leave the bones prominent and bare – or as if blobs of putty had been arranged on the jaw and cheekbones of a skull, then covered with white pancake make-up. Later he was to say 'a man', but in fact he was never sure whether it belonged to a man or a woman. Of the body beneath it he caught only confused impressions – a pale brown raincoat, thin shoulders, a leather case or bag. A hand, its knuckles reddened and enlarged by years of work or illness, offered him the book. He took it without thinking: imagined he heard someone say in a contemptuous, dismissive voice, 'Narcissus' or 'Narcissus Fire': lost sight of the figure in the crowd pressing towards the ticket barrier.

He stared at the book in his hand. He was suddenly convinced that there must be some other way to live. What he meant by this he couldn't think; except that it wasn't what you would normally mean. He had to catch the train, or he would have dropped the book into the nearest waste bin. When he got out at the other end it was in his pocket.

'All at once,' he now thinks of saying to the girl at his table, 'you can't make head or tail of anything, can you?'

As he opens his mouth to speak she smiles at him and pinches out the candle flame. He sees how the naked small of her back would curve up out of the waistband of her skirt, how astonishingly real and human its warmth would make her seem to him. But the book is in his pocket – though its cover has fallen off long since, he thinks it was a paperback, quite an old one from the '30s or '40s – and he knows he will be going home to read it. It is Ebert's belief that understanding ought to come by epiphany rather than by increments: it has never occurred to him how completely this might limit his intellectual reach. Behind him the waitress says, 'Whose was the plain chocolate mousse?'

3: Sophia's Gift

Every story is a cup so empty it can be drunk from again and again.

Once or twice a week she brings a man home to room 236 at the Central Hotel. If men see too much of her face they sometimes become puzzled and unkind, so out of consideration she keeps it turned away when she can, and on the way home tries as often as possible to be looking at something on the other side of the road: an old bicycle propped against a wall, the brightly lit shop window where a display of popular wedding stationery seems to merge indistinguishably with the cigarette ends and chip wrappers on the pavement outside. She always leaves the door of the room open a crack, so there will be no need for a light.

Tonight she is with a man called Dave.

When they get inside the room he won't lie down. He has been drinking whisky and Coke, so she has to struggle with his clothes as well as her own. 'I love you, Dave,' she says, kissing his face. 'At least do something to help,' she says. 'Dave, I love you.' He keeps trying to find the light switch. Eventually he manages to put one of the bedside lamps on. Please don't change your mind now, she thinks, and looks away so quickly that the tendons stand out in her neck. But he only says, 'Women!' and switches the light out himself. Then he falls on to the bed, where – after trying to lever her legs apart, unaware that they have become fastened together at the knees by the muddle of tights and underwear she hasn't had time to push down any further – he makes a few disconnected movements, comes with a groan between her closed thighs, and falls asleep. 'No, wait,' she is still whispering, 'you're not –'. She holds his head tenderly.

Dave's semen is drying in the warm hotel air, tautening a patch of her skin. A hotel is so comfortable, she thinks: if you had really wanted to do that I could have helped you, and now we could be having a bath together or anything. Sophia stares at the diffuse line of light round the open door. The last train has come in, and now the station concourse is so quiet you can hear someone's shoes squeaking across the polished floor. This faint dry sound reminds her of her holiday in Norway: the sound of feet on the shiny museum floors of Oslo, which smell of care and polish and respect.

She loves pictures. At the Munchmuseet she was careful to see *Consolation*, *Madonna*, and *The Mountain Path;* at the Nasjonal Galleriet, *Den Sarede Engell.* A friend took her to the Vikingskipmuseet so she should have a chance to see the Oseberg Ship before she left. He showed her a runic inscription scratched on a piece of black wood one thousand years old. 'It means,' he told her, '"Mankind knows so little".' He was a quiet man, a little younger than herself and determined to entertain her, who sold books in Scandinavia for a firm of English academic publishers, and lectured at the Universitet on the early film documentarists with their theories of 'camera eye' and 'redemption of reality'. He had made short films for a living, and still wrote scripts. 'I read everything about this once,' he said. 'I think that's what it means.' The old ships, their planks laid together in bunches of hurtling curves like diagrams of a slipstream, sailed round her through the dim light of the museum, ignoring her.

'It's hard to imagine them buried,' she said. 'How they must have flown across the sea!'

'A boat like this was built only for funerals I'm afraid.'

Later she had to wait for him in the darkened cafeteria of one of the university buildings. There, a boy with long red hair played desultorily on an out-of-tune piano; after a moment he got up with an exclamation of impatience and went out into the corridor. Outside, the rain was falling into a courtyard the high brick walls of which, though quite new, looked authentically old and tranquil. To foster this impression weeds had been allowed to grow between the unworn cobbles. The rain turned to hail, then after a moment of violence passed over; the fountain bubbled up. Yellow roses and dark earth. The red-haired boy came in again and said with Norwegian irony, 'I suppose we are all waiting for something!'

That was the last day of the holiday. When they drove back to her friend's home along the coast it was late. On one side of the Drammensveien the moon hung diffused and dark orange, bloated like a bag; on the other, the morning light, clean and green. The moon, though, would not set; and the dawn, endlessly promised, was endlessly incomplete. She was so tired and happy. They had stayed on in the cafés of Tingvallakaia, which at half past two every morning begin to empty themselves of couples so drunk they could only look straight ahead.

The next day, through the scratched and smeary window of a British Airways 757, she caught sight of the great granite rock of Kolsas. Because she had stared at it so often from the balcony of his flat, she was eager for it to be the last thing she saw in Norway. Touching her face gently at the airport, he had promised her: 'This is not a birthmark. It's a map.'

4: The Precious Discoveries of the Senses

At three in the morning Peter Ebert makes himself a cup of tea.

The hotel is quiet. At this time of night you might hear a door open then close, a muffled laugh from another room: but though the lights burn in the carpeted corridors, no one is walking along them. The central heating touches your skin gently and evenly. Ebert loves the sense of freedom this gives him; he loves nothing better than to be awake at night and let the hotel press round him its padded silence.

At six, grey light comes through the curtain, and he opens his window. Cold air spills over his feet; pigeons clatter away between the buildings, a sound unannounced and without issue; somewhere out of sight a pink and gold dawn is colouring the edges of the statues in the city's hilly little parks. Ebert rubs his hands over his eyes.

At nine o'clock he telephones his office.

'Another puzzle,' he thinks as he waits for his secretary to answer, 'is the *title*.'

What sort of book has he been given? Peter Ebert is unable to say. It lies open on the table in front of him amid a litter of crumpled hotel notepaper, empty cups, and torn sachets of non-dairy creamer: a hundred and thirty pages which end in the middle of a sentence – 'the precious discoveries of the senses –'. Even the surviving text is incomplete. Some pages are missing, others have been torn in half longitudinally, to leave only curious groups of words: 'years of swill', 'the subsoil account' and 'comically little value'.

Everyone who has owned it has stained and defaced it with his humanity, thinks Ebert. They have annotated it in pencil too faint to read, spattered it with food, slashed it in straight careful lines with a razor blade on a wet Monday in a bus station. They've sweated into it and worse whilst reading listlessly, sick in bed in Nottingham or Manchester. They've rubbed tomato sauce into it in thumbprints, and left impacted in its central creases cigarette ash like the grey flock which bursts from padded bags. Its outer pages are a pissy yellow colour, glazed with grease yet furry from being handled, their corners rounded-off and thick as felt. Its spine is rotten. All that remains of its title pages is a blank leaf on which is printed centrally in bold letters *EON HEART*; and even there they have spilled bleach or semen on it, Ebert thinks, so that 'eon' is only part of a word which might as easily have read 'Simeon' as 'Pantheon'.

'I'm not coming in today,' he says suddenly into the telephone. Then: 'Tell him no.'

His eye has been caught by the words, '. . . the little Fennec with its beautiful ears!'

Last night, though he had no idea what they meant, he gave a shiver of delight every time he read these words.

'To make the little white Fennec, butterflies mated themselves to foxes, fluttering into their uplifted faces in the desert air at evening. The faces of the foxes were like flowers to them, they circled closer.'

Ebert's hotel room looks out on a deep, four-sided yard built in Victorian Gothic, with pointed windows, peaked gables and brick finials. The lower part of the yard – where, less than thirty years ago, traffic still went in and out – has become choked with small buildings. Wires sag aimlessly from wall to wall above them, rotten ladders run over their roofs. Where hotel guests once stepped down from cars and taxis, moss thickens the rusting gutters. Where laughter once flew up like birds, everything is indescribably filthy. Every flat surface – even the collars which hold the drainpipes against the walls – is covered with a soft roll of pigeon shit, which hangs beneath each window ledge like a cream-coloured beard.

When he first got the book home, his excitement was so intense that he could feel the whole of his upper body rocking slightly and rhythmically to the beat of his heart. All the way home he had looked forward to the moment when he could open it. At every junction the familiar streets had seemed to lurch into new arrangements, as if he was seeing them after a long absence or from an unexpected angle.

5: 'As if by Moonlight'

'If my face was a map,' Sophia wonders, 'what kind of country would it reveal?'

An island, with other islands outlying, in a warm sea.

From its central highlands fissures and ridges radiate, mapped with jungle: green velour sleeves which fall right down to the tide. Coral snakes curl up like strings of lacquered beads, water lizards bask in the sun, macaws thicken the noon sky in flocks. Up there in the highlands the light slants between the trees in distinct beams. At night you dream you are down in the island's fever-haunted valleys, where the aboriginals – painted ash-white with blackened eye-sockets – pursue you without mercy to the shore. 'While the currents are generally labyrinthine,' the guidebooks promise, 'the water unforgiving and wine-dark, you can sometimes find a shallow bay filled with water of an intense blue.'

She stares into the make-up mirror.

'I'm like a whitewashed wall,' she decides. 'Should I go to the zoo?'

On the way she thinks of Dave, who never got in touch.

The streets smell of burning rubber, and cold has made the air transparent. You can see every building in the city centre – every duct and aluminium window frame, the gilded iron on every old bridge – from miles away, and sense the river flowing grey and gelid to the sea. At the zoo a few Japanese and Italian tourists shiver from cage to cage, photographing one another while waste paper and empty peanut shells blow about their ankles. Wherever you go in the zoo you can hear the strange, carrying, bird-like cry of the lar gibbons.

These coffee-coloured animals huddle like lookouts among the metal struts in the ceiling of their tall cage. They hold their delicate hands curved in front of them as if the joints are painful. Their eyes look bruised. They face steadily into the cold wind and cry out as though there is some message in it they cannot understand, only celebrate. Sophia can't bear this. To escape them she takes the underpass to the Nocturnal Mammal House, thinking:

'If my face is a map, it must never show a wilderness –'

All down the west coast of the island at night glitter the lights of a modern city five miles long, its towers like black and gold cigarette packets standing on end. In its shopping malls fluorescent light catches the surfaces of hard and soft designer goods: matte plastics, foams of lace and oyster satin, the precise curves of cars and shoes and shoulder pads. This city is well known for the scent of Anaïs-Anaïs in the streets; stacked video screens in the cocktail lounges; and, down by the sea-front, where men push past you smelling of sweat and Chinese food, neon of green, red or frosty blue. Music pulses from its amusement arcades and night clubs. In the jazz bars they serve only Black Heart rum, and you can hear the intricate bass and saxophone lines twenty miles out to sea.

'It's none of these things,' she admits to herself. She laughs.

'My face is the map to an island off the coast of Norway. A few quiet people from Oslo live there at weekends, in coloured wooden houses. To get there you first catch a train to Sandvika, where a bank of wildflowers comes right down to the station platform.'

The further you go into the Mammal House, with its walls of undressed brick, the darker it gets. The Moonlight World itself is illuminated only by the dim yellow lamps in each specimen compartment. Its air is full of the recorded blips and warbles of nocturnal insects or birds. Groups of people come and go preoccupiedly in front of the animals; pause silhouetted on the edge of vision; vanish murmuring round an unexpected corner. It is quite crowded: attracted immediately by the most beautiful miniature fox with creamy beige fur, soft thick tail and enormous ears, Sophia finds herself standing next to a young man.

'Isn't it lovely?' she exclaims, for something to say.

But he seems less interested in the fox than its compartment, in which has been reconstructed – with a bit of stone, brushwood, and the skull of a camel embedded in fine sand – a dreary little corner of some desert. The fox trots so intelligently about this lost or reduced territory! You can feel its warmth and liveliness even when it curls up and goes to sleep. At first Sophia is delighted like this by every animal she sees – lemurs, echidnae like soft toys, civet cats and desert mice. But soon the air feels too warm. It smells increasingly like sawdust and urine. The animals, she notices suddenly, often move in agitated, repetitive patterns behind the smeary, finger-printed glass. A child, laughing shrilly, makes claws of its hands and runs up and down in front of a puzzled cat.

On her way out, Sophia has to pass the young man.

'Still looking?' she calls, but he doesn't seem to hear. In the feeble light from the compartment she can see how tight he grips the plastic rail; how drawn his face is, how wide and tired his eyes. He takes out a notebook and begins to write intently in it. He is copying down the details of the animal, which are recorded on a small plaque.

6: In Omber Grove

Whatever else it may be, *EON HEART* is the record of a journey, made some time during the last fifty or sixty years, into one of the less-travelled countries of the world. And often a plain record, too:

'For four miles round the bay at Enchidoche,' the author tells his readers, 'where the deeper water runs inshore, will be found meat-packing plants and sheds which, until recently, were used for drying fish.' He includes specific sailing instructions – 'Half a mile from Tharasalla Point, sandbars and wrecks show themselves at half tide. We went in boldly and got ten feet of clearance at low water. Keep Mutton Rock in line with the derelict flensing factory on Auxilliadora Island and it will take you clear of the sand' – though they are not for major ports; and clear sketches in pen and ink of items of special interest:

'A diadem of yellow and blue macaw feathers, with the Clan Sign.'

Yet this country is never referred to by name. And if, in its original condition, Peter Ebert's copy contained a map, it has been lost with the title pages. The surviving text, a description of the interior, speaks only of villages, minor towns and rivers too small for any atlas to record. The kinds of clues it might offer are obscured by the author's style:

Exploration, anthropology, natural history. Metaphysics, poetry and fear. A travel book should be about all these. But then it must whirl itself away beyond them; and, at once runaway boat and racing current, plunge between the dark walls of its own silence until it becomes only a spume of visions and metaphors – so that its reader, gripped by the vertigo of new experiences, is compelled to close it suddenly and walk away in an attempt to control his own excitement. In short, it must address our *desire*.

– or lost among the partly torn pages, stains and defacings, of which Ebert has now compiled a list so exhaustive it defeats any use he might make of it. 'p43: two words of text heavily deleted in red ballpoint pen, and another word – perhaps "fugazi" – inserted above.' 'p53/9 missing.' 'p60 detached, folded in half, and reinserted between pp75/6. Scrawled across it in black marker pen the words, "Mary I can't believe this. See you at ten." This unsigned, and the ink has deeply penetrated the paper.'

Peter no longer eats out in the evenings. He has exchanged his room at the Midland Hotel for a cheaper one in a boarding house a short way out of the city centre. From his window he can now see: a short stretch of cracked, littered pavement (Omber Grove), curving away to a junction (with Quex Road); a unisex hairdresser's called *Nueva Swing*; and a newsagent owned by an old man with the acronym FUGA tattooed on the inside of his left wrist. Though Peter still wears the expensive, generously cut suits and striped shirts you would expect to see at the Doric Restaurant, he no longer shaves every day and even forgets to wash. Obsessed by a puzzle his intelligence is unequal to, he has resigned from his job, and goes agitatedly from one lending library to another, from reference library to museum, looking for a complete copy of the book.

He has often wondered why it was given to him, speculating, 'It's not uncommon for a commuter to pass on, say, a newspaper he's finished with.' But when he reviews the circumstances of the gift – the crowd, the train, that white face with its shiny lumps of flesh – he understands that this is too simple an answer. His notebook describes a visit to the zoo, concluding disappointedly:

'After all, the Fennec is only a kind of fox.'

Every morning the pale light throws on to the wall of his room the shadow of a tree outside in Omber Grove. At first this image is so clear and sharp that Ebert can make out the patches of condensation on the window pane and construct the whole depth of the tree – its nearer branches sharp and black, the further ones less and less distinct. Later it fades until you have to work just to see it. Before it vanishes altogether it seems more like a product of the wall than of optics: as if, lighted by a very faint inner radiance, the wall has offered some memory of its own as a curio, as an almost random pattern. Someone pushes a pram down the street outside.

7: *The Truth Which Most Contradicts Itself*

Sophia often gets up late and walks about the city in her fur coat, watching the afternoon light die out of the residential streets. From the recreation grounds come the shouts and whistles, the tragic howls of some football game. At this time of year, with the sun setting at half past three behind a frieze of bare sycamores, the big red-brick houses round the parks have a comfortable November style: yew, holly and privet make their gardens mysterious, their lighted front rooms warm and inviting, as if Christmas had already come.

On the pavement one woman says to another:

'He's had no proper dinner then?'

'No, he's like a whitewashed wall. Eating chocolate all the time, well it's no good, is it? Just no good at all. All he thinks about is that CD.'

This reminds Sophia of Oslo. The phrase 'en koppe caffe og en koppe sjokolade' comes back to her very clearly.

'The morning we went to Toyen,' she thinks, 'to the Munchmuseet, we sat in an upstairs café. He looked into his cup and said in a lugubrious, Norwegian voice, "Nothing lasts forever!" and we laughed.'

Whenever she recalls something like this a shiver of excitement runs through her, itself an echo of the excitement she felt every moment in those days. 'Nothing lasts, especially a cup of chocolate!' He was so clever at mimicking himself. Her own cup, she remembers, was decorated with three thin horizontal lines: pink, maroon, pastel blue. 'They seemed so precise and yet so fragile against the bluish-white depths of the china. I was afraid to move the saucer in case they rippled and broke.' She felt the tendency of all things to quiver without warning and fall away from perfection. But as long as she left her coffee untouched, and the sun continued to pour in so brightly across the marble table-top, the world would remain fixed. It would maintain its exact edges.

At Oslo airport, waiting for the flight back, she bought a box of matches. On its label an attractive little landscape – a tree, some low hills, a lake – was silhouetted in black against an ochre ground. 'Bruks-Eske,' ran the legend. She had no idea what it meant. 'Hjelpestikker.' For a long time she kept it on the make-up table in 236. It was an impulse of love not so much for him, she recognised, as for Oslo itself: she never used the matches, but the box could make her think so suddenly of the view from Holmenkollen, or the seagulls in Pipervika harbour, that everything seemed to rush out of her and empty itself away like water.

'En koppe caffe og en koppe sjokolade: that's what we had.'

Though which of them gave the order to the waitress she is no longer sure. Weakened and tranquillised by these memories, Sophia stands in the middle of the pavement,

42

staring helplessly over some railings at a strip of grass strewn with fallen leaves where two dogs are running in opposite circles in the gathering dark. Then, wondering what people must think of her, she walks off quickly towards the city centre and goes into the first bar she finds.

'Black Heart rum, please.'

Leaving it two or three hours later, she wishes she could fly up into the trembling meniscus of light over the city. Some rain has fallen and the air is warmer. High up there are a few clouds like ribs. From above, she imagines, they must look like something drawn on a transparency between the aeroplane and the earth.

'I did think it would last forever,' she admits. 'I did think it would.'

8: Peter Ebert's Gift

Meanwhile Ebert lurches about the city, the EON HEART clutched to his chest, now in one hand, now in the other. The streets are glassed with rain, the long cotton coat he often wore to the Doric is sodden and filthy, his route has become as habitual as any dosser's. By seven or eight a.m. he's on the pavement outside the Midland Hotel where he used to live. He spends much of the morning at Regent's, shuffling his feet in the cold draughts under the great Victorian vault. At lunchtime he takes himself off to one or another of the city's little parks. He has stopped pretending that by this means he can 'understand' the book. Neither is he driven any longer by the urge to revisit, venue by venue, the stages of his own descent – the platform where he was given it, the libraries in which he searched for it, the rooms in which he copied it out. Instead he reads the book to himself for itself. Mid-afternoon finds him in the Natural History Museum, moving his lips over the words 'fly down mass' (p62) or returning to the most resistant passage of all:

After all why *should* our goal be the reinstatement of an illusory 'exact' relationship between events and words? If you probe in the ashes you will never learn anything about the fire: by the time the ashes can be handled the meaning has passed on. Every adventure is a cup so empty it can be drunk from again and again and again. Every adventure is so perfect it verges on silence. (p112)

His hair has gone grey.

Perhaps from all this reading, his eyes are inflamed, caked at the corners, deeper-set than he remembers. If he is ever frightened it is not when he smells his own breath in the morning. Or when in the mirror he sees a man twenty years older than the one who, in an unguarded moment a month or two ago, accepted a book just because it was offered him. These shocks soon pass. He slides them over his real fear, that he will begin to read the book aloud to passers-by. There are days when every park bench is a pulpit. He feels himself begin to speak. If he did, how could he bear their contempt?

Regent's Station, 4.30: commuters prowl uneasily beneath its scrolled iron girders in the bitter cold. The arrivals board makes a fluttering, disappointed noise and a train is wiped off as they watch. In his turn, Ebert watches them, looking for the one he could talk to; makes off, limping, just in time. He has the intolerable sense of being at a locus, where something is struggling to be revealed.

'I –'

Every adventure verges on silence.

Trapped by the rhetoric of the *EON HEART* he sees how impossible it will be to say anything ever again, and by nightfall finds himself standing on an obscure corner in the pool of light outside the *New Venus* dry cleaner's. Across the road a few market stalls are closing down for the night. There is a smell of rain, leather, soapsuds, food; in a gust of wind the plastic over the stalls shifts uneasily; a tortoiseshell cat is staring intently down a drain. Inside the *New Venus* a woman in a fur coat is arguing with the proprietor.

'What colour were the trousers?'

'There weren't any trousers,' she repeats tiredly.

Ebert sees a tall untidy woman with brown hair and wide shoulders, whose age is hard to guess because her face is turned away from him. Beneath the bulky fur, which is itself in need of a clean, her body has heavy, relaxed qualities, as if she has always been comfortable with it. Her shoes are scuffed, black suede peeling off to reveal the plastic heel; and wet pavements have left little pale splashes of mud on her stockings. In one hand she holds a pair of gloves, in the other a carrier bag printed with the name of a well known off-licence.

'Ah,' says the proprietor, an elderly Asian. '*No* trousers.'

He takes her ticket and stares at it for some moments.

'One white shirt. Two pullovers. A blue dress,' she reminds him. 'You said I could have them before six.' But the proprietor can find none of these garments on the rack behind the counter. Instead he keeps offering her quite different ones.

'This?'

'No.'

'This?'

Making a gesture of disgust she walks quickly to the door. Ebert, who has been following their exchange as if it represented some warm real world from which he is now endlessly separated by the existence of the book, turns guiltily away from the window. He hears the door of the *New Venus* swing open. In a gust of heated, solvent-laden air she crosses the road. Heels click, bottles clink. Before he can stop himself Ebert has pushed his way between the market stalls and is hurrying after her. Bare electric bulbs illuminate his face, her retreating back. Spoiled vegetables slither under their feet. He hears himself call out.

'Wait! I was given a book!' And then, managing at last to touch her arm shyly, 'Please let me read you this –'

Horrified by his fatal loss of self-control, and hallucinating in his anxiety to escape before he can add anything more, a strong smell of rum, Ebert dodges away from her and runs blindly into a brick wall.

9: *The Hearts of Things*

'All at once you can't make head or tail of anything, can you?'

Tonight Sophia is with a man whose name she doesn't know. This has happened before, if not often. When they got back to the Central Hotel the bar was still open.

'Would you like a drink?'

'It's kind of you,' he said. 'No.'

He was so preoccupied she found it easy to keep her face turned away from him. While she collected her room key he sat on the edge of a chair in the foyer, staring down between his shoes at the design in the carpet as though he were trying to see past it. Every time the door opened, a cold draught came into the foyer and he looked up suddenly. He was thinner than she'd thought, and his coat was ruined.

'I hope you didn't hurt yourself too much,' she apologised. 'I thought you were the man from the dry cleaner's. I was so angry with him!'

'It's a relief to talk to someone,' he said obscurely.

'Didn't I once see you at the zoo?'

He passed his hand puzzledly across his face.

Now they are up in 236, with the door a little open so that the room is filled with a brown light. She has helped him off with his coat. He doesn't say much, but sits there on the bed, leaning forward with his hands between his knees. She likes his face, which though young is so tired it seems all bone, stubble, grey eyes; which is incapable of taking shelter; which admits desire but never alleviation. She wants to touch it gently round the eyes and cheeks, and at the same time say, 'You can just sleep if that's what you'd like. I mean, we don't have to do anything at first.' She can imagine herself saying just those words: 'I mean.' Then a couple go past in the corridor outside, talking and laughing quietly. At this a shiver runs through him and he pulls away from her.

'All at once you can't make head or tail of anything –'

Out of the pocket of his coat comes an old book; and before she has time to realise what he is going to do, he has reached out and switched on the bedside light –

– To Peter Ebert the lamp seems brighter than it can possibly be, a kind of lightning flash that splits the air diagonally between them to reveal the appalling rose-coloured map which obscures her face.

He recalls the words, 'Instants of self-awareness too confused to be of any use.'

The book has become agitated in his hands, leafing through its own pages with increasing hysteria until they flicker and blur like destinations on the 'departures' board at Regent's Station. In slow motion Sophia averts her face from the light, turning her head to the left and dropping it forward and down so that her chin will be tucked protectively into the hollow of the clavicle on that side. Before she can complete this characteristic passive gesture, it seems to Ebert that the EON HEART has left his hands and embedded itself in her face. As it is sucked away, a white arc hangs fluorescing in its wake, overlapping images of an open book fossilised in the very air of the room.

Sophia opens to it like a flower –

– Every story is so perfect it verges on silence: in this moment none of us can ever be sure whether the map receives the book or is received by it. The light flares up, room 236 is filled with the strange, carrying, bird-like cry of the lar gibbons, while a voice repeats endlessly: 'It's lovely. It's so lovely –'

– It isn't a dream. The book lies on the bed, its accumulated defacements glowing like stigmata. With the light dying out of the air between them, Peter and Sophia are flung apart. They will find one another again confidently enough. She will be surprised by the heat of his skin and whisper, 'I only felt the slightest touch.' The way the hollow of her back curves up out of the waistband of her slip will make her seem astonishingly real and human to him. Just before dawn there will steal over the 'entresol' floor of the Central Hotel that silence which enfolds lovers and lovers' cries and is only deepened by them.

Aware of it pressing upon them its padded warmth, they will go to the window of 236 and smile out at the city – five miles of coloured neon where the jungle comes down to the sea, buildings like elegant black and gold cigarette packets standing on end, music from the amusement arcades trailing out like lights across the water: the smell of Black Heart rum and the scent of Anaïs-Anaïs in the streets.

Sophia will sit before the mirror in the morning, while Peter reads (already planning how to pass the book on, in some jazz bar or pizzeria) and then scribbles on the fly-leaf, just under the title in that intense, endlessly expectant white space –

Take me aside. Tell me a sign.
Send me a neon heart. Seek me inside.

1988

I Did It

YOU KNOW HOW IT IS. Chelsea lose two-nil at home to Portsmouth, and you want to go home and bury an axe in your face. You want to do it, there and then, bury it in your face. You tell your friends, they never believe you. Normally, you'd think twice. What sort of sound would it make? That puts you off. But this time, 'Two-nil,' you think. 'Christ, that's it, I'm doing it. This time I really am. Chunk. Axe in the face.'

It's easily done. Some people do that and it isn't even football.

Alex did it.

Alex did it and then phoned Nicola.

He said: 'I did it. I said I would, and I have.'

'Is that you, Alex?' she said.

'Don't you even recognise my voice any more?'

'I haven't got time for this,' she said.

She rang off.

Alex rang back. He said: 'You never believed I'd do it.'

'Wrong, Alex,' she said. 'I wished you would.'

'I'm coming to see you.'

'No you're not.'

'I'm coming for lunch,' he said. 'One o'clock.'

He got himself into the Audi and drove from Islington to Soho, where he waited outside her building. There was a sweet April wind. Alex breathed it deeply, feeling nothing he had expected to, only a delighted tranquillity. He did notice that he had quite an appetite. When Nicola came out of the building she stopped and stared at him.

'Still as beautiful as ever,' said Alex, though privately he thought she had put on weight.

'Christ, Alex, you sick fuck.'

'Good, isn't it?' said Alex. 'I hit myself in the face with it until it stuck. It was quite hard to do that.'

'Christ.'

'I had to use a mirror. I kept swinging it in the wrong direction.' He laughed rather wildly. 'And they call it the easy way out!'

'Well I'm not coming to lunch with you like that,' she said.

Later, Alex saw her in a West London restaurant with Chris. They looked happy. Alex, who was less happy, had to turn his face sideways before he could press it up against the glass. Nicola and Chris, he saw, were eating respectively a layered sandwich of hand-rolled buffalo mozzarella with chargrilled vegetables; and bruschetta of seared baby squid. They were drinking red, but Alex couldn't make out the label. It was probably house red. Chris wiped his mouth on a napkin. He smiled. He leaned forward to lightly touch the inside of Nicola's arm above the wrist. Alex waited until they came out of the restaurant and then jumped in front of Nicola waving his arms.

'Like it? It's your *fault*.'

'It's a very female thing,' Nicola was explaining to Chris, 'like giving birth with wolves.'

She said: 'Alex, I'm not having this.'

Chris looked embarrassed.

'Lost your tongue, Chris?' Alex asked him. 'I've lost mine.'

Alex wasn't one hundred per cent certain Chris's name was Chris. Everyone who lived in West London was called Chris, and that was the name he thought he remembered: but he did admit it could easily have been Sam, or Ben. He phoned Nicola up at one o'clock in the morning. 'Chris there with you?'

'Alex, leave me alone.'

'Is it Chris? I had the idea it might be Sam.'

'Alex, I'm getting an injunction.'

'I've had some photographs taken,' Alex said. 'Give one to Chris. It's his fault too.'

'Alex –'

'Is it Chris? They all have the kinds of names you give Border collies. Sam. Mick. Bill. Ben.'

'– for God's sake leave me alone.'

Alex said: 'Bill and Ben, eh?'

He said: 'I did it for you, Nicola.' And he burst into tears.

Nicola did it next.

'You'll be pleased to know I've done it too,' she said. 'You made me, Alex. Chris couldn't bear you following us about.' It was her turn to burst into tears. 'Alex, he left me for some scrawny little twenty-year-old, and it's your fault. How does that make you feel, Alex?'

It made Alex feel annoyed.

'You've got no imagination of your own,' he said. 'Women never have.'

Nicola laughed nastily. 'I'm coming round to show you, Alex.'

'Show Chris,' said Alex, and hung up.

People all over London are walking about with axes buried in their faces. You see them on tubes and buses, you never know why they did it. It might be that their whole family died in a nuclear incident on a visit to Poland. But it's more likely that they have recently been stood up, or that last night they had to talk to Yuri the comics expert at the Academy Club:

'Nobody would ban *Lady Chatterley's Lover* these days. They just don't have time to read it. Visual images are a different thing.'

Chunk. Axe in the face.

*

The moment Nicola started following Chris, Alex stopped following Nicola.

It happened this way:

One morning he woke with a terrific headache. In the bathroom he was surprised by the thought: Is it a good axe? He also thought: Is an axe too much of a statement? Finally he thought: I'm not sure I ever liked this anyway. He examined his face, turning it right and then left, careful to stand back from the mirror. The axe was off-centre, and twisted a bit where it had bounced off his top gum. That had always spoilt it for him, as had the effect it gave of a harelip. He shaved round the axe and looked at it again.

'No. No good.'

Midday, he phoned Nicola.

'I've had it out,' he said.

'Why should I care?'

'They have to lever quite hard,' Alex told her, 'when they're loosening it. It's a very male, a very physical experience. How would I describe it?'

'I didn't ask.'

Alex thought for a minute.

'It's a bit like having your wisdom tooth done,' he explained. 'You know?'

He said: 'Now it's out, I feel great!'

Nicola put the phone down.

Chris told Nicola, as kindly as he could:

'Nicola, you need counselling.'

The very next time she phoned him, he hung up, although not before she had heard her replacement in the background, calling:

'Chris, is that the Mad Bitch? Come and fuck me afterwards! Chris? Chris?'

She phoned Alex.

'Alex, I'm so miserable.'

'Get a life,' advised Alex.

He said: 'I have.'

That was the low point, they now agree. Shortly afterwards they were accepted for joint counselling at Islington Relate. As soon as they felt able to talk over their differences without the help of a third party, they arranged to meet in the Bar Italia on Frith Street. It was a Saturday evening at the beginning of September. Nicola wore her long silver one-sleeved dress from Amanda Wakeley on Fulham Road, and carried an Anya Hindmarch bag with a diamante clasp. She was a little late. She found Alex watching Italian football on the Bar Italia TV: Juventus v AC Milan.

'Aren't you cold in that?' he asked Nicola. He said: 'You look very nice.'

The counselling service had persuaded Nicola to have her axe out. She felt a little nervous, a little exposed, without it; and she was shocked and upset to see that Alex's was back. He had planted it squarely in the middle of his face. This time he had thought about it properly and gone for a good practical Stanley with a black rubber grip. He looked tired.

'Alex! *Who is it?*'

'What?'

'Alex, *that!*'

'This? Oh, this is just Manchester United losing to City,' laughed Alex. 'I'll get over it.'

1996

Running Down

LYALL WAS NEVER MORE than an acquaintance of mine even at Cambridge, where we shared a room and might have been described as 'close'; in fact, there were times when we found it difficult to disguise our dislike for one another. Nevertheless, we clung together, embittered and hurt – neither of us could make any warm contact with our contemporaries. To be honest: no one else would put up with us, so we put up with each other. It's common enough. Even now, Cambridge is all comfortable November mists, nostalgic ancient quadrangles, the conspiracy of the choir practising at King's – pure, ecstatic and a constant wound to the outsider. It was inevitable that Lyall and I should press those wounds together to achieve some sort of sour blood-fraternity. I suppose that's hard to understand; but it must be a common enough human compulsion.

Lyall was tall and ectomorphic, with a manner already measured, academic, middle-aged. His face was long and equine, its watery eyes, pursed mouth and raw cheeks accusatory, as if he blamed the world outside for his own desperate awkwardness. He did: and affected a callow but remorseless cynicism to cover it. He was a brilliant student, but comically accident-prone – constantly scratched and bruised, his clothes stained with oil and ink and food. His background (he had been brought up by two impoverished, determined maiden ladies in Bath) chafed the tender flesh of my own early experience under the bleak shadow of the southern end of the Pennines – the open-coffin funerals of a failing industrial town, a savage unemployment, Methodism.

We must have made a strange pair in those endless winter fogs: Lyall as thin as a stick, hopeless in the tweed jacket and college scarf his aunts insisted he wear, his inflamed nose always running, his wrists and ankles protruding dismally from the awful clothes; and myself, short of leg, barrel-chested and heavily muscled about the shoulders and ridiculous long arms for the solitary climbing and fell-walking that had in adolescence become my passionate escape from the back-terraces of the North. In those days, before the Dru accident, I could do a hundred press-ups with a fifty-pound pack on my back. I was sullen, dark, aggressive, and so terrified of being nicknamed 'Ape' by the fragile, intellectual young women of the modern languages faculty that no one but Lyall ever had the miserable chance. God knows why we do these things to ourselves.

So: it was a temporary alliance. I have memories of Lyall's high, complaining voice, his ruthless wit and feral disappointment as we separated on the last day of the last term. He took a poor Honours, due to an unfortunate bicycle accident a week before Finals: but mine was poorer (although somewhat ameliorated by the offer of a junior instructorship I'd received from an Outward Bound school in Kenya). His handclasp was curt, mine cursory. We were both faintly relieved, I think.

We never sought each other out. I believe he tried several jobs in the provinces before becoming the junior personnel officer of a small manufacturing firm in London, which was where I met him again, quite by chance, some two or three years later.

A week off the boat from North Africa – and finding it almost as difficult to adapt to the dirty chill of late autumn in the city as to accept bacon at a hundred pence a pound after Kenya's steak at twenty-five the kilo – I was wandering rather morosely about in the West End, wondering if I could afford to go into a cinema and waste another evening, when I spotted him teetering at a kerb trying to hail a taxi. Two ignored him while I watched. He hadn't changed much: his ghastly college scarf was now tucked into the neck of a thin raincoat, and he was carrying one of those wretched little plastic 'executive' cases. The contemptuous grooves round his mouth had deepened.

'Oh, hallo, Egerton,' he said off-handedly, staring away from me down the road. He looked drunk. One of his hands was inexpertly bandaged with a great wad of dirty white gauze. He fiddled with his case. 'Why on earth did *you* come back to this rat-hole? I'd have thought you were better off out of it.'

I felt like a deserter returning to some doomed ship only to find its captain still alive and brooding alone over the white water and foul ground: but I was surprised to be remembered at all, and, when he finally captured his taxi, I agreed to go home with him.

It turned out that he'd been in another taxi when it became involved in some minor fracas with a pedestrian, and had to get out. 'I should have been home bloody hours ago,' he said sourly. That was all: and by the time we reached his flat I was beginning to regret an impulse which had basically been one of sympathy. There was an argument with the driver, too, over a malfunctioning meter. It was always like that with Lyall. But Holloway isn't Cambridge.

He had two poky, unwelcoming rooms at the top of a large furnished house. The place had a sink, a filthy gas-stove and some carpets glazed with ancient grease: it was littered with dirty crocks, empty milk bottles, every kind of rubbish conceivable; everything in it seemed to be damaged and old; it was indescribably cheerless.

When I declined the offer of a can of soup (partly because he was at pains to let me see he had nothing else in the cupboard where he kept his food, and partly out of horror at that mephitic stove) he shrugged ungraciously, sat cross-legged on the floor among the old newspapers and political pamphlets – he seemed to have become interested in some popular nationalist organisation, to the extent anyway of scrawling 'Rubbish!' or 'A reasonable assumption' in the margins of some of the stuff – and ate it ravenously straight out of the pan. He was preoccupied by some slight he'd received at work. 'Bloody jumped-up filing clerks,' he explained, 'every one of them. You'd better sit on the bed, Egerton. There's nothing else, so you needn't bother to look for it.'

Later, he insisted on going out to an off-licence and fetching back some half-pint bottles of stout. This produced a parody of fellowship, strung with gaunt silences. We really had nothing in common anymore, especially since Lyall would mention Cambridge only in the cryptic, barbed asides of which he was so fond.

But he seemed determined; and I took it as a desperate attempt on his part to achieve some sort of contact, some sort of human feeling among all that cold squalor. His loneliness was apparent – in deference to it, I talked; and I was quite happy to fall in with his mood until I realised that he had adopted a most curious conversational procedure.

This consisted in first eliciting from me some reminiscence of my time in Africa, then blatantly ignoring me as I talked – flicking through the pages of a girlie magazine, picking up books only to toss them aside again, staring out of the un-curtained windows at the ominous pall of sodium light outside; even whistling or humming. He took to breaking in on my anecdotes to say, apropos of nothing, 'I really ought to have that scarf cleaned,' or, 'What's that racket in the street? Damned lunatics,' and then when (perfectly relieved to escape from what had become an agonizing monologue) I made some answering remark about the London air or traffic, demanding:

'What? Oh, go on, go on, you mustn't pay me any attention.'

I talked desperately. I found myself becoming more and more determined to overcome his scarcely-veiled sneers and capture his attention, inventing at one point an adventure on Mount Nyiru that I simply hadn't had – although it did happen to a fellow instructor of mine shortly after his arrival at the school.

It was an eerie experience. What satisfaction he could have had from it, I can't imagine.

'Fairly pleased with yourself then, are you?' he said suddenly. He went on to repeat it to himself, rocking to and fro. 'Fairly pleased –' And he laughed.

In the end, I got up and made some excuse, a train, a matter of a hotel key: what else could I have done?

He leapt immediately to his feet, the most ludicrous expression of regret on his face. 'Wait, Egerton!' he said. He glanced desperately round the room. 'Look here,' he said, 'you can't go without finishing the last bottle, can you?' I shrugged. 'I'll only chuck it out. I'll just –' He lurched about, kicking up drifts of rubbish. He hadn't taken that flimsy raincoat off all night. 'I can't seem –'

'Let me.' And I took the bottle away from him.

I bought my knife at Frank Davies' in Ambleside, more than twenty years ago. Among its extensible, obsessive gadgets is a thing like a claw, for levering off the caps of bottles. I'd used it a thousand times before that night; more. I latched it on to the cap with my right hand, holding the neck of the bottle with my left. An odd thing happened. The cap resisted; I pulled hard; the bottle broke in my hand, producing a murderous fork of brown glass.

Beer welled up over a deep and painful gash between my thumb and forefinger, pink and frothy. I stared at it. 'Christ.'

But if the accident was odd, Lyall's reaction was odder.

He groaned. Then he began to laugh. I sucked at the wound, staring helplessly at him over my hand. He turned away, fell on his knees in front of his bed and beat his hands on it. 'Bugger off, Egerton!' he croaked. His laughter turned suddenly into great heaving sobs. 'Get out of my sight!' I stood looking stupidly down at him for a moment, at the thin shoulders crawling beneath that dirty raincoat, the miserable drift of *Guardian*s and girlie magazines and Patriotic Front literature: then turned and stumbled down the stairs like a blind man.

It wasn't until I'd slammed the outside door that the full realisation of what had happened hit me. I sat down for a minute among the dented bins and rotting planks of the concrete area, shivering in what I suppose must have been shock. I remember trying to read what was daubed on the door. Then an upstairs window was flung open, and I could hear him again, half laughing, half sobbing. I got up and went down the street; he leant out of the window and shouted after me.

I was terrified that he might follow me, to some lighted, crowded tube station, still laughing and shouting. He'd been expecting that accident all evening; he'd been waiting all evening for it.

For a couple of weeks after that, a thin, surly ghost, he haunted me through the city. I kept imagining him on escalators, staring bitterly through the dirty glass at the breasts of the girls trapped in the advertisement cases; a question mark made of cynical and lonely ectoplasm.

Why he chose to live in squalor; why he had shouted 'You aren't the first, Egerton, and you won't be the bloody last!' as I fled past the broken milk machines and dreary frontages of his street; how he – or anyone – could have predicted the incident of the last bottle: all questions I never expected to have answered, since I intended to avoid him like the plague if I ever caught sight of him again. I had four stitches put in my hand.

Then the Chamonix climbing school post I had been waiting for came free, and I forgot him in the subsequent rush of preparation.

He stayed forgotten during a decade which ended for me – along with a lot of other things – on a stiffish overhang some way up the Dru, in a wind I can still feel on sleepless nights, like a razor at the bone.

When I left Chamonix I could still walk (many can't after the amputation of a great toe), but I left counting only losses. The English were just then becoming unpopular on the Continent – but I returned to Britain more out of the lairing instinct of a hurt animal than as a response to some fairly good-humoured jostling outside Snell's sports shop. I simply couldn't stand to be in the same country as the Alps.

At home, I took a job in the English department of a crowded comprehensive school in Wandsworth; hobbled round classrooms for a year or so, no more bored than the children who had to sit day after day in front of me; while on Saturday mornings I received, at the Hampstead hospital, treatment for the lingering effect of the frost-bite on my fingers and remaining toes.

I found quickly that walking returned to me something of what I'd lost to a bit of frayed webbing and a twelve-hour Alpine night. During the long vacations that are the sole reward of the indifferent teacher, I rediscovered the Pennines, the Grampians, Snowdonia – and found that while Capel Curig and Sergeant Man are no substitute for the Aiguille Verte group, I could at least recapture something of what I'd felt there in my Cambridge days and before. I walked alone, despite the lesson of the Dru (which I am still paying for in a more literal way: French mountain rescue is efficient, but it can cost you twenty years of whatever sort of life you have left to you; up there, many people pray *not* to be taken off the mountain); and I discouraged that obsessive desire to converse which seems to afflict hikers.

It was on one of these holidays that I heard next from Lyall.

I was staying in the 'Three Peaks' district north and west of Settle, and beginning to find its long impressionistic sweeps of moorland arduous and unrewarding. Lyall's letter caught up with me after a day spent stumping half-heartedly over Scales Moor in the kind of morose warm drizzle only Yorkshire can produce. I was sufficiently browned-off on returning, I recall, to assassinate a perfectly good pair of boots by leaving them too long on top of Mrs. Bailey's kitchen stove.

So the surge of sentiment which took hold of me when I recognised Lyall's miserly handwriting may be put down to this: I was soaked to the skin, and receptive.

The letter had been forwarded from Chamonix (which led me to wonder if he'd been as drunk as he seemed on the night of the accident – or as indifferent), and again from my digs in Wandsworth: a round trip of absurd length for something which bore a Westmorland postmark. That in itself was curious; but it was the contents that kept me some time from my shepherd's pie.

It seemed that Lyall's maiden ladies had finally succumbed, within two months of one another and despite all that Bath could do, to the inroads of heart-disease; leaving him – 'Almost as an afterthought,' as he described it, 'among two reams of sound advice –' a property in the Langdale Valley. He had nothing good to say of the place, but was 'hard up' and couldn't afford to sell it. He had 'funked' his personnel officership in London because the place had begun to 'stink of appeasement'–

an apparently political comment I couldn't unravel, although by now, like all of us, I knew a little more about the aims of the Patriotic Front. He had married: this, I found almost incredible.

He suggested with a sort of contemptuous bonhomie that if I was 'tired of grubbing about on the Continental muckheap', I might do an old friend the favour of dropping by to see him.

There was something else there; he was his usual mixture of cold formality and old colloquialisms; 'It's not much to ask' and 'Please yourself of course' were there; but underneath it all I sensed again the desperation I had witnessed in that squalid flat twelve or thirteen years before – a horrified sense of his own condition, like a sick man with a mirror. And his last sentence was in the form of an admission he had, I'm quite sure, never in his life made before:

'Since you seem to like that sort of mucking about,' he finished, 'I thought we might walk up some of those precious hills of yours together. It's what I need to cheer me up.'

That, tempered no doubt by a twin curiosity as to the nature of his inheritance and the temperament of his unnamed wife, decided me. I packed my rucksack that night, and in the morning left Mrs. Bailey's inestimable boarding house to its long contemplation of Ingleborough Common. Why I was so quick to respond to him, I don't know; and if I'd suspected one half of the events that were to follow my decision, I would have been content with any amount of rain, moss and moorland.

Ingleborough Hill itself is a snare and a delusion, since a full third of its imposing height is attained by way of an endless gentle slope bare of interest and a punishment to the ankles: but that morning it thrust up into the weather like a warning – three hundred million years of geological time lost without trace in the unconformity between its base and its flat summit, from which the spectre of the brigand Celt chuckles down at that of his bemused, drenched Roman foe.

The Ambleside bus was empty but for a few peaky, pinch-faced children in darned pullovers and cracked shoes. Their eyes were large and austere and dignified, but for all that they taunted the driver unmercifully until they spilled out to ravage the self-involved streets of Kendal, leaving him to remark, 'It don't bother the kids, though, does it?' It didn't seem to bother him much, either. He was a city man, he went on to explain, and you had to admit that things were easier out here.

In the thirty or so miles that separate Ingleton from Ambleside, geomorphology takes hold of the landscape and gives it a cruel wrench; and the moorland – where a five-hour walk may mean, if you are lucky, a vertical gain of a few hundred feet – gives way to a mass of threatening peaks among which for his effort a man may rise two thousand feet in half a mile of forward travel. If I saw the crowding, the steepness, of those hills as Alpine, it may be that the memory dulls in proportion to the wound's ripening, no more.

The weather, too, is prone to startling mutation in that journey between Yorkshire and Westmorland, and I found the Langdales stuporous under a heatwave of a week's standing (it works, as often as not, the other way round). Ambleside was lifeless. Being too early for the valley bus, and tiring finally of Frank Davies' display window, I decided to walk to Lyall's 'property'.

Heat vibrated from the greenstone walls of the new cottages at Skelwith Bridge, and the Force was muted. A peculiar diffused light hung over the fellsides, browning the haunted fern; Elterwater and Chapel were quiet, deserted; the sky was like brass. I had some conversation with a hard-eyed pony in the paddock by the Co-op forecourt when I stopped to drink a can of mineral water; but none with the proprietor, who was languid even among the cool of his breakfast cereals and string.

Outside Chapel I took to the shade of the trees and discovered a dead hare, the flies quite silent and enervated as they crawled over its face; a little further on, in the dark well of shadow at the base of the drystone, a motionless adder, eyeless and dried up. The valley had undergone some deterioration in the fifteen years since I had last seen it: shortly after I got my first sight of the Bowfell crags and Mickleden (the Rosset Gill path a trembling vertical scar in the haze), I came upon the rusting corpse of a motor car that had run off the difficult narrow road and into the beck.

Here and there, drystone scattered in similar incidents simply lay in the pasture, white clumps infested by nettles, like heaps of skulls; and when I came finally to the address Lyall had given me, I found the fellside below Raw Pike blackened up to the five hundred foot line by fire. I didn't know then what I began to suspect later; I saw it all in terms of the children on the Ambleside bus, the price of bacon in Wandsworth – symptomatic of another kind of disorder.

And none of it prepared me for Lyall's 'property', a low, shambling affair of local stone, facing directly on to the road; the main cottage having two rooms on each floor, and a couple of ancillary buildings leaning up against it as if they would prefer not to but had no choice.

It was amazingly dilapidated. Much of the glass at the front had been replaced by inaccurately cut oblongs of hardboard; something seemed to have been spilt out of one of the upper windows to dry as an unpleasant brown smear on the stone. The barn roofs sagged, and wanted slates. Uncovered rafters are an agony and here crude patches of corrugated iron did little to mitigate it. One corner of the cottage had been battered repeatedly by confused motorists returning at night from the pubs of Ambleside to the National Trust campsite at the head of the valley; the same fire that had wasted the fern on the slope above had charred and cracked it; small stones and mortar made a litter of the road.

I untied the binder twine that fastened the gate and wandered round, knocking shyly on doors and calling out. The valley, bludgeoned into stillness by the sun, gave back lethargic echoes.

Road-walking tires my mutilated foot quite quickly. I keep a stick clipped to my pack where an ice axe would normally go, and try to have as little recourse to it as possible: the first two miles had forced it in me that day. I knocked down a few nettles with it, watched the sap evaporate. Two or three minute figures were working their way slowly down the Band, heat and light resonating ecstatically from the 2,900-foot contour behind them. I sat on an upturned water trough, blinking, and cursing Lyall for his absence.

I'd been there for perhaps a quarter of an hour, wondering if I could hear the valley bus, when he came out of the house, swirling dirty water round an enamel bowl.

'Good God!' he exclaimed sarcastically, and the stuff in the bowl slopped down the front of his trousers. 'The famous Alpinist deigns to visit.' He shot the water carelessly into the nettles. 'Why the hell didn't you knock, Egerton? Shy?' I had the impression that he'd been watching me ever since I arrived. It wouldn't have been beyond him.

'You'd better come in,' he said, staring off into the distance, 'now you're here.'

The intervening years had made him a parody of himself – lined and raw, all bone and raging, unconscious self-concern; he'd developed a stoop, a 'dowager's hump', during his London days; a small burn on his neck seemed to be giving him trouble, and he kept his head at a constant slight angle to ease the inflammation caused by his collar. He remembered I was there, nodded at my stick. An old cruelty heliographed out like the light from the peaks.

'Your fine mountaineering cronies won't be so interested in you now, then? Not that I'd have thought that thing stopped you buying their beer.'

It may have been true. I honestly hadn't thought of it until then. 'I've learnt to live with it,' I said, as lightly as I could.

He paused in the doorway – Lyall always walked ahead – and looked me up and down. 'You don't know the half of it, Egerton,' he said. 'You never will.' Then, sharply: 'Are you coming in, or not?' The crags of Bowfell broadcast their heat across Mickleden, and the Pikes gave it back like a thin, high song of triumph.

What the outer dilapidation of the cottage led me to expect, I don't know: but it was nothing to what I found inside; and despite all that has happened since it still unnerves me to think of that place.

Plaster had fallen from the ceiling of the grim cubby-hole of a kitchen, and still lay on the cracked tile floor; an atrocious wallpaper meant to represent blond Swedish panelling, put up by the maiden ladies or one of their tenants in an attempt to modernise, bellied slackly off the walls. In the living room there was only plaster, and one wall had actually fissured enough to admit a thin, wandering line of sunlight – just as well, since the windows let in very little. Across this tenuous wafer of illumination, motes danced madly; and the place stank.

All the furniture was scarred and loose-jointed. Everywhere, objects: table-lamps, ashtrays and paltry little ornaments of greenstone: and nothing whole. Everything he owned had become grubby and tired and used in a way that only time uses things, so that it looked as if it had been broken thirty years before: a litter of last month's paperbacked thrillers, spilling with broken spines and dull covers and an atmosphere of the second-hand shop from the bookcases; gramophone records underfoot, scratched and warped and covered in bits of dried food from the dinner plates, with their remains of week-old meals, scattered over the carpet.

It was as if some new shift of his personality, some radical escalation of his *morgue* and his bitterness, had coated everything about him with a grease of hopelessness and age. I was appalled; and he must have sensed it, because he grinned savagely and said:

'Don't twitch your nose like that, Egerton. Sit down, if you can find something that won't offend your lily-white bum.' But he must have regretted it almost immediately – making tea with an air of apology that was the nearest he ever came to the real thing, he admitted, 'I don't know what I'm doing in this hole. I don't seem to be any better off than I was.' He had got a job correcting publishers' proofs, but it gave him nothing, 'Not even much of a living.' While I drank my tea, he stared at the floor.

I got nothing but the weather from him for about half an hour. Then he said suddenly: 'I haven't seen – what was his name? – *Oxlade* – lately. You remember him. The guitarist.'

I was astonished. Probably the last time either of us had seen Oxlade was at Cambridge, just before he went down in the middle of his second year to sing with some sort of band; and then Lyall had loathed the man even more than the music, if that were possible.

I chuckled embarrassedly. All I could think of to say was, 'No. I suppose not.' This threw him into a temper.

'Christ, Egerton,' he complained, 'I'm doing my bit. You might join in. We've got little enough in common –'

'I'm sorry,' I began, 'I –'

'You've brought some bloody funny habits home with you, I must say.' He was silent again for a moment, hunched forward in his seat looking at something between his feet. He raised his eyes and said quietly: 'We're stuck with each other, Egerton. You need me again now. That's why you came crawling back here.' This with a dreadful flatness of tone.

I looked for my rucksack. 'There's a place where I can camp further up the valley,' I told him stiffly; perhaps because I suspected he was correct.

We were both on our feet when a large vehicle drew up in the road outside, darkening the room further and filling it with a smell of dust and diesel oil; airbrakes hissed. It was the valley bus, and down from it stepped Lyall's wife. Lyall, tensed in the gloom, seemed to shrug a little – we both welcomed the interruption. 'Look, Egerton –' he said.

He went to let her in.

She was a tall, haggard woman, ten or even fifteen years older than him and wearing a headscarf tied in a strangely dated fashion. Her legs were swollen, and one of them was bandaged below the knee. From under the headscarf escaped thin wisps of brownish hair, framing a quiet, passive face. They greeted one another disinterestedly; she nodded briefly at me, her lips a thin line, and went immediately into the kitchen, swaying a little as if suffering from the heat. She was carrying two huge shopping bags.

'You didn't tell me we'd run out of coffee,' she called. When she returned, it was to throw a couple of paperbacks on the floor in front of him. 'There weren't any papers,' she said. 'Only the local one.' She went upstairs, and I didn't see her again that day. Lyall hadn't introduced her, and I don't think he ever told me her name.

I didn't want to stay, but he insisted. 'Forget all that,' he said. Later, he opened some cans into a saucepan. While we ate, I stuck to Cambridge, the safe topic, and was glad to see his customary sense of the ridiculous steadily replacing the earnestness with which he'd introduced the subject of Oxlade. Afterwards, 'Let me do the washing up,' I offered: and so cleared enough floor space to unroll my sleeping bag. Nobody had unpacked the shopping; I couldn't coax more than a trickle from the kitchen taps. Lyall looked cynically on.

After he'd gone to bed, I heard them arguing in tight suppressed voices. The sound carried all over the house – hypnotic but meaningless. The darkness was stuffy and electrical, and I hadn't got rid of the smell.

They were up and sparring covertly over some domestic lapse before I got out of my sleeping bag the following morning – the woman throwing things round the sink, Lyall prowling restlessly out into the garden and back again. If my presence had acted as a brake the night before, it was clearly losing its effect; by the time breakfast was ready, they were nagging openly at one another over the eggs. I would have been more embarrassed if the argument had not been over who was to unpack yesterday's shopping.

'I emptied the bloody Elsan yesterday,' said Lyall defensively. 'You do the shopping, not me.'

'For God's sake who eats it?'

I drank some reconstituted orange juice and bent my head over my plate. The woman laughed a bit wildly and retreated into the kitchen. 'For God's sake who *eats* it?' mimicked Lyall, ignoring me. I heard her scraping something into the sink tidy. There was a sudden sharp intake of breath. A moment later she reappeared, holding up her left hand. Blood was trickling slowly down the wrist.

'I'm sorry,' she said desperately. 'I cut it on a tin-lid. I couldn't help it.'

'Oh, *Christ!*' shouted Lyall. He smashed his fist down on the table, jumped to his feet and stalked out.

She looked bemusedly after him. 'Where are you going?' she called.

The cut was a ragged lip running across the base of her thumb, shallow but unpleasant. Worried by the grey tinge to her sallow, ageing face, I made her sit down while I rummaged through the place looking for some sort of dressing. In the end, I had to raid my pack for a bit of plaster. When I got back to her she was slumped head-down on the table, her thin bony shoulders trembling. I saw to her hand, wishing Lyall would come back. While I was doing it, she said:

'You wonder why I stay here, don't you?'

The palm of her hand was cross-hatched with other, older scars. I might have been tempted to chuckle at the thought of these two sour accident-prones, trapped together in their crumbling backwater and taking miserable revenges on one another, if I hadn't had recollections of my own – chilly images of London in late autumn, the pall of sodium light outside Lyall's poky rooms, the last bottle of beer.

'Lyall's hard to live with,' I temporised. I didn't want her confidences, any more than I wanted his. 'At Cambridge –'

She took hold of my wrist and squeezed it with a queer fervour. 'It's because he needs someone.' I shrugged. She hung on. 'I love him, you know,' she said challengingly. I tried to free my wrist. 'So do you,' she pressed. 'You could be anywhere but here, but you're his best friend –'

'Look,' I said angrily, 'you're making this very difficult. Do you want your hand bandaged or not?' And when she simply stared: 'Lyall just invited me to stay here. We knew each other at Cambridge, that's all. Hasn't he told you that?'

She shook her head. 'No.' Colour had come back into her face. 'He needs help. I made him write to you. He thinks –' Her mouth thinned; she seemed to withdraw. 'Let him tell you himself.' She looked down at her hand. 'Thank you,' she said formally.

I spent the rest of the day sitting on the water trough, staring out across the valley at quite another range of hills and wondering who I'd meet if I went to one of the hotels for a drink. At about midday she came out of the house, squinting into the sunlight.

'I'm sorry about this morning,' she said. I muttered something, and drew her attention to a hawk of some kind hanging in the updraught over Raw Pike. She glanced at it impatiently. 'I don't know anything about birds. I was in social work.' She made a vague motion that took in the whole valley, the hot inverted bowl of the sky. 'Sometimes I blame this place, but it isn't that.' She had come out to say something else, but

I gave her no encouragement. Perhaps I should have done. 'Do you want any lunch?' she said.

Lyall returned with the valley bus.

'I suppose she's been talking to you,' he said. He avoided my eyes. A little bit disgusted by the whole thing, I walked up to the New Dungeon Ghyll and spent the evening drinking beer. The place was full of tourists who'd been running up and down Mill Gill all day in tennis shoes, making the rest of us look like old men. When I got back, Lyall and his wife were in bed, the eternal dull complaint rising and falling soporifically through the cottage. I was half asleep when the woman suddenly shouted:

'I'm twenty-five years old! *Twenty-five years!* What's happening? What's happened to me?'

After that, I got up and paced around until dawn, thinking.

Heat pumped down the valley from the secret fastnesses of Flat Crags, from the dry fall at Hell Ghyll; up in the high gullies, the rock sang with it. Further down, the hanging Langdale oakwoods were sapless, submissive – heat had them by the throat. A sense of imminence filled the unlovely living room of the Lyall cottage, reeked on the stairs, fingered out from the bedroom. Lyall took to staring for hours at the crack in the wall, hands clasped between his knees. His wife was quiet and tense. Her despairing cry in the dark still hung between them.

Into this strange stasis or prostration, like a low, insistent voice, a thousand small accidents introduced themselves: the insect bite, the hand slipping on the can-opener, a loss of balance on the stair – cuts, rashes, saucepans dropped, items lost or broken; a constant, ludicrous, nerve-wracking communication from the realm of random incidence. For half a day the kitchen taps refused to give water of any sort, then leaked a slow, rusty liquor even when turned off; four slates fell from the roof in an afternoon of motionless air;

Lyall's wife suddenly became allergic to the sun, and walked about disfigured.

Lyall's response to these events was divided equally between irritation and apathy. He brooded. Several times he took me aside as if to broach some mutually embarrassing subject, and on each occasion failed. I couldn't help him: the raging contempt of his Cambridge days, applied with as much rigour to his own motives as to those of others, was by now a memory. Out in one of the barns, cutting a piece of zinc to mend the roof, he said, 'Don't you ever regret your childhood, Egerton?'

I didn't think I did; I didn't think childhood meant much after a certain age. I had to shout this over the screech of the hacksaw. He watched my lips for a while, like a botanist with an interesting but fairly common specimen, then stopped working.

'In Bath, you know,' he said, brushing his lank hair off his face, 'it was all so clear-cut. A sort of model of the future, with neat sharp edges; English, Classics, Cambridge; and after that, God knows what – the Foreign Service, if the old dears had a thought in their heads.' He laughed bitterly. 'I had to play the piano.' He held up the hand with the dirty ball of bandage on the thumb. 'With this.' He looked disgusted for a moment, but when he turned away, his eyes were watering.

'I was really rather good at it.'

This picture of the young Lyall, shut in some faded Regency drawing room with a piano (his limbs protruding amazed and raw from the tubular worsted shorts and red blazer his maiden ladies would doubtless have insisted upon), was ludicrous enough. He compounded it by yearning, 'We never deserve the future, Egerton. They never tell us what it's going to be like.'

When I tried to laugh him out of it, he went angrily off with, 'You might show a bit of interest in someone else's problems. It'd take your mind off your precious bloody foot.'

He came back to the house late, with a half-empty bottle of brandy. God knows what fells he had been staggering across, red-faced and watery-eyed, his shirt pulled open to the waist. His wife and I had been listening to Bach; when he entered the room, she glanced at me and went straight upstairs. Lyall cocked his head, laughed, kicked out at the radiogram. 'All that bloody Lovelace we had, eh?' he said, making some equation I couldn't follow.

'I don't know what I am, Egerton,' he went on, pulling a chair up close to mine. 'You don't, either. We'll never know the half of it,' he said companionably. 'Eh?' He was bent on baring his soul (or so I imagined): yearning for the emotional storm I was equally determined to avoid – Cambridge, recrimination, the maudlin reaffirmation of our interdependence. 'Have a bloody drink, Egerton,' he demanded.

'I think you ought to have some coffee,' I said. 'I'll make you some.' I went into the kitchen.

'You bloody prig,' he said quietly.

When I went back, he had gone upstairs. I listened for a moment, but could hear nothing. In the end I drank the coffee myself and went to bed. That night was one of vast heat and discomfort: the rancid smell I had noticed on my first day in the cottage oozed from the furniture as if the heat were rendering from the stuffing of the cushions some foul grease no scrubbing brush could touch; my sleeping bag was sticky and intolerable, and no amount of force would move the windows; I lay for hours in an exhausted doze poisoned by nightmares and incoherent, half-conscious fantasies.

Groaning from upstairs disturbed that dreary reverie. A sleepy moan, the dull thump of feet on the bedroom floor; something fell over. There was a moment of perfect silence, then Lyall saying loudly, 'Oh Christ, I'm *sorry* then.' Somebody came stumbling down through the thick, stale darkness of the staircase. My watch had stopped.

'Egerton?' called Lyall, bumping about in the dark.

'Egerton? Egerton?'

He sounded like a dead child discovering that eternity is some buzzing, languorous dream of Bath. I heard him cough once or twice into the sink; then the brandy bottle gurgled, fell on to the kitchen tiles and was smashed. 'Oh God,' whispered Lyall. 'Do you ever have nightmares, Egerton? Real ones, where you might just as well be awake?' I felt him coming closer through that ancient velvet darkness. 'All this is my fault, you know.' He swallowed loudly. He tried to touch my shoulder.

'You could get another job,' I suggested cautiously, moving away. 'The proofreading doesn't seem to make you much.'

'When we came here, this place was perfect. Now look at it.' There was a pause, as he scratched irritably about for the light switch. He failed to find it. 'It's a slum, *and I'm doing it.* What difference can a job make?'

'Look,' I said, 'I don't quite understand.' I couldn't bear the confines of the sleeping bag anymore, but out there in the dark I was as lost as Lyall. I perched on what I hoped was the arm of a chair. 'You'd better tell me about it,' I invited, since there seemed to be no alternative; and added, feeling disgusted with myself even as I did it, 'Old chap.' I needn't have worried. He hardly noticed.

'Everything I touch falls to pieces,' he said. 'It's been happening since I was a kid.' Then, with a dull attempt at dignity – 'It's held me back, of course: I'd have had a First if it hadn't been for that bloody bicycle; the last job went down the shute with the office duplicator; I can't even get on a bus without it smashing into something.'

'Everybody feels like that at some time or another,' I said. 'In the Alps –'

'Bugger the Alps, Egerton!' he hissed. 'Listen to me for once!'

His mind was a back drain, it was an attic with a trap full of dry, eviscerated mice. In it he'd stored up every incident of his childhood – a nursery *faux pas*, a blocked lavatory bowl, a favourite animal run down in the street – making no distinction between the act and the accident, between the cup and the lip. With a kind of quiet hysteria in his voice, he detailed every anticlimax of his maturity – each imagined slight carefully catalogued, each spillage, each coin lost among the rubbish beneath a basement grid; every single inkblot gathered and sorted into a relentless, unselective system of culpability.

It was nonsensical and terrifying. Typists, tutors and maiden ladies, his victims and pursuers, haunted him through that attic; *I* haunted him, it seemed, for he ended with: 'It was me that cut your hand in London, Egerton, not the bottle. I couldn't help it. Something flows out of me, and I can't control it anymore –

'Look at this place. Look at it!' And he began to sob.

A dim, cobwebby light was filtering through the remaining panes of glass, greying his face, his scrawny, hopeless body. I have a horror of confession; I was angry with him for burdening me, and at the same time full of an awful empty pity; what could I have said to him? – That I thought he was mad? Self-concern makes us all mad. All I could do then was pat his shoulder reassuringly.

'Look,' I said, 'it's getting light, Lyall. Let's both have a bit of sleep. We can work it out later. You've obviously got a bit depressed, that's all. You'll feel better now.'

He stiffened. One moment he was blubbering helplessly, the next he had said quite clearly, 'I might have known. You've had it easy all your life, you bloody pompous bastard –'

I got to my feet. I thought of Chamonix, and the razor of wind that shaves the Aiguilles. I should have kept my temper; instead, I simply felt relieved to have a reason for losing it. I waited for a moment before saying, 'Nobody paid my way through Cambridge, Lyall.' Then, deliberately, 'For God's sake pull yourself together. You're not a child any more. And you never were a Jonah – just a bloody great bag of self-pity.'

He was hitting me the moment I turned away. I fell over the chair, upset more by the things he was screaming than by his clumsy attempts to re-enact some schoolyard fight of twenty years before. 'Christ, Lyall, don't be silly!' I shouted. I got the chair between us, but he roared and knocked it away. I made a grab for his windmilling arms; found myself backed into a corner. I got a knock on my cheek which stung my pride. 'You little fucker,' I said, and hit him in the stomach. He fell down, belching and coughing.

I pulled him back into the room and stood over him. His wife discovered us there in our underpants. 'What's the matter?' she pleaded, befuddled with sleep and staring at my mutilated foot. Lyall said something filthy. 'You'd better look after the baby,' I told her viciously. And then that old terrible boyhood cry of triumph. 'He shouldn't start things he can't finish.'

I got dressed and packed my rucksack, Lyall sniffing and moaning throughout. As I left, the woman was kneeling over him, wiping his runny nose – but she was gazing up at me. 'No!' I said. 'No more. Not from me. He needs a bloody doctor –' Turning in the doorway: 'Why did you have to lie to him about your age? Couldn't *you* get anybody, either?' I felt a little sick.

It might have ended there, I might have taken away the simplest and most comforting solution to the enigma of Lyall, if I hadn't decided that while (for the second, or, now I could admit it, the third time in my life) I never wanted to see him again, I didn't intend to let him ruin the week or so of holiday I had left to me. It was unthinkable to return to Wandsworth with only that sordid squabble to remember through the winter.

So instead of catching the bus back to Ambleside I moved up the valley to the National Trust site, put up my little Ultimate tent, and for a week at least had some recompense for my stay beneath Raw Pike; pottering about in the silent, stone-choked ghylls of Oxendale, where nobody ever seems to go; drowsing among the glacial moraines of Stake Pass, where dragonflies clatter mournfully through the brittle reed-stems and the path tumbles down its spur into the Langstrath like an invitation; watching the evening climbers on Gimmer, coloured motes against the archaic face of the rock, infinitely slow-moving and precarious.

It was a peculiar time. The heatwave, rather than abating, merely consolidated its grip and moved into its third week, during which temperatures of a hundred degrees were recorded in Keswick. Dead sheep dotted the fells like *roches moutonnées*, and in dry gullies gaped silently over bleached pebbles. A middle-aged couple on a coach-outing for the blind wandered somehow on to the screes at Wastwater, to be discovered on the 1,700-foot line by an astonished rescue team and brought down suffering from heat prostration and amnesia. Mickleden Beck diminished to a trickle – at the dam beneath Stickle Breast, exhausted birds littered the old waterline, staring passively up at the quivering peaks.

The campsite was empty, and curiously lethargic. A handful of climbers from Durham University had set up in one field, some boys on an Outward Bound exercise in the other: but there were none of the great blue-and-orange canvas palaces which normally spread their wings beneath Side Pike all summer long, none of the children who in a moment of boredom trip over your guylines on their way to pee secretly in the brook. After dark each night, a few of us clustered round the warden's caravan to hear the ten o'clock national news, while heat-lightning played round Pike o' Stickle then danced gleefully away across Martcrag Moor. Under a fat moon, the valley was greenish and ingenuous, like an ill-lit diorama.

Despite any anger – or perhaps because of it – I couldn't exorcise the Lyalls, and their dreamlike embrace of inadvertency and pain continued to fascinate me. I even broke an excursion to Blea Rigg and Codale to sit on the fellside for half an hour and muse over the cottage, small and precise in the valley; but from up there it was uncommunicative. One of the barn roofs had sagged; there was fresh rubble in the road; the whole place had an air of abandonment and stupefaction in the heat. Where was Lyall? – Prowling hungrily through the Ambleside bookshops, haggling sourly over the price of a paperback thriller now that he couldn't get *The Times*?

And the woman – what elusive thoughts, what trancelike afternoons, staring out into the sunlight and the nettles? Her calm was mysterious. Lyall was destroying her, but she stayed; she was a liar – but there was something dreadfully apt in her vision, her metaphor of entropy. If this seems a detached, academic attitude to her essential misery, it was not one I was able to hold for long. The heatwave mounted past bearing; the valley lay smashed and submissive beneath it; and eight days after my brawl with Lyall, on a night when events human and geological seemed to reach almost consciously towards union, I was forced from the speculative view.

Sleep was impossible. Later than usual, we gathered round the warden's radio. But for the vibrant greenish haze in the sky, it might have been day. Sweat poured off us. Confused by the evil half-light and the heat rolling out of Mickleden, a pair of wrens were piping miserably and intermittently from the undergrowth by the brook, where a thousand insects hung in the air over an inch of slow water.

With oil-tariff revelations compromising the minority government, public anger mounting over the French agricultural betrayal, and the constant spectre of the Patriotic Front demanding proportional representation from the wings of an already shaky parliament, the political organism had begun to look like some fossil survivor of another age. That night, it seemed to wake up suddenly to its situation; it thrashed and bled in the malarial air of the twentieth century, and over the transistor we followed its final throes; the government fell, and something became extinct in Britain while we slapped our necks to kill midges.

After the announcement, a group of the Durham students hung uneasily about in the wedge of yellow light issuing from the warden's door, speechless and shrugging. Later, they probed the bleeding gum cautiously, in undertones, while the warden's wife made tea and the radio mumbled unconvincingly into the night. They seemed reluctant to separate and cross the empty site to empty tents, alone.

It was one of them who, turning eventually to go, drew our attention to a curious noise in the night – a low, spasmodic bubbling, like some thick liquid simmering up out of a hole in the ground. We cocked our heads, laughed at him, and he deferred shyly to our judgment that it was only the brook on the stones beneath the little bridge. But shortly afterwards it came again, closer; and then a third time, not twenty yards away across the car park.

'There's someone out there,' he said wonderingly. He was a tall, wispy lad with a thin yellow beard and large feet, his face young and concerned and decent even in that peculiar beryline gloom. When we laughed at him again, he said gently, 'I think I'll go and have a look, though.' The gate creaked open, we heard his boots on the gravel. With an edgy grin, one of his friends explained to us. 'Too much ale tonight.' Silence.

Then, 'Oh my God,' he said in a surprised voice. 'You'd better come and do something,' he called, and gave himself up suddenly to a fit of choking and coughing. We found him sitting on the gravel with his head between his knees. He had vomited extensively. On the ground in front of him lay Lyall's wife.

'How did she walk?' he whispered. 'Oh, how did she walk?' He wrapped his arms round his knees and rocked himself to and fro.

She was hideously burnt. Her clothes were inseparable from the charred flesh in which they had become embedded; one ruined eye glared sightlessly out of a massive swelling of the facial tissue; plasma leaked from the less damaged areas, and she stank of the oven. Whatever fear or determination had driven her from under the shadow of Raw Pike now kept her conscious, staring passively upwards from her good eye, her body quivering gently with shock.

'Egerton,' she said, 'Egerton, Egerton, Egerton –'

I knelt over her.

'– Egerton, Egerton –'

'Someone get that bloody Land Rover across here,' said the warden thickly.

'What happened?' I said. She lay like a blackened log, staring up at the sky. She shuddered convulsively. 'Where's Lyall?'

'–Egerton, Egerton, Egerton, Egerton –'

'I'm here.'

But she was dead.

I staggered away to squirt up a thin, painful stream of bile. The warden followed me. 'Did she know you?' he said. 'Where did she come from? What's happened?' I wiped my mouth. How could I tell? She had come to get help from me, but not for herself. I hang on to that thought, even now. With some idea of protecting Lyall, at least until I could get to him, I said, 'I've never seen her before in my life. Look, I've got to go. Excuse me.'

I felt him staring after me. The Land Rover was manoeuvring nervously round the car park, but now they had nowhere to take her. The boy from Durham was asking himself, over and over again, 'How did she *get* here?' He appealed to his friends, but they were shaken and grey-faced, and they didn't know what to say.

It was past midnight when I left the campsite. An almost constant flicker of heat-lightning lent a macabre formality to the lane, the hills and the drystone walls – like subjects in some steel engraving or high-contrast photograph, they were perfectly defined but quite unreal. At Middlefell Farm the lights were all out. Some sheep stared at me from a paddock, their sides heaving and their eyes unearthly.

I lurched along under that hot green sky for forty minutes, but it seemed longer. Like a fool, I kept looking for signs of the woman's blind, agonised flight: had she fallen here, and dragged herself a little way? – And there, had it seemed impossible to drive the quivering insensate hulk a yard further? I was brought up short, stupid and horrified, by every smear of melted tar on the road; yet I ignored the only real event of the journey.

I had stopped for a moment to put my back against a drystone and massage the cramped calf of my left leg. A curlew was fluting tentatively from the deep Gothic cleft of Dungeon Ghyll. I had been gazing vacantly down the valley for perhaps half a minute, trying to control my erratic breathing, when the sky over Ambleside seemed to pulse suddenly, as if some curious shift of energy states had taken place. Simultaneously, the road lurched beneath me.

I felt it distinctly: a brief, queasy swaying motion. And when I touched the wall behind me, a faint tremor was in it, a fading vibration. I was dazed through lack of proper sleep; I was obsessed – and knew it – by the grim odyssey of Lyall's wife: I put the tremor down to dizziness, and attributed that strange transitional flicker of the air to a flare of lightning somewhere over Troutbeck, a flash partially occluded by the mass of the fells between. But when I moved on, the peculiar hue of the sky was brighter; and although the event seemed to have no meaning at the time, it was to prove of central significance in the culminating nightmare.

The smoke was visible from quite a long way off, drifting filmy and exhausted up the fellside, clinging to the spongy ash and shrivelled bracken stems of that previous fire, to be trapped by an inversion about a hundred feet below Raw Pike and spread out in a thin cloudbank the colour of watered milk.

Lyall's cottage was ruined. Both barns were down in a heap of lamp-blacked stone, here and there an unconsumed rafter or beam sticking up out of the mess; the roof of the main building had caved in, taking the upper floor with it, so that there remained only a shell full of smoking slates and white soft ash. It radiated an intense heat, and the odd glowing cinder raced erratically up from it on the updraughts, but the fire *per se* had burnt itself out long before.

The wreckage was curiously uncompact. An explosion, probably of the kitchen gas-cylinders, had flung rubble into the nettle patch; and for some reason most of the face of the building lay in the road.

There among a tangle of smashed window frames and furniture, motionless in contemplation of the wreck and looking infinitely lonely, stood the long, ungainly figure of Lyall. His tweed jacket had gone through at the elbows, his trousers were charred and filthy, and his shoes were falling to pieces, as if he'd been trampling about in the embers looking for something. I began to shout his name long before I reached him. He studied my limping, hasty progress down the road for a moment; then, as I got close, seemed to lose interest.

'Lyall!' I called. 'Are you all right?'

I kicked my way through the rubbish and shook his shoulder. He watched a swirl of ash dance over the deep embers. Something popped and cracked comfortably down in that hot pit. When he faced me, his eyes, red and sore, glowed out of his stubbled, smoke-blackened face with another kind of heat. But his voice was quite inoffensive when he said, 'Hello Egerton. I didn't get much stuff out, you see.' Stacked neatly in the road a few yards off were twenty or thirty charred paperbacks. 'She came to fetch you, then?'

He stared absently at the ruin. I had expected to find something more than a drowsy child, parching its skin in some reverie over the remains of a garden bonfire. I was sickened.

'Lyall, you bloody moron!' I shouted. 'She's *dead*!' He moved his shoulders slightly, stared on. I caught hold of his arm and shook him. He was relaxed, unresistant. 'Did you send her away in that condition? Are you mad? She was burnt to pieces!' I might have been talking to myself. 'What's been *happening* here?'

When he finally pulled up out of the dry trap of ashes, it was to shake his head slowly and say, 'What? I don't know.' He gaped, he blinked, he whispered, 'She was getting so old. It was my fault –' He seemed about to explain something, but never did. That open-mouthed pain, that terrible passive acceptance of guilt, was probably the last glimpse I had of Lyall the human being. Had he, at some point during the dreadful events of that night, actually faced and recognised the corroding power of his self-concern? At the time I thought I understood it all – and standing uselessly amid all that rubble I needed to believe he had.

'I'm sorry,' I said.

At this the most inhuman paroxysm of misery and loathing took hold of his swollen, grimy features. 'Fuck you, Egerton!' he cried. He threw off my hand. For a second, I was physically afraid, and backed quickly away from him. He followed me, with, 'What's it got to do with you? What's any of it got to do with you?' Then, quieter, 'I can't seem to –'

The spasm passed. He looked down at his blistered hands as if seeing them for the first time. He laughed. His eyes flickered over me, cruel as heat-lightning. 'Bugger off back home, then, Egerton, if you feel like that,' he said. He put his hands in his trouser pockets and stirred the rubble with his toe. '*I* didn't break the bloody piano, and I'll tell the old bitch I didn't –' He whirled away and strode off rapidly across the scorched fellside, stopping only to pick up an armful of books and call: 'I'm sick of all this filthy rubbish anyway.'

Smoke wreathed round him. I saw him turn north and begin to climb.

With this absurd transition into the dimension of height began what must surely be the most extraordinary episode of the entire business. Lyall stalked away from me up the fell. Amazed, I shouted after him. When he ignored me, I could only follow: he may or may not have had suicidal intentions, but he was certainly mad; in either case, if only out of common humanity, I couldn't just stand there and watch him go.

It might have been better if I had.

He made straight for Raw Pike, and then, his torso seeming to drift legless above the pall of white smoke that hung beneath the outcrop, bore west to begin a traverse which took us into the deep and difficult gullies between Whitegill Crag and Mill Gill. Here, he seemed to become lost for a while, and I gained on him.

He blundered about those stony vegetation-choked clefts like a sick animal, trying to scale waterslides or scrape his way up the low but steep rock walls. His shoes had fallen off his feet, and he was leaving a damp, urgent trail. He ignored me if I called his name, but he was quite aware of my presence, and took a patent delight in picking at his emotional scabs, real or imagined, whenever I got close enough to hear him. His voice drifted eerily down the defiles. The piano seemed to preoccupy him.

'*I* never broke it,' I heard, in a self-congratulatory tone, then: 'Nowhere near it, Miss,' mumbled as part of a dialogue in which he took both parts. She didn't believe him, of course, and he became progressively more sullen. Later, groping for a handhold three feet above his head, he burst out angrily, 'You can tell him I *won't* be responsible for the bloody things. Staff loss isn't *my* problem.' His hold turned out to be a clump of shallow-rooted heather, which came out when he put his weight on it. He laughed. 'Go and lick her arse then –'

In this way, he visited almost every period of his life. He met his wife down by the Thames, in a filthy March wind; later, they whispered to one another at night in his Holloway flat. He conjured up mutual acquaintances from Cambridge, and set them posturing like the dowdy flamingos they had undoubtedly been. And once my own voice startled me, echoing pompously over the fells as part of some student dispute which must have seemed excruciatingly important at the time, and which I still can't remember.

When he finally broke out on to the east bank of Mill Gill, he stared back at me for a moment as if reassuring himself that I was still there. He even nodded to me, with a sort of grim approval. Then he lurched unsteadily through the bracken to the ghyll itself and dropped his paperbacks into it one by one, looking over his shoulder each time to see if I was watching. He crouched there like a child, studying each bright jacket as it slipped beneath the surface of the water and was whirled away. His shoulders were moving, but I couldn't tell whether he was laughing or crying.

It was during the latter part of this unburdening that the earth began to shake again – and this time in earnest. I sensed rather than saw that energetic transition of the air. The whole sky pulsed, flickered with lightning, seemed to stabilise. Then, with an enormous rustling noise, the fell beneath my feet shifted and heaved, lifting itself into a long curved wave which raced away from me up the slopes to explode against the dark rock of Tarn Crag in a shower of small stones and up-rooted bracken.

I tottered about, shouting, 'Lyall! Lyall!' until a second, more powerful shock threw me off my feet and sent me rolling twenty or thirty feet down towards the road.

Mill Gill gaped. The last paperback vanished. A groan came up out of the earth. Abruptly, the air was full of loose soil and rock-chippings, mud and spray from the banks of the ghyll. Lyall stared up through it at the throbbing sky; spun round and set off up the path to Stickle Tarn at a terrific rate, his long legs pumping up and down. Rocks blundered and rumbled round him – he brandished his fist at the hills. 'Lyall, for God's sake come back!' I begged, but my voice was sucked away into the filthy air, and all I could see of him was a dim untiring figure, splashing across the ghyll where Tarn Crag blocks the direct route.

I put my head down into the murk and scrambled upward. Black water vomited suddenly down the ghyll, full of dead sheep and matted vegetation. Through the spray of a new waterfall I had a glimpse of Lyall waving his arms about and croaking demented challenges at a landscape that changed even as he opened his mouth. Twice, I got quite close behind him; once, I grabbed his arm, but he only thrashed about and shouted, 'Bugger off home, Egerton!' over the booming of the water.

Five hundred feet of ascent opened up the gully and spread Stickle Tarn before us, the colour of lead: fifty acres of sullen water simmering in its dammed-up glacial bowl. Up there on the 1500-foot line, out of the confines of the ghyll, it was quieter and the earth seemed less agitated. But the dam was cracked; a hot wind rumbled through the high passes and gusted across the cirque; and up out of the black screes on the far bank of the tarn there loomed like a threat the massive, seamed face of the Borrowdale Volcanics –

Pavey Ark lowered down at us: the highest sheer drop in the Central Fells, four hundred and eighty million years old – impassive, unbending, orogenetic. A constant stream of material was pouring like fine dust from the bilberry terraces at its summit two thousand feet above sea level, crushed volcanic agglomerate whirling and smoking across the face; while, down by the water, larger rocks dislodged from the uneasy heights bounced a hundred feet into the air in explosions of scree.

Lyall stood stock-still, staring up at it.

Beside him, the dam creaked and flexed. A ton of water spilled over the parapet and roared away down Mill Gill. He paid it not the slightest attention, simply stood there, drenched and muddy, moving his head fractionally from side to side as he traced one by one the scars of that horrific cliff, like a man following a page of print with his index finger; Great Gully, unclimbable without equipment, Gwynne's Chimney, Little Gully, and, tumbling from the western pinnacle to the base of East Buttress, the long precipitous grooves and terraces of Jack's Rake.

He was looking for a way up.

'Lyall,' I said, 'haven't you come far enough?'

He shrugged. Without a word, he set off round the margin of the tarn.

I'm convinced that following him further would have done no good: he had been determined on this course perhaps as far back as Cambridge, certainly since his crisis of self-confidence in the cottage. Anyway, my foot had become unbearably painful: it was as much as I could do to catch up with him halfway round the tarn, and, by actually grabbing the tail of his jacket, force him to stop.

We struggled stupidly for a moment, tottering in and out of the warm shallows – the Ark towering above us like a repository of all uncommitted Ordovician time. Lyall disengaged himself and ran off a little way. He put his head on one side and regarded me warily, chest heaving.

Then he nodded to himself, returned, and, keeping well out of my reach, said quite amiably, 'I'm going up, Egerton. It's too late to stop me, you know.' Something detached itself from the cliff and fell into the tarn like a small bomb going off. He spun round, screaming and waving his fist. 'Leave me alone! Fuck off!' He watched the water subside. He showed his teeth. 'Listen, you bastard,' he said quietly: 'Why don't you just chuck yourself in that?' And he pointed to the torrent rumbling over the dam and down Mill Gill. 'For all the help you've ever been to me, you might as well –'

He began to walk away. He stopped, tore at his hair, made

an apologetic gesture in my direction. His face crumpled, and the Lyall I had beaten up in the living room of his own house looked out of it. 'I can't seem to stop going up, Egerton,' he whispered, 'I can't seem to stop doing it –'

But when I stepped forward, he shook with laughter. 'That got you going, you bloody oaf!' he gasped. And he stumbled off towards the screes.

It really would have done no good to go with him. Once or twice on the long walk back to the dam, I actually turned and began to follow him again. But it was useless: by then, distance and the Ark had made of him a small mechanical toy. I called for him to wait, but he couldn't have heard me; in the end, I made my way up the northern slopes of Tarn Crag (I had to cross the dam to do it – I waited for a lull, but even so my feet were in six inches of fast water as I went over, and my skin crawled with every step) and from there watched his inevitable ascent.

He crabbed about at the base of the Great Gully for a while, presumably looking for a way up; when this proved impractical, he made a high easterly traverse of the screes and vanished into the shadow of East Buttress: to reappear ten minutes later, inching his way up Jack's Rake – an infinitely tiny, vulnerable mote against the face.

I didn't really imagine he would do it. God knows why I chose that moment to be 'sensible' about him. I sat down and unlaced my boots, petulantly determined to see him through what was after all a rather childish adventure, and then say nothing about it when the cliff itself had sent him chastened away. There was so little excuse for this that it seems mad now, of course: the Ark was shaking and shifting, the very air about it groaned and rang with heat; St. Elmo's fire writhed along its great humped outline. How on earth I expected him to survive, I don't know.

He was invisible for minutes at a time even on the easy stretch up to the ash tree at the entrance of Rake End

Chimney, inundated by that curtain of debris blowing across the sheer walls above him. He tried confusedly to scale the chimney; failed; trudged doggedly on up, the temperature rising as he went. A smell of dust and lightning filled the air. Negotiating the fifty-degree slope of the second pitch, he was forced to cling to the rock for nearly half an hour while tons of rubble thundered past him and into the tarn below. He should have been crushed; he must have been injured in some way, for it took him almost as long to complete fifteen yards of fairly simple scrambling along the Easy Terrace.

Perhaps I remembered too late that Lyall was a human being; but from that point on, I could no longer minimise the obsession that had driven him up there. When some internal rupture of the cliff flooded the channels above him and turned the Rake into a high-level drainage culvert, I could hear only that despairing mumble in the cottage at night, the voice of his wife; when he windmilled his arms against the rush of water, regained his balance and crawled on up, insensate and determined, I bit my lip until it bled. Perhaps it's never too late.

In some peculiar way the Ark too seemed to respond to his efforts: two thousand feet up, spidering across the Great Gully and heading for the summit wall, he moved into quietude; the boulder slides diminished, the cliff stood heavy and passive, like a cow in heat. Down below, on Tarn Crag, the earth ceased to tremble. Stickle Tarn calmed, and lay like a vat of molten beryl, reflecting the vibrant, acid sky; there were no more shadows, and, when I took off my shirt to dip it in the Tarn Crag pool, I felt no movement of the air. Hundreds of small birds were rustling uncomfortably about in the heather; while up above the blind, blunt head of Harrison Stickle, one hawk wheeled in slow, magnificent circles.

Twenty minutes after his successful negotiation of the Great Gully intersection, Lyall crossed the summit wall. There I lost him for a short period. What he did there, I have no clue. Perhaps he simply wandered among the strange nodular boulders and shallow rock pools of the region. But if any transition took place, if his sour and ludicrous metaphysic received its final unimaginable blessing, it must have come there, between summit wall and summit cairn, between the cup and the lip, while I fretted and stalked below.

All this aside: suddenly, the peaks about me flared and wavered ecstatically; and he was standing by the cairn—

He was almost invisible: but I can imagine him there, with his arms upraised, his raw wrists poking out of the sleeves of his tweed jacket: no more unengaging or desperate, no stranger than he had ever been among the evening mists of Cambridge or the broken milk machines of Holloway: except that, now, static electricity is playing over him like fire, and his mouth is open in a great disgusted shout that reaches me quite clearly through the still, haunted air –

For a moment, everything seemed to pause. The sky broadcast a heat triumphant – a long, high, crystalline song, taken up and echoed by summit after summit, from Wetherlam and the Coniston Old Man, from Scafell Pike and the unbearable resonant fastnesses of Glaramara, never fading. For a moment, Lyall stood transfigured, perched between his own madness and the madness of an old geography. Then, as his cry died away to leave the cry of the sky supreme, a series of huge cracks and ruptures spread out across the cliff face from beneath his feet; and, with a sound like the tearing of vast lace, the whole immense façade of Pavey Ark began to slide slowly into the tarn beneath.

Dust plumed half a mile into the air; on a mounting roar the cliff, like an old sick woman, fell to its knees in the cirque; the high bilberry terraces poised themselves for a long instant, then, lowering themselves gently down, evaporated into dust. Millions of tons of displaced water smashed the dam and went howling down Mill Gill, crashing from wall to wall; to spill – black and invincible, capped with a dirty grey spume – across the valley and break like a giant sea against the lower slopes of

Oak Howe and Side Pike. Before the Ark had finished its weary slide, the valley road was no more, the New Hotel and Side House were rubbish on a long wave – and that pit of ashes, Lyall's house, was extinguished forever.

I watched the ruin without believing it. I remember saying something like, 'For God's sake, Lyall –' Then I turned and ran for my life over the quaking crag, east towards the safety of Blea Rigg and the fell route to an Ambleside I was almost frightened to reach. As I went, an ordinary darkness was filtering across the sky; a cool wind sprang up; and there were rain clouds already racing in from the Irish Sea along a stormy front.

Even allowing for the new unreliability of the press, exoteric explanations of the Great Langdale earth movement – activity renewed among the Borrowdale Volcanics after nearly five hundred million years; the unplanned landing of some enormous Russian space probe – seem ridiculous to me. Beyond the discovery of that poor woman, there were no witnesses other than myself in the immediate area. Was *Lyall*, then, responsible for the destruction of Pavey Ark?

It seems incredible: and yet, in the face of his death, insignificant. He carried his own entropy around with him, which makes him seem monstrous, perhaps; I don't know. He believed in an executive misery, and that should be enough for any of us. It hardly matters to me now. Other events swept it away almost immediately.

As I stumbled through the dim, panicky streets of Ambleside in the aftermath of the earthquake, the Patriotic Front was issuing from dusty suburban drill halls and Boy Scout huts all over the country; and by noon England, seventy years too late, was taking her first hesitant but heady steps into this century of violence. Grouped about the warden's radio in the still, stupefied night, we could have guessed at something of the sort. I understand now why the

Durham students were so affected: students have suffered more than most as the Front tightens its political grip.

In dreams, I blame Lyall for that, too; equate the death of reason with the collapse of Pavey Ark; and watch England crawl past me over and again in the guise of a burnt woman on her desperate journey to the head of a valley that turns out every time to be impassive and arid. But awake I am more reasonable, and I have a job at the new sports shop in Chamonix. It's no hardship to sell other climbers their perlon and pitons – although the younger ones will keep going up alone, against all advice. Like many of the more fortunate refugees I have been allowed to take a limited French nationality; I even have a second-class passport, but I doubt if I shall ever go back.

Walking about the town, I still hate to look up, in case the cruel and naked peaks surprise me from between the house-tops: but the pain of that wound is at least explicable, whereas Lyall –

Everyone who ever met Lyall contributed in some small way to his death. It might have been averted perhaps, if, in some Cambridge mist of long ago, I had only come upon the right thing to say; and I behaved very badly towards him later: but it seems as futile to judge myself on that account as to be continually interpreting and reinterpreting the moment at which I was forced to realise that one man's raw and gaping self-concern had brought down a mountain.

And I prefer to picture Stickle Tarn not as it looked from the 1,600-foot contour during Lyall's final access of rage and despair, but as I remember it from my Cambridge days and before – a wide, cold pool in the shadow of an ancient and beautiful cliff, where on grey windy days a seabird you can never identify seems always to be trawling twenty feet above the water in search of something it probably can't even define to itself.

1975

Land Locked

THERE'S NO EVIL IN the story, only loss and confusion.

Palinurus the Navigator fell off the boat and forgot his signature skill. Panic attacks, anxiety attacks and depressive episodes followed. 'You don't ask a builder,' he remembered trying to explain to someone, 'if an arch is the truth about something. That isn't the point.' For a moment before sunset, light levels were distributed strangely across the landscape, so that the coastal hills seemed closer than the house. 'You can either build an arch or you can't.' After that he drove from town to town up the coast, deteriorating all the way and no one heard from him again.

Her journey was literally at right angles to his. Though she had never learned to drive, she found that after she had eaten a cab driver it came easily to her, along with the local language. She left not long after him, heading north, following the steady rise of the land: but while the Navigator clung to the coast, always keeping the sea to his left, she headed for the interior, seeking out middle-class landscapes with simple founding assumptions. A glass of wine in the evening; a toddler on the patio in the failing light; people waiting unexpectantly to find themselves in their real lives – or unexpectantly trying to outlive the wrong lives – all of their lives. Often, she found them surrounded by a detritus of their own acts of abjection, symbolised in collections of rediscovered personal possessions from which they felt alienated. They often remarked that they wondered why they had these objects. She kept a geranium in a pot in the back of the car; reached behind her now and then, while driving, to crush a leaf.

Palinurus had two repeating dreams. In the first, as he went overboard, the water had an ugly look – dark and speedy but also with something to it of stagnant harbours, scenes you might find yourself in when you were already dead: shallow in places; black mudbanks in static water with a cream of chemicals all over; overlooked by shipping containers; a viscidness, a meniscus full of petroleum rainbows and bobbing faecal matter; bent cans, plastics large and small. Small islands of ruderal scrub. Whole dead animals with slick fur and no eyes. Like that one minute, anyway, but the next changing direction to accelerate and rush past, then – grey and waveless, bowed tight at the surface, here and there pulsing, like the worst currents, the big cold rips and eddies of a body of true coastal water – carry you off in the night. That moment, felled by the tiller, woken so abruptly from one nightmare into the next, Palinurus knew he'd had it. Yet he hadn't, and through luck and coincidence made it somehow to the shore. That was the unexpected thing about it all, he reported: it wasn't by any means the end.

She felt some sort of relief to be out of the salt sea. But a life on land had no credibility as far as she was concerned; it was just something to laugh about. Meanwhile, she could see that he was still not sure he hadn't, in fact, died. Their conversations from then on were frequent, but always brief. She might sit with her feet in a half-filled bucket and her shoulders in the sunlight from the window, asking him about the things she could see. From the outset he had left her to her own devices in the evening, while he went from bar to bar along the seafront telling the story to old friends who didn't believe it.

The rooms she stayed in during her drive inland were often full of a strong old-fashioned scent she associated with the seafront barber-shops – although it might equally have been confectionary. It was on the edge between perfume and citrus and also – since there was no one but her in the room – seemed liminal in its actual nature, that is, both there and not there. A little later it was gone. She would get up and walk about in a restless way, not exactly sniffing the air but holding it in her nose then breathing out slowly, lifting her head like an animal bringing into play an olfactory organ human beings don't have. Sometimes she thought she could still smell the scent, but more often she couldn't. Later she would realise it was herself.

Palinurus' second repeating dream was essentially one of kinesis. It was a relic: the bodily memory of another time, other levels of confidence, and awareness. But given the slightest encouragement, it spilled out of the night and took him over, as if it had been down there waiting since the accident. Understanding yourself, he thought, is always a meaningless joke. But sometimes you can't help wanting to make personal contact with who you are, or in this case who you used to be. You get lost a few times. You give up. It's scary at first. That's when you remember that the dream has a lizardlike, ironic look in its eye. Shortly after falling off the boat, though, he had begun to feel liberated. 'I enjoyed it!' he insisted, the final time they talked. In return she asked him how much of that elation – that relief – was a diversion. How much of his embrace of what he now called possibility was a covert replay of the final voyage? He said he didn't want to talk about that. Navigation was a broken process for him, he'd taken it up too early and now he felt free.

In the last room she took, they gave her a fruit that tasted like slightly sweetened rubber, which she ate slowly, keeping away the many small flies with one hand. A girl watched her carefully as she ate, her expressions changing as if she were eating it herself. 'Yum,' said the girl. And: 'We plant them every year, so they come up.' This seemed too literal to mean anything. Why else would you plant anything, if not for it to come up? So instead of trying to answer she looked out of the window at a man on a little tractor, going up and down in the short, sloping field below the house. He had a dog that ran about untiringly, up and down the shallow furrows, which were dark to begin with but dried out in minutes; it stopped at every corner to stand and stare around as if it had never stood there before.

Alone in the room again, she found a glass bowl full of water and sunlight, throwing onto the wall every flickering, shimmering, debatable pattern she knew. Who had pulled who ashore? Given the situation, neither of them would ever be sure. The sea had had an ugly look that night; but there is no evil in the story, only a misunderstood gesture, the saturations of self-deception. He's dead and she's marooned. He never leaves his dream; she won't, now, ever leave that room. It is a comedy, a brief confusion followed by both persons getting, in a sense, what they want. For instance, he often reassures himself as he travels the coast, 'To what degree does 'navigator' only mean 'someone going somewhere'?' While she thinks: Why do I love the light here so much?

2020

Yummie

IN HIS LATE FIFTIES Short experienced some kind of cardiac problem, a brief but painful event which landed him in an Accident and Emergency unit in East London. From A&E he was processed to Acute Assessment, where they took his blood pressure at two-hourly intervals but otherwise didn't seem to know what to do with him. Everyone was very kind.

His second night on the ward, he stood in the corridor where it was cooler and looked out over a strip of grass. An iron staircase was off to one side. He could see bollards; what he imagined was a car park; behind that a few trees quite dense and dark against the sky. He rested his forehead against the cold glass of the fire door. Propane tanks, portacabin offices, everything lighted grey and blue. He had a short clear glimpse of himself opening the door and walking out. It wouldn't have required a decision; to some degree, in fact, he felt it had already happened. That glimpse had lobed itself off immediately, becoming its own world. He could see himself moving away between the trees, tentatively at first but with increasing confidence.

Late the next evening, a bed came free in Coronary Care, a wheelchair ride away across the architectural and procedural grain of the hospital, from clean and new to grimy and old, past stacks of mysterious materials, parks of apparently abandoned medical electronics and radiology machines, and into a narrow slot deep in the original building. 3am, he found himself awake again. Someone further along the slot was moaning. Someone else had a cough, long and retching, full of sad self-disgust.

'Make no mistake about this,' the consultant advised him next morning: 'You've had a heart attack.'

Short, who had never believed anything else, waited to hear more; but that seemed to be it. The procedure he now underwent was an experience very much like an amusement ride. He was placed carefully on a narrow table. The nurse gave him an injection of diazepam she described as 'the equivalent of three good gin-and-tonics', while someone else demonstrated the bank of cameras that would image his heart. The table stretched away in front of him, elongated, bluish. The cameras then groaned and slid about, pressing down into his space. Soon, off to one side, someone was putting in a lot of effort to push something like an old-fashioned drain-rod up the femoral artery and deep into his body. It was a struggle. He had the distant sense of being smashed and pummelled about. He couldn't feel anything, but sometimes their voices made him nervous. 'He'll have a bit of a bruise,' someone warned; someone else said they would put some pressure on that. Every so often they asked him if he felt ok. 'I don't know what I feel,' Short answered. In fact he felt violated but excited. He felt as if he was whizzing along some blue-lit track, he could come off the rails at any time but thanks to the diazepam he wouldn't mind.

'I'm quite enjoying it,' he said.

They laughed at that, but when he heard himself say he thought there might be a sensation in his heart – not a pain precisely, but some sort of feeling he couldn't quite describe – there was a silence then the thud of some more powerful drug hitting his system like a car running over a cattle grid.

Back on the ward, he felt embarrassingly optimistic, though a list of possible changes to his life (scribbled under the heading 'Opportunities' in the blank space next to the Guardian crossword puzzle) proved vague; turning out when he consulted it later to be couched in the self-improvement languages of the 1980s. How, for instance, could Short be 'kinder' to himself? What might that actually mean? Deep in the night, Coronary Care became a site of hallucination, like the woods in a fairytale: he was woken by a child's cough, sometimes seeming to issue from a ward directly beneath this one, sometimes from the wall of monitors and tubes behind his bed. It was a careful, precise little sound, urgent yet determined to attract no attention. Towards dawn a tall languid-looking man of his father's generation stood in the corridor by the fire door, calling, 'Yummie? Yummie?' in tones pitched between puzzlement and command. His head was almost entirely round, his expression in some way surprised. He looked Short up and down, made eye contact and said, 'Let's not be mistaken! You will have a hell of a bruise!'

An empty trolley clattered past unseen behind them.

'Are you even here,' Short whispered. 'Because Yummie is not a name.'

'Those chickens,' the man said, 'waiting outside for you now? They are your chickens. You deny them, but I see they follow you with great persistence.'

Though no chickens were visible, he was right: if Acute Assessment had been like the lobby of a cheap but comfortable hotel – air too hot, coffee bearable, quiet conversations at reception – Coronary Care was where events played out the way Short had been taught to fear. It wasn't the bottom of things by any means, but it was the beginning of the bottom of things. Those chickens, having come home to roost, would eye him now and until the end, heads on one side, mad little combs flopping.

The next day, he was discharged.

'Isn't it a bit soon?' he asked the rehab nurse.

'You'll be fine,' she said.

She said people often felt a little anxious. But it really was a safe, easy, walk in, walk out procedure, and he could plan for a good outcome. She asked him if she could take him through some leaflets. 'For instance,' she pointed out, lowering her voice, 'as soon as you can manage two flights of stairs you can have sexual activity.' There was also a list of foods he should avoid. Short had a look at it. Before the attack, his diet had been sourced almost wholly from the red end of the scale. He wondered what he would eat.

'I don't drink much alcohol anyway,' he said.

She gave him a number to call if he needed any further advice. 'If you're worried about anything at all,' she said, 'just ring.'

He wrote 'sexual activity' in his notebook.

'That seems fine,' he said.

Soon afterwards he found himself wearing his own clothes, carrying a two-day-old copy of the Guardian and some hospital toothpaste in a plastic bag, waiting for a cab to come down through the traffic and turn on to the hospital apron. When he got home he was exhausted just from leaning forward and telling the cabby how to get where they were going. He lay down on the sofa and pulled a blanket up over him and went to sleep. When he woke up it was on the edge of being dark. The street outside was quiet. The light in Short's room had a kind of sixty-year-old smokiness, as if he was looking at things through nicotine-stained glass. The door of the room was open, and the man he had met in the hospital corridor now stood at the window, holding the net curtain back with one long hand so he could stare down into the street. He was whispering, 'Yummie? Yummie?' to himself.

I'm moving forward into something here, Short thought: but I don't know what it is. He fell asleep again. The next day he rang the number the rehab nurse had given him and told her: 'I don't think I'm half as well as I feel.'

'People often report a sense of vulnerability,' the nurse explained. 'It's nothing to be ashamed of.'

'Do they report a man with a round head?' Short said.

'Let's get you to come in and have your blood pressure taken.'

In an attempt to normalise himself, Short walked around his neighbourhood, not far at first, twenty minutes here, twenty minutes there. He knew it well, but there are always a few little corners of a neighbourhood you don't know. You always meant to explore them: today, perhaps, you do. Or in the end you glance into that short curving street – with its blackened gap halfway along where a woodyard used to be, or the Memorial Hall with the three tall cemented-up windows and stopped clock – and decide again that it only connects to some other street and then another after that. All the pubs down there, you suspect, have yellowed, patchy ceilings and a feeling of grease under the fingertips wherever you touch.

At home he slept a lot, dreaming repeatedly of his angioplasty – the bunker-like underground theatre, the table too narrow to rest on comfortably, the banks of cameras, the lively technicians and nurses in their colourful thyroid protectors, the air dark but also displaying a slight bluish-grey fluorescence in the corners as if it had absorbed the radioactive dyes from Short's bloodstream. 'How are you getting on,' someone would ask, 'in your ongoing struggle with the world of appearances?' Short's responses became increasingly facetious. He was embarrassed for himself. He woke sweating, his pulse a hundred and fifty beats a minute, experiencing such premonitions of disaster that he had to get up and move around the room. In these moments of unconscious hindsight, the essentially violent nature of the procedure – the feeling of racing feet-first forward on rails under a weird light while your heart is reamed, plumbed, measured to its full physical depth and found wanting – was only heightened. By day he thought he felt a little better. His blood pressure remained too high.

'Whatever you say,' Short told the man in his room, 'Yummie isn't a name.'

'Who are you to tell me that?' the man said. 'It was your mother's name, and her mother's before her. It was your sister's name.'

Short was becoming embittered with the whole thing.

'I never had a sister,' he said. 'How did you get in here?'

'I'm always here. I was here before they christened your father, and before they christened your mother, and before they buried the poor unstained sister you say you never had.' His eyes were as round as his head, entirely without expression and yet somehow both confiding and expectant, as if he knew Short would soon admit to something. 'The poor sister,' he repeated, with a sentimental emphasis. When Short failed to answer – because this was not a past he could recognise, let alone own or identify with in any degree – he waved one hand dismissively and seemed to fade a little. 'How are you getting on with those chickens?' he said. 'Yummie.'

Short made another appointment at Rehab and told them, 'I think my medication might need adjusting.'

'How do you think of me?' the heart nurse said.

'I think of you as the heart nurse,' Short said.

'Well, I am a nurse,' she said. 'But my name's Linda.'

'Then I'll think of you as Sister Linda.'

They laughed and Short left with his new leaflets. A minute or two later he went back down the corridor to her office and stood in the doorway and said: 'I'm supposed to talk when I'm walking?'

'We recommend that,' she said. 'We need you to exercise,

but we need you just to make sure your breathing stays inside the range: if you can walk and talk, you're inside the range, you know your heart is fine.'

'I can't think of anything to say.'

She stared at him. 'Well, for instance, you can just have a nice conversation with the other person.'

'The other person,' Short said: 'OK.'

He wrote 'other person' in his notebook.

'I'm usually on my own,' he said. In fact, he was hearing voices in his room at night. One voice would say, 'You're accepting more, aren't you?' and after a pause another would answer, 'Oh yes, yes, I'm accepting more. Definitely. I'm able to accept much more now.' They sounded like an old couple, talking in the tea room at a garden centre. Short couldn't quite locate them, or tell if they were male or female. They seemed to originate quite high up, in a region of discoloured wallpaper, then, in the weeks that followed, still invisible, lower themselves down until they were able to occupy the room proper, pulling themselves about quietly but jerkily between the larger items of furniture, murmuring, 'Two funerals and now another house move. No wonder I can't take anything in,' or, 'Look at this one, dear. He's young enough.'

Once he had noticed them, he noticed others. Sometimes he woke in the night and it was quite a hubbub in there. They were everywhere. They were looking for the toilet. They had opinions about Catholicism and walking. Short had the feeling that they gathered round him while he slept, looking down at him considerately and with concern. Perhaps they even discussed him, and these fits and starts of language were the only way they could express what they knew. As their conversation decayed further, into a mumbled repetition he could hear only as 'Yummie, yummie, yummie,' he would see the tall, calm, round-headed figure waiting by the window, pulling back the curtain to look out, smiling a little. One night it whispered: 'Research shows how rats dream repeatedly of the maze they have not yet solved.' Short woke up with a sharp pain on the left side of his chest and called an ambulance.

'The paramedics said I was fine,' he told Sister Linda at his next appointment. 'They said it wasn't the right kind of pain. They were very kind.'

'I should hope they were,' she said.

'It was just a moment of panic,' Short admitted. He tried to think of a way to qualify that, but could only add: 'My parents were the same.'

'You're due for the three-month echocardiogram anyway.'

On his way to Sonography, Short became lost in the hospital basement; then the technicians didn't want to admit he was in the cubicle with them, but carried on checking their equipment as if they were waiting for some more significant version of him to arrive. After a brief glimpse of what looked like a translucent marine animal pulsing and clutching inside his chest, Short kept his gaze directed away from the monitors. He couldn't so easily ignore the swashy emphysemic whisper produced by this monster, surfacing in his life as if from the depths of a Hollywood ocean. He went back upstairs to Rehab and asked the nurse, 'Have you heard that noise? It's like a 1950s Hotpoint washing machine. Do you remember those?'

She stared at him, then down at the echocardiogram result.

'This is all good,' she said. 'You can take it from me. You can look for a very positive outcome with results like this.'

'So, a heart sounds like obsolete white goods.'

'Really, no one's surprised if you have some anxiety.'

That night he dreamed that a great hoard of household rubbish – broken beds, cheap soiled mattresses, used unpaired shoes stuffed into plastic shopping bags – covered the floor of his room. It smelled of urine. It smelled like a slot deep in the old hospital building. The ceiling was off, and the ceiling of the room above that, and the one above that too: all the way to the roof, which was also off. The room was open to the night sky.

In some way, Short's original procedure was still going on. The cameras whirred and shook above him. The walls, bluish with radioactive dyes and ruined by moonlight, were crawling with slow old people pulling themselves head-down towards the floor. 'Where's the toilet here?' they whispered. 'I think it's over that way, dear.' The tweed jackets of the men, the old fashioned wool skirts of the women, fell around their heads, muffling their dull talk; while by the window, Yummie the watchman kept his eye on the street below.

'Why are you doing this?' Short said.

'You think you are alive. Have a closer look. These people were victims of that thought too. People come home from a visit and discover they've never left. Or they have a wall knocked down in their attic and find this behind it. Do you see?'

'I don't see, no.'

'People imagine there will be no upshot from this, no discovery, that it will be the end of the story. Or so they hope.'

'Another thing,' Short said: 'I don't want you here.'

'Good luck with that.'

That was a low point, Short was forced to admit; but afterwards his life seemed to improve. He found another room, not far from the hospital. He went to the gym every two or three days. From being a zone of anxiety, the weekly act of transferring his medication from its calendar-packaging into the dispenser became a comforting regime. Bisoprolol, losartan potassium, atorvastatin, lansoprazole like a cheap holiday destination in the Canary Islands: their side effects were legion, though in three months Short had suffered only a sudden but unimpressive swelling of the inner lip. He bought himself a blood pressure monitor. The clutch of its cuff was like a reassuring hand on his upper arm, although inevitably it reminded him of things he didn't want to remember. Once a major organ has failed you – or you have failed it – your relations with the world become more tentative, more grateful and fragile. He had never liked to feel the beat of his heart. Other emotional reactions he experienced: a kind of protective reluctance; easily-triggered startle reflex; fear that every internal sensation might be the symptom of another event.

'But there's something else too,' he told Sister Linda. He experienced it as 'a kind of lifting up away from life and towards it at the same time. You can't avoid it anymore, so all you're left with is to engage it.'

'I'm not sure I follow you,' she said.

'The other thing is I'm determined to be kinder to myself.'

By day he walked the streets – chatting out loud to no one, maintaining a brisk pace but always checking that his heart rate remained safely within the range – or toured the supermarket aisles foraging for products at the green end of the scale. At night he watched on-demand television; worked on the Guardian crossword puzzle he had begun in hospital. He had to admit now that he had enjoyed his stay there, the warmth at night, the regular coming and going of the staff by day. He had felt safe for the first time in his life. He went through his belongings until he found the toothpaste and toothbrush he had brought back with him from Coronary Care, laying them out on top of his chest of drawers where he could see them, along with a pair of red non-slip ward socks still in their packaging. While he was doing that, Yummie climbed slowly down the wall behind him and said:

'You needn't think collecting a lot of old rubbish will help. They all thought that.'

'Those chickens you used to mention,' Short said: 'I never saw them. How are they now? I often think of you on the street, waiting outside the hospices and care homes in all weathers. I worry on your behalf.'

'Worry about yourself,' said Yummie, 'not me. That's my advice.'

2017

The Causeway

'NOBODY HAS BEEN HERE for a hundred years. Why should you take an interest?'

Crome didn't know. He had been bored with travel and almost frightened by the immense distance of his home.

'You can get sick of stars,' he said.

'We can't be helped, you know. You should go back where you came.' She swept an arm vaguely across an arc of sky attributing to him several unlikely points of origin. The Heavy Stars: surely she didn't think he came from there. Firelit, her face was beautiful, strange.

'People have tried. We don't want you here. Don't you see we are ashamed?'

He got up, planning to turn his back on her abruptly, evince some powerful emotion, shock her.

'The migration begins tomorrow,' she said.

He sighed, walked away a few paces.

'You should leave before then,' she called after him calmly.

He thought it might be some kind of adolescent pose, evidence of uncertainty. He looked back at her thin, appealing form behind the fir: her robe was tinted orange by the dying flames, and a heat shimmer distorted her. He shrugged.

'I'm going to take you away from here whether you want to go or not,' he said. 'This entire planet is a madhouse.'

There were things he didn't quite understand, but even after a week of her evasions, he was sure she had no husband.

A little after dawn the next morning, lured by the continuing enigma of the causeway, Crome flew his queer machine over to the coast.

It was a hundred-kilometre trip, and the landscape was as quietly resigned as its inhabitants. Low hills, worn drumlins, coarse grass and bracken, the odd thorn or bullace bent by the prevailing wind: it was tired and passive, sparsely populated, and prone to slow, drizzling rains. He found it vastly irritating.

The causeway he had discovered as he made his final braking run some weeks before. Its apparent length had impressed him immediately, but he had been too occupied with his instruments to give it attention. Since then he had come to believe it crossed some thousands of kilometres of ocean, linking two large continents. But he preferred to leave that simply as a possibility, and he had never flown its length.

The villagers could not be persuaded to talk about it. He knew they hadn't built it. Settling the machine above the tideline, he gazed blankly through a porthole; tapped his fingers for a moment, three against four. These visits were an indulgence: not that he had any reason to feel guilty.

It was a shingle beach, a vista of grey ovoid pebbles stretching to the uneasy sea. The wind blew his hair into his face, the pebbles scraped and shifted beneath his feet. Black gulls were squabbling over the terminal massif of the causeway; circling, mewling, dipping down to the access ramp hidden among the dunes; furious quanta of energy in a static panorama.

He began as always by trying to make some sense out of the immense age of the structure, poking desultorily about where the great uneven granite blocks grew out of the bedrock of the shore. Far back in the gaps between the stones were traces of old, crude mortar. The thing reared thirty metres above him, its shadow cold. He was overpowered by Time, and soon grew tired.

He prised some small crustaceans away from the green, slimy surface beneath the high-water line, but later threw them into the water.

He wandered through the dunes to the access ramp and found that the gulls had been mobbing a larger bird. Its white feathers were bloody and disordered, its metre-and-a-half span of wing limp and ineffectual. He wondered why it had not escaped by flying. He thought once that it moved – saw himself washing it in the sea, taking it back to the village as a present for the girl – but it was quite dead.

Up on top, the wind seemed to pluck harder at his clothes, and if he looked down suddenly, he tended to lose his balance.

The road itself had a much smoother surface than the rest of the structure, a completed look. He stood at the exact spot where the ramp became horizontal, and stared down the long grey perspective.

I am standing at the very beginning, he thought. Right here.

The road had a slightly convex surface and no walls. There were cracks, but he could ignore them, particularly in the middle-distance, where they vanished in the haze. The causeway was enormous beneath his feet, but as it moved out across the sea it dwindled to a thread, a tenuous link with the barely perceptible horizon.

The sea was choppy.

He saw something that made him hurry back down the ramp.

Seaward of the shingle where he had grounded the machine, the retreating tide had exposed a strip of sand. Along it, from the south, meandered a line of footprints, dark and haphazard against the glistening surface. They were already losing definition as the waterlogged sand sank back into a plane.

An old, hunched figure was making its way hesitantly over the pebbles. There was nothing male or female about its long dirty coat, or the way the wind plucked at it. It stopped every so often to stoop awkwardly, grub about, and put something in a wicker basket beneath its arm. Reaching Crome's machine, it halted abruptly; took a pace back, peering.

After a moment, it set the basket down, spat, and shook its fist irritably at the obstruction.

Crome's boots thudded on the access ramp – each footfall exploding along his bones – and sprayed grey sand as he entered the dunes, his arms cartwheeling.

'Oy!' he shouted.

He looked down and saw that he was going to tread on the dead bird. He tried to change direction in mid-stride: fell heavily and rolled down the side of the dune, marram whipping his face. When he had picked himself up, he found that the figure with the basket had gone, and left no footprints in the shingle. He crushed several small, active dune bugs that had got into his clothing.

He lifted the machine on its chemical engines, trawled north and south along the beach, and made four or five passes over the causeway environs. Nothing was moving there but the marram and the mad, speedy gulls, so he flew back to the village to clarify what the girl had told him the night before. Below him, the land was lost, diffused by drizzle, a watercolour applied too wet.

He closed the portholes.

The village was empty. A few sheep huddled in an irregular field and panicked when he landed. A discarded length of unbleached cloth looped down one street in the wind; in another, a cat stalked something he couldn't quite see. Hunched into his clothes against the rain, he quartered the place, carrying a small, powered megaphone.

'Halloo!' he shouted. There were no answers, and the buildings hardly echoed.

The villagers were defined here, in the absence of tension between village and landscape. The single-storey barns and cottages were comfortably weathered, their edges blurred by accumulations of moss and lichen. Crome shivered, wishing for a less vernacular architecture, a severity of line that might provide a reply to the organic dreariness of the landscape, if not a defence against it.

The cat had vanished.

All the dwellings were carefully shut up, neat and deserted, dim and chilly inside. He entered every other one – knocking loudly on each door before he opened it – and found nothing more to do than fiddle with domestic implements or poke through chests of clean, abandoned linen. In the girl's home, there was no message for him.

Soot stirred and rustled in the chimney as he examined some of her personal garments. He put his megaphone down by a wooden cruet that stood on the scrubbed table and compared them as expressions of purpose.

Along the ledge above the fireplace marched a curious little procession of clay figures, crudely painted in bright colours.

Where have they all gone? he thought. He felt offended to discover she had been telling the truth about that.

The cat reappeared as he left, rubbing itself briefly against his leg. It purred as he walked away, and slipped into her house without looking after him. 'You're too late.' Rain dripped steadily into stone sinks outside each cottage, soft water for washing the healthy, peasant hair of the women.

During the latter part of the morning, he discovered that the migration was general: drifting in and out of low cloud cover, he watched the moorland villages emptying themselves smoothly on to the major road of the province via a loose network of unsurfaced lanes. After two or three hours a caravan several kilometres long had formed beneath him, a long blind animal moving very slowly towards the sea.

While the girl and her fellow villagers remained a separate unit, he hovered above them; but by twilight the caravan had absorbed them, and he was forced down. A fine rain hissed across the heath on an easterly wind, beading the dull shell of his machine, like condensation on a black grape. Migrants streamed past him as he stood shivering by the road.

Their faces were empty and similar, their gait uniform; they were dressed in coarse wool; some of them carried small bundles. They rarely spoke among themselves, and affected not to notice him at all. (Originally he had parked the machine in the centre of the road ahead of them, hoping to focus attention on his arrival: but they had simply split into two columns and flowed past on either side, scattering silently when he throttled up and lifted off again.) It was a dull pilgrimage. The children that gazed incuriously at him or the machine would look away as soon as he smiled. A dull pilgrimage, he thought.

Three-quarters of the caravan passed.

'Here I am!' he shouted.

Her expression was calm and contained, in repose despite a frame of damp, stringy hair: it recalled vividly the tired, bucolic fatalism of the older villagers. She raised her arm briefly to wipe rain from the hollows of her cheeks; ignored him. She was entirely involved with walking. Her robe clung wetly to the small of her back, like the paint on a cheap Madonna.

A village boy was walking at her left side, a big, graceless adolescent wearing bulky agricultural sabots. The nape of his neck was red and soft. He kept reaching back there with blunt fingers to scratch at an incipient boil.

Crome hurried along and fell into step on her right. He caught her arm.

'It's me.'

'Please go away. I told you we can't be –'

'All right,' he admitted, 'I'm not interested in the rest of them. Why on earth are you going off with them like this?'

'It's just something we do.'

'Here,' said the boy suddenly, craning his neck to peer at Crome. 'Why don't you pee off? You can see she doesn't want to listen to that stuff.' His lips were thick and strong. Curly yellow hairs sprouted in clumps from his chin and cheekbones.

'Look –' Crome tugged at the girl's sleeve '–leave this stupid procession. It's all right for these people.' He indicated the boy.

She shook his hand away. 'No.'

'You heard her,' said the boy. 'Bugger off.' He touched her shoulder possessively. He pointed a belligerent finger at Crome, showed his teeth. 'We don't want you here. She doesn't want you, either. Sorry.'

'Christ!' shouted Crome. 'Who is this? What is he to you?' He waved his arms.

Tonelessly, she said, 'This is Gabriel.'

The boy blushed and grinned stupidly. 'Yes.' He licked his lips. 'And don't hurry back,' he told Crome.

'You said nothing about this to me. Why haven't I seen him before? Oh, for God's sake stop fooling about. Come on.' He had lost patience with her. 'He's a village idiot!'

Gabriel worked his lips around and spat. He stepped agilely round to Crome's side of the girl, dusting his hands. 'Do you want it willing, or not?' he hissed. He clutched at Crome's clothing and dragged him bodily out of the column. 'It makes no bloody difference to me, then.'

The migrants behind milled about. One of them stumbled over Crome's feet. They closed the gap and walked, hardly looking at him.

Out on the peat-moss he tore himself loose. The wind cut at him. The boy came very close. 'How do you want it? Well then?' He grinned. Ropes of spittle linked his upper and lower incisors. His face was pink and healthy. He rolled up his sleeves, flexed his knees, and tested his footing on the moss.

'I'm not sure what you mean,' said Crome.

'You wet little sod.'

Gabriel drew one foot back and lashed out. It was so quick: the heavy wooden sabot hit Crome just below the knee. His leg gave way abruptly as the blow shuddered along his bones. He yelled involuntarily and fell forward into the moss. He squirmed and looked up. The boy was grinning at him. 'Want any more? I've hurt strong men with these clogs.' He laughed.

Crome let his head settle back. Brackish water squeezed out of the moss ran into his mouth. His shin wasn't broken, but the whole leg was trembling violently. He had wet himself. He knew the girl was standing over him, too.

'I watched you for a week,' he said. 'You had nobody in the village.'

'He's been away.'

Gabriel came between them. 'You quite sure you don't want any more of that?' And, when Crome had looked away ritually, shaking his head (full of fear but thinking, you arrogant bastard): 'Fair enough then.'

He nodded equably and took the girl's arm.

Crome rubbed his bad leg, stood up. He let them move off a little way in the direction of the procession, then followed, limping. His light boots made very little noise on the moss. He locked both his hands together and swung them into the nape of the boy's red neck. Then he stumbled the half-kilometre to his queer vehicle, looking back through the rain and the gathering dark to watch humiliated as the girl knelt over her collapsed youth.

The migrants were still walking, unpoliced and orderly; impassive. All through the night, they registered on his detectors: the populations of outlying villages, coming on late but steady behind the main body.

He kept track of the caravan, although by now he was quite certain of its destination. The obsessive plodding of the villagers moved him to a mixture of fury and elation; an emotion which, paradoxically, affected him most when they stopped.

At noon, he would fly low over their heads as they lit their cooking fires, putting the machine through hesitation rolls and daring outside loops; when he went transonic they fell down like curious little wooden dolls, hands clamped over their ears. After nightfall, he hovered beneath the cloudbase injecting powdered cerium into his exhaust venturi and firing off red parachute flares.

But he grew bored as they came within striking distance of the coast. On the third day since his discovery of the abandoned village, he returned to the causeway.

Down where the tide slapped the granite, spindrift rose in fast spectral arcs; up over the access-ramp the gulls spun and side-slipped furiously, shedding feathers; but the causeway buttresses and the immense roadway absorbed all that – they glistened, they hummed faintly with accumulated Time.

Recalling his last experience on the shore, Crome resumed his search for the old beachcomber, scouring the sand for footprints. He found nothing.

He decided on stealth, he hid behind a buttress.

He caught the sod throwing stones at his machine.

'Stop that!' he shouted, as the vehicle's hull rang sullenly.

Coat flapping and cracking wildly in the wind, the beachcomber ignored him. Gnarled, liver-spotted hands scrabbled energetically in the shingle. Crome left his cover, came closer, and the previous sexual ambivalence of the figure resolved: it was a man, with chin-whiskers and a rheumy eye.

'Come off it!' Crome yelled. 'I want you!'

The old man twitched. He looked challengingly at Crome, and threw another stone, the billowing coat lending his motions a mad energy. He cackled and turned to escape. His basket lay on the shingle: he tried to pick it up on the move, stumbled, and fell down in a vile storm of rags and flailing limbs. He looked up at Crome, panting.

'You wouldn't hurt an old man?'

Crome helped him up.

'I just wanted to ask you some things.'

'Oh, ah.' His teeth were brown and sticky. His hands ran over him like tired piebald crabs, picking at his thighs and crotch. He bent down, clutched his basket firmly to his chest. He eyed Crome slyly. 'You wouldn't *steal* from an old man?'

'No. Look, you must have lived here for years. What do you know about the causeway?'

He squinted. 'Eh? Oh, that. I know all about that, all right.'

He plucked at Crome's sleeve, drew him close and whispered: 'You come a long way, then?' He chuckled. 'Oh, I could tell you some tales about *that*. Pee your pants.' He wiped his nose on the back of his hand. 'Ah.'

'Yes?' said Crome.

'What? Now you look here at this, for instance –' He offered Crome his basket. 'You're an honest lad. Take a look at this.'

It was full of white pebbles. They were uniformly ovoid and smooth. They averaged six or seven centimetres long. Wet sand adhered to some of them.

'These here,' he said, 'is eggs.'

He seemed to notice Crome's machine again.

He grimaced and spat at it. He shook both fists. When Crome stepped forward to prevent him from picking up another stone, a vacant, silly look of fear crossed his face. He dropped the basket and ran off, reaching the nearest dune without looking back. He scrambled up it with amazing agility.

'Bloody *eggs*!' he shouted, and vanished.

Crome stirred some of the spilt pebbles with his foot. He looked bitterly round at the inert landscape. He went back to the machine and modified some equipment.

Up on the causeway.

During the evening, the wind had risen and cleared the cloud cover, revealing odd configurations of stars. One moon came up, hazed faintly by wisps of fast-travelling cirrostratus. The tide rose and bit the shingle. The wind gave the darkness a sense of motion, but the causeway was heavy, inorganic. Moonlit, the cracks in the roadway made a strange, communicative web. Crome, standing on the access–ramp, felt that given time he might have understood.

Behind him, a mechanical voice was counting out seconds.

At *sixty* the causeway groaned and shuddered.

Two kilometres ahead, the road lifted itself into a one-in-one gradient, bent like a neck, and flew apart. Bits of masonry floated upward, silhouetted against an inverted cone of white light. Crome threw his tools into the sea. The wave-front of the explosion rocked him. Smoke and dust streamed past like weed in a shallow river.

He shook his head.

In the moment before the demolition charge fired he had imagined he could see along the whole, immense length of the causeway to the opposing shore; as if he had the power to overcome horizons.

He lifted off into the turbulence above the area of collapse. The machine yawed, spun slowly: dirty steam shrouded it as the sea boiled through a thirty-metre gap in the ancient masonry.

He turned his back and flew inland at Mach 2, trailing more concussions.

That night he further limited the options of the column, visiting the moorland with plastic explosives and improvised detonators. He mined key roads and bridges until just before dawn, working in the fitful red glare of the erupting villages.

In the dark hinterland there was nothing wholly human. Crome found a six-kilometre animal nosing hesitantly at the dunes, directed by some uncomfortable instinct to find a way through. Its head broke suddenly into a hundred component parts as it felt about for the route buried in the shifting sands. It changed shape uneasily; impatient; hurt by internal goads.

By the time he had settled the machine on the shingle the road had been rediscovered: with a curious gritty rustling of feet, the main body of the column was spilling on to the access-ramp of the causeway. Faces disturbed him, passing in the pre-dawn chill. The children were alien, tired. He suspected that the column had been moving all night.

The wind hissed in the marram. A faint band of viridian light appeared above the eastern horizon. It struck wickedly off the line of a jaw, the side of a neck, limned the causeway buttresses like dawn in an underworld.

It was still too dark to see well. Crome waited for the girl. He mistook other women for her; stopped them; found himself staring horrified into unknown peasant eyes. They were strong, they pulled away from him without a word. Growing frightened of them, he clambered up the side of a tall dune to wait out the inevitable confusion and retreat. He decided to approach the girl with his final offer somewhere on the return journey.

The sky paled. High chains of cloud broke free of the horizon and came on purposefully, reflecting magenta and burnt orange. Seabirds began dogfighting above the causeway, wailing as they shot the blackened gap left by Crome's bomb.

The column hesitated. It compacted itself into a third of its original length. Crome sniggered. Along the submerged dune road came a few infirm stragglers, murmuring dully. They wedged themselves on to the access-ramp, pushing against the motionless backs of the main body. Their legs attempted walking motions. Some of them collapsed.

Two kilometres out, the leaders of the caravan faced a heavy sea. They moved their heads bemusedly from side to side, squinting at the mad black gulls.

'Why aren't you migrating?' called Crome derisively.

He raced down to the machine and found his little electric megaphone.

'Why aren't you?' he boomed. He laughed.

He was floundering back up the face of the dune for a better look when the first of the villagers stepped calmly off the lip of the cavity and fell into the water; by the time he had reached the top the column was moving again, faster and faster.

1971

Colonising the Future

HUMANITY: YOU'RE WELCOME TO find your own. An epistemic shift reveals that everything is mathematics. Discoveries on the 'Fano Plane' reveal that mathematics is not a set of rules but the structure underneath everything. Division algebras control all nature's 'laws': eight degrees of freedom can be used to generate one neutrino, one electron, three up quarks and three down quarks. Is the Fano Plane 'real'? Or a self-referential cabalistic diagram? It makes no difference, the inhabitants of the near future discover. They continue to experience themselves and their context. A sunrise is still a sunrise.

Humanity & the rapture: In the future we expected to ingest a single dose of tailored viruses and nanomachines, which would effect the most amazing change. We would almost instantly be quite different from, say, our parents. It was a good prediction except that, all the time, we were already in the future. We still are. Every day, as we ingest our untailored paste of environmental microplastics, hormones and other transformative pollutants, we move a little further in, losing a little more of what it used to mean to be human and gaining a little more of what it means now.

Humanity & the past: Automotive components are discovered by fossil hunting holidaymakers, embedded in the 'Black Ven' strata of England's Jurassic Coast. In early footage of these unlikely finds (mainly engine blocks and suspension items from the late 1980s, held aloft in the rain by jubilant amateur palaeontologists) we see that they are not rusty but genuinely fossilised. Originally dismissed as corroded items from some recent RTA on the slopes above, they are in fact temporal anomalies which redefine concepts like 'the Anthropocene' and send palaeontology back to revise its understanding of the earliest drawings from the Precambrian fossil beds of the Burgess Shale.

Humanity loses its way: Palinurus the navigator fell off the boat into the Underworld and forgot his only talent. Lost inland – inside the land – he came to believe he had successfully rejected the Orphic adventure. But as usual things were tangled up together, and every route led downwards or opened its own can of snakes. 'Whatever art is,' he would propose later, 'it's not about the past; whatever science is, it is not about the future.' What if both these categories were bankrupt, and the world was always the present, and there was some other grid that could be laid over things?

Humanity: new kinds of medicine. 'Before I abandoned vaccination, I had so many eating disorders and breakdowns I couldn't count them. I felt no one was seeing my point of view. It was such a relief when I understood I could let my children make a future they felt was theirs, take their chances in the marvellous lottery of disease. Now bravery and good genes, rapture and singularity, intertwine. Now the whole family can float back into the future they deserve. Float away on a golden haze. Futures are everywhere and when you are human you can just have everything you want.'

Humanity at night: Two visitors board the sole remaining inland funicular railway in Great Brexit. New to the country, they sit in a front seat. They love the view: the dark walls of the steep sandstone gorge, the lights of the town above. A minute or two later they receive extensive injuries from 'an unknown source'. Understanding that the present administration won't help them, they post images of their wounds on social media. The present is the future. The present is the past. Every instant, these images seem to be saying, we lose a little of what we might be and regain more of what we always were.

Humanity: Palinurus & the fish. 'The vast fish swims along. It never hurries. It never stops. You will never exhaust the fish. Nothing that happens around it makes a difference to it. Whenever you wake you're aware of the fish swimming. If anxiety is a word that can be used in this context, any anxiety here is yours. The fish will never crush you! It will never even notice you! It's cold out there in the dark; it's dark. Nothing is changed by night or swimming. It's clear you are not the fish. The only certainty is that one day you will begin to understand what that means.'

Humanity, age & death: It's not that we get older, it's that the age of things becomes so hard to understand. New objects have an artificiality to them, in their colours that always suggest chemicals or toys; or they resemble items from two hundred years ago, the uses of which have been forgotten. Plastic, shiny & inert, lighted immovably from inside today's preferred surface, shiny or matt, is easily understood. You might as well pick up a stone, although it would be heavier. Yet here is the voice as always, telling you something you wanted to know before you knew you wanted to know it.

Humanity, death & burial: For some time after the new custom took hold, there was confusion on the more crowded motorways, the environs of which had become as hallowed as any English churchyard before them. Bouquets blew & burst across the tarmac in celebratory Instagrams & YouTube footage. On the grass banks at Brentwood & Corbets Tay, out of the grey central glare of the midnight carriageway, processions of the dead were glimpsed, shadowy and irritable, swaying down towards realities they thought they had been able to leave behind They were, as WG Sebald put it so succinctly, 'usually a little shorter than they had been in life…'

Humanity & the animals: A chair had been left out in the rain, at a distance from the garden pond but facing it across the lawn as if someone had been watching the water all night but didn't, perhaps, want to get too close. A little light fell on the cobbled path, glistened along the arms of the chair. None fell on the yellow irises around the pond; or on the tall poppies by the hedge, with their bent Victorian necks and papery flowers. Eighteen hours later, the jackdaws arrived in the woods around the house. It had been a long flight.

2020

The Machine in Shaft Ten

ALTHOUGH I WAS LATER to become intimately involved with Professor Nicholas Bruton and the final, fatal events at the base of Shaft Ten, I was prevented by a series of personal disasters from taking much interest in the original announcement of his curious discovery at the centre of the earth. A copy of *National Geographic* containing the professor's immaculate geological proof of the presence of an 'emotion converter' buried at the core of our planet lay unread on my desk for a month; and, I am ashamed to say, the international scientific uproar precipitated in the early weeks of 197 – by the sinking of the 'B' series of exploratory shafts – passed me by. One is morally entitled, I believe, to some life of one's own, even to the detriment of one's public self.

I did, however, hear the end of a broadcast talk given by the professor, soon after the appearance of the *National Geographic* article, to an audience made up of interested parties from the English scientific community. I feel that 'interested' may not be the best word to use in this context: their behaviour was undignified, and made listening rather difficult. Despite that, I found myself fascinated by his conclusions.

'Thus, gentlemen,' he said, 'I can see no alternative to a radical readjustment of Man's view of himself and his universe.

'I have shown – beyond doubt, I believe – that our emotions, subsequent to their processing at the core of the earth, are converted to an essentially radiological energy and projected into space, in the direction of the sun.

'We have no descriptive systems capable of dealing with whatever changes they effect there. We must, however, as my recently published work shows, view this as an artificial process; and, more important, *a process of very long-standing indeed*.

'Gentlemen, we have no option but to assume that the joys and miseries of Man are fuel for some gigantic cosmic machine; that, since our evolution as an emotion-bearing species, we have been *used*; that our most public triumphs and our most sordid personal tragedies may be the oil that runs the galactic bakery van.

'How does it feel, gentlemen, to be a resource?'

My resignation from the Cabinet had only recently come into effect: finding it difficult to shake off old habits, I wondered how my ex-colleagues would react to the news (Fairbairn took the government to the country, and was promptly thrown out on his ear). Beyond that, I was unconcerned by the machine at the centre of the earth until I received, in the July of that year, a visit from the professor himself.

By then, of course, his work had been verified, and his credibility as an investigator completely restored.

Social and religious hysteria was at a peak: fifty new administrations and a hundred novel creeds had sprung up during the week following Shaft Ten's attainment of 'machine-zero' (perhaps the most amazing feature of this whole affair was the speed at which a successful shaft was sunk). The few rational observers who remained in the world were left to reflect cynically that, even when convinced of the true purpose of his ideological conflicts – 'emotional sumps' in the growing terminology of the machine – Man could find no more original method of expressing himself than to multiply them.

Several small wars, dormant for some time, rampaged over South East Asia and the Middle East with refreshed ferocity. I feared privately that the emotion converter would suffer an overload of faith and patriotism, triggering some immense metaphysical catastrophe as its capacitors exhausted themselves into the surrounding magma.

A change had come about in the professor's attitude to his discovery: he was no longer interested in pure science, he explained as I ushered him into the study of my summer home at Lympne, but in something he called 'action'.

I remember very few of the impressions I received at that first meeting; they are obscured by later images of him, clothed and equipped for his descent of Shaft Ten. I can recall being almost repelled by his physiology. He was a peculiarly small man with an immense, sad head (I believe that, earlier in his career, he had written a paper which offered new light on the physical characteristics of Darwin, da Vinci, and Socrates – all three were, it seems, less than five feet tall) and his features were birdlike to an exaggerated degree, too well-defined for the comfort of his friends and a gift to his enemies.

'Frankly,' he said, 'I've come to you for finance.' I found this surprising. I had imagined that, in his present commanding situation, he would have access to considerable finances as soon as he decided on a line of research he felt worthwhile. 'There are,' he told me, 'more important things than research.' He looked down at his tiny blunt hands for a moment. 'We didn't deserve this, Lutkin,' he said. 'Any of us.' He seemed to be uncomfortable with the sentiment. 'There is a way to stop it, though, you know,' he went on, quite defiantly. 'I'm sure *you* don't like living with that thing down there, any more than I do.'

He was making a transition common in that decade: the fumbling shift from concern for abstracts to a more active involvement with the results of his work. When he refused to tell me the nature of the scheme he wished me to support, I politely but firmly refused to commit myself. But the vanity of the failed public figure, the half-conscious realisation that if I helped him I would retrieve my position as a substantial contributor to the mainstream of events, weakened my rejection severely.

Two days later, he called again, and left with my promise of limited support (ceiling to be decided by myself), in exchange for an assurance that I would accompany him on any expedition to the centre of the earth.

At the end of July my personal affairs adjusted themselves most equably, and, my time being once more my own, I studied the news media daily. The professor had dropped sharply out of the public gaze, and I learned very little of him beyond that he had shut himself away somewhere in Cumberland, and refused to make comment even on the wealth of material being generated by the investigatory teams at the base of Shaft Ten. Extant newsreel films of his retreat in Honister Pass show a square stone cottage set among sombre, desolate hills.

Most of the news through August and the beginning of September was of a steady social and moral adjustment which can perhaps best be expressed in the decline of the authoritative religions. A complex front of Druidic and neo-Mayan cults swept out of centres as widely dissimilar as Peach Valley, California and St. Anne's, England; all had basically apocalyptic premises and a solar orientation. But the religion of the decade began in Chile, when a minor nihilist and political agitator named Estanislao persuaded two thousand people to drown themselves in the Pacific Ocean.

The Roman Catholic Church was the major casualty of this period. Estanislao's queer religion of despair spread rapidly across Latin America, and, later, the world; Pope Pius declared him the Antichrist, and was assassinated by a sensible Bolivian while blessing a crowd in Lima, Peru. Massive, silent mobs gathered to hear Estanislao and his disciple announce that since man was incapable of independent action and decision-making, all that was left to him was to choose the manner of his own death as unemotionally as possible, thus depriving the machine of its raw materials.

As I have said, I saw nothing of the professor, but in October he began to draw regularly on the Lloyds account I had opened in his name, and he continued to make his presence felt in this manner until late December. I received one letter from him, hastily-written in a somewhat stilted tone. He was worried, he informed me, that local hysteria would prematurely end his preparations: bands of armed agricultural workers were active in the area of Keswick, destroying machinery and isolated houses; would I therefore authorise his purchase of a quantity of small arms, so that his staff might protect themselves?

'D' notices, and a heavy security blanket then in effect, prevented any public report of such guerrilla activity. I was not anxious to subscribe to any programme of violence, and asked Bruton if he could not finish his work in the south. There was a space of some days before he replied by telephone. I noticed immediately an alteration in the character of his voice, a side product, I assumed, of his successfully completing the transition I have mentioned above. He was adamant in his demand for the weapons, and I was duly presented with an invoice from a well-known private arms dealer. I felt nervous, but resigned.

In January, almost a year after the discovery of the machine, I received a cryptic telegram dispatched from Keswick. Two days later I was in train for Retford in Nottinghamshire, and the head of Shaft Ten.

The 'B' series of shafts had created their own microclimate, a result of the volcanic failure of Shafts Four through Six. Consequently, most of the county lacked the blanket of January snow that covered the rest of the Midlands, and over its flat, once-productive beet-fields hung a warm, oppressive mist. A small Vesuvian cone reared up from the site of the teacher-training college disaster at Eaton, East Retford. Classic basalt formations had inundated the colliery town of Worksop. Immense long-chain protein molecules had been observed forming in the heated pools of waste chemicals discharged by the shaft projects among the suburban lava flows of Retford.

Bruton telephoned soon after I had booked into my hotel. He limited himself to rather brusque directions for finding Shaft Ten and instructions as to the type of clothing I should wear: when I pressed him for further information, he resorted to obscurity. That was at approximately ten o'clock in the evening; it seemed rather strange to me that we were to begin the descent almost at once. I ate a light meal, and, to quell my growing nervousness about the coming incredible journey into the underworld, decided to walk to the head of the shaft.

Faint volcanic flares lit the Ordsall Road as I went, and through breaks in the mist I could see electrical will-o'-the-wisps dancing round the summit of the Eaton cone. The service buildings for the shaft were located on the corpse of Ordsall Wood; a few remaining bitter trees were outlined against the massive pre-cast concrete sheds that housed the shaft-refrigeration turbines. In the darkness the ground vibrated palpably; subsonics from the deeper levels of the shaft itself trembled in my bones.

I stood beyond the arc-lights that surrounded the check-point gates, sweating in the heat of the nearest extractor-outlet, amazed by Man's ability to construct such enormous extensions of himself despite the tyranny of his most basic psychological processes. Had we not been bred specifically as a power source for the emotion converter, what might we not have accomplished? Two large Land Rovers drew up behind me and disgorged the professor and his staff.

At our first meeting, the watery-eyed scientist in Bruton's skull had been retreating under pressure from other elements of the man's personality: now he had vanished completely, and the tiny figure standing before me, dressed in a closely-fitting black overall, was composed, self-assured and powerful. The disproportion of his big, avian head no longer invited caricature – it was still desperately ugly, but a tremendous change had occurred behind his eyes. He was carrying a light shoulder pack, across which was strapped one of the machine pistols he had ordered in December.

I was dismayed. 'Look here, Bruton,' I said, 'you don't need that thing.' A glance at the dozen or so men who lounged on the vehicles behind him confirmed that they were similarly armed.

'I'm sorry, Lutkin,' he said, 'but things aren't quite what you've taken them to be. I should have explained. There never were any Luddites in Keswick. At least, not while I was there. I'm sorry. It was an unpardonable deception –' Here, he shook his head apologetically, and I noticed that he was in need of a barber '– but the only chance I had to get the stuff. No Grants Committee would have considered it; that's why I had to have you.'

'You must do without me from now on, professor,' I said. I was sick with anger. I turned my back on him and made to walk off in the direction of the town. He put a surprisingly powerful hand on my arm.

'I can't allow you to do that. Look, Lutkin, I told you that there was a way to stop the thing, and there is: but did you seriously expect that I would be permitted to just go down and turn it off?'

Abruptly, I realised that he was correct. Millions of man-hours of international co-operation had gone into the sinking of the shafts. More important, the shaft-projects were the sole still-centre in a political chaos: without them, the tenuous unity achieved for the first time ever by the major powers would evaporate. Sensing an advantage, he went on:

'And we deserve this chance, Lutkin. We deserve the opportunity to make our first gesture of independence since the Pliocene, to become self-determining at least as far as the limits that were originally built into us. Cornelius is right: that thing down there is bloody *insufferable*.

'We can't let it go on leaching.' A curious pause. Then: 'Whatever the repercussions.'

It was that peculiar choice of expression – with its Miltonic implications of cosmic rebellion – that convinced me then, and which haunts me now.

Bruton looked across at the head of Shaft Ten, and when he spoke again there was such a wealth of bitterness and despair in his voice that I hated to imagine what sort of dreams he had lived with since his discovery of the nature of the machine. However accidentally, he had impelled the human race to confront its own clown-like glorification of its metaphysical inferiority – and I think he felt the resultant terrifying sense of impotent rage more than anybody.

'With any luck,' he said, 'when we have finished here, Man will have no place or purpose at all. We've lived too long with them. We deserve the dignity of pointlessness.'

You will have seen the videotapes of our assault on the main gates, made automatically by the closed-circuit security system and retrieved later, at great personal risk, by Colonel C. R. S. Marsden of the Sherwood Foresters. Nothing would be accomplished by my adding to that record, although I would like to say that the so-called 'atrocities' Thompson and Frost claim to have detected on the poor-quality tapes from Camera Five simply did not take place. This is a deliberate slur on the professor's memory. We lost five men – not two, as Frost has suggested recently – and left the remaining ten to hold the head of the shaft open for our retreat.

'The odd thing,' Bruton said, as he operated the mechanisms of the elevator and the pressure doors of the cage sealed themselves behind us, 'is that I could have got in quite easily on my own. I'm well-respected here, you see. But they wouldn't have let this in without an inspection.' He had brought with him a heavy wooden crate, some three feet long by two square, and now tapped it significantly. 'I could have got in quite easily without it.' There was a tone of irony in his voice which repelled me even though it did not stem from any callous trait of his. I stared at his parrot-like, powder-burned face for some seconds, and he looked away.

The descent was uneventful and, apart from Bruton's terse advice on the proper use of the various instruments of personal comfort installed in the life cage, carried out in silence – if the vast humming and hissing of the shaft refrigeration can be termed 'silence'. The atmosphere of the cage rapidly became hot and stifling. I found myself swallowing almost constantly to relieve the unpleasant sensation in my ears. None of the awe I had previously felt towards Shaft Ten survived that journey. I don't know what I had expected: echoing fallopian tunnels recalling to my genetic memory the similar pre-womb excursion, perhaps – or simply some sight of the magma that boiled and roared around the shaft – some sense, anyway, that this was a forbidding Plutonian descent, carried out at great and immediately visible risk.

The reason for the professor's peculiar timing of the raid became apparent when we reached the complex of interconnecting vaults and passages that honeycombed the magma around the emotion converter, and found them deserted. Machine-zero was a high, cathedral vault, its organic-plastic walls constructed to resonate in sympathy with the shifting phases of the machine's cycle. Into this shivering, gently-lit space we lugged Bruton's box.

I had planned at this point in the narrative to introduce some illustrations of the more salient and enigmatic portions of the machine, but I find I am unable to obtain copyright. Most of you will have to hand, however, at least one of the many colourful diagrams of the mapped areas that have appeared in the Sunday supplements. I find the *Sunday Times* photographic essay the most comprehensive and accurate of these.

From machine-zero, the professor and I moved to the area usually labelled 'induction chamber' (Frost persists in using the obsolete Plattner notation 'primary capacitor': the area was later proved, of course, not to be a capacitor of any kind). By leaving it through Subsidiary Fornices 6 & 7, we avoided the little-understood lobes of material that choked the main archway. Achieving Access Point Three, we dragged our burden into the major staging vault which surrounded the heart of the machine. To find oneself standing a mere eighty feet (a higher figure may be given in some diagrams) from the exact geometrical centre of the earth is an exhilarating experience.

The soft fluctuating light that filled the vault lent the organic surfaces of the machine a delicate pastel tint, and reflected dully from the huge grapelike extrusions that had made their appearance on its walls after the sinking of Shaft Ten – so that the whole thing resembled a giant, alien fruit, ripe, but marred by parasitic organisms. In operation, the converter generated a constant musical chord, six separate vibrations on two notes comprising a 'modal' E. For a moment I stood, exultant yet tranquillised, feeling for the first time the mystical thrill I had expected of my journey.

But Bruton was inured to the effects of the machine. As soon as his box was put down, he prised open its lid, and from it took several small grey blocks of a waxy substance, apparently *plastique*; various pieces of detonating apparatus; and a woodcutter's axe with a long curved wooden shaft. 'You can do nothing here, Lutkin,' he told me. 'You might be more useful up on the surface.'

'Allow me at least to stay until you go up,' I said, hurt that I had been used as nothing more than a pack-animal. He shrugged, took a firm grip on the axe and began to swing it against a spot on the machine he had been at some pains to locate. I could see no difference between it and the surrounding areas.

He had soon cut a sizeable hole in the 'rind' of the converter, and about a pound and a half of rose-tinted, fleshy substance, dry and firm like the meat of a mushroom, lay on the floor of the chamber. Quickly, he packed explosive into the cavity, wired it up, and moved to another spot about five yards away to repeat the procedure. I experienced a peculiar, dreamlike curiosity as he worked, and moved about the central vault, relaxed by its rosy hues. By the time he had finished mining at equal intervals around the circumference of the machine, I was deep in an examination of one of the tumours I have noted above, fascinated by the veinlike structures of a pale gold colour that lay just beneath its surface. I heard a sharp metallic *click* behind me, and turned to find Bruton pressing a full magazine into his machine-pistol.

'Thanks for your help, Lutkin,' he said. 'It's time you went.'

I looked at the gun.

'Aren't you coming?' I asked foolishly.

He shook his head.

'But you'll be killed when it –'

He interrupted with a jerk of the machine-pistol barrel.

'You must get up there and tell them they have precisely fifty minutes to get clear of the head of the shaft and begin the evacuation of the town. I have allowed a small margin of error, but it would not be wise to let them know that.

'There will be a good deal of volcanism.'

'Tell whoever is in charge up there now that if you or any of my staff who are still alive are injured, or if they send anyone down the shaft, I will simply bypass the time-fuse and detonate the stuff at once.'

'Why are you doing this?' I said.

I could not understand him at the time. I left him under the threat of the gun (I cannot say whether he really intended to shoot me if I refused to leave him), but not because of it, and he knew that. By the time I had reached the access-point of the chamber, he had put it down and lost all interest in it. 'Professor!' I called. 'Don't be silly!' He pretended not to hear.

My last glimpse of him was as a tiny, madly-whirling figure swinging the axe again and again into the flesh of the emotion converter. His long white hair was damp with sweat, and on his pitiful, ugly face was an expression of what I can only describe as methodical ferocity. Since he had finished the work of mining, I could see no reason for that action. I realise now that he hated the machine, which seems paradoxical.

The events that followed my return to the surface are public knowledge.

The professor's prediction of volcanic disturbances was more than borne out. But thanks to the untiring efforts of Colonel Marsden – who had arrived with the Foresters shortly after our attack on the gates – we got out of the Shaft Ten buildings in advance of the *plastique* explosion and managed to move half the inhabitants of Retford before the greater explosion of the machine itself drowned the town under a lake of lava. For many days, Shaft Ten flung thousands of megatons of magma into the air every hour, and the crash evacuation of what is now the Nottingham Lava Plain was only partially successful.

My present position of trust came about largely as the result of a mistake on the part of Colonel Marsden. He was quite uninterested in politics, devoted to his career, and had forgotten that I no longer had a place in the House. My appearance at the head of Shaft Ten led him to think that I had been engaged in some official attempt to dissuade the professor from his anarchic attack on the machine. 'Negotiation never works with buggers like that, sir,' he said to me. I see no point in hiding the true reason for my presence there: the massive public support for the professor's act of defiance that has risen in the last year leads me to believe that the electorate will regard my honest admission with sympathy.

The human race is now, as the professor wished, entirely devoid of purpose. Recruitments to Estanislao's faith have fallen off recently, which seems to suggest that the survivors of his 'global suicide' programme – partly-realised during the hysteria which swept the world soon after the Retford eruption – are aware of the self-contradiction implicit in its creed. An ideology of despair is as emotional as any other.

Lately, I discover myself giving more and more attention to Bruton's words at the head of Shaft Ten. I envisage the entire nation, indeed, the entire human race, waiting unrepentant for whatever reprisals the builders of the machine may initiate. We have no meaning – and thus, thankfully, no more illusions – left to lose.

1972

A Young Man's Journey to Viriconium

ON THE DAY OF the enthronement of the new archbishop, the 'badly decomposed' body of a man was found on the roof of York Minster by a TV technician. He had been missing for eight months from a local hospital. He had fallen, it was said, from the tower; but no one had any idea how he had come to be there. I heard this on the local radio station in the day; what excited me about it was that they never repeated the item, and no mention of it was made either on the national broadcasts later in the day, or in the coverage of the ceremony itself. Mr Ambrayses was less impressed.

'A chance in a thousand it will be of any use to us,' he estimated. 'One in a thousand.'

I went to York anyway, and he came with me for some reason of his own – he paid visits to a second-hand bookshop and a taxidermist's. The streets were daubed with political slogans; even while the ceremony was going on, council employees were working hard along the route of the procession to paint them out. The man on the roof, I discovered, had been missing from an ordinary surgical unit, so I had made the journey for nothing as Mr Ambrayses predicted. What interested us at that time was any event connected with a mental or – especially – a geriatric home.

'We all want Viriconium,' Mr Ambrayses was fond of saying. 'But it is the old who want it most!' That night on the way home he added, 'No one here needs it. Do you see?'

The 11.52 Leeds stopping train was full of teenagers. The older boys looked confused and violent in their short haircuts, faces and jaws thrown forward, purple and white with cold; the girls watched them slyly, shrieked with laughter, then looked down and picked at their fingerless gloves. They stuck their heads out of the windows and shouted 'Fuck off!' into the rush of air. Later when we got off the train we saw them hopping backwards and forwards over a metal barrier in the sodium light, unfathomable and energetic as grasshoppers in the sun. Sensing my disappointment Mr Ambrayses said gently, 'On occasion we all want to go there so badly that we will invent a clue.'

'I'm not old,' I said.

Mr Ambrayses had lived next door to me for two years. At first I was only aware of him when I was trying to watch the news. A body under a coloured blanket, slumped at the foot of a corrugated iron fence; the camera moving in on a small red smear like a nose-bleed cleaned up with lavatory paper, then as if puzzledly on to helicopters, rubble, someone important being ushered into a building, a woman walking past the end of a street. Immediately Mr Ambrayses's low appreciative laughter would come 'Hur hur hur' through the thin partition wall, so that I lost the thread. 'Hur hur,' he would laugh, and I felt as if I was watching a television in a foreign country. He liked only the variety shows and situation comedies.

His laughter seemed to sensitise me to him, and I began to see him everywhere, like a new word I had learned: in his garden where the concrete paths, glazed with rain, reflected the sky; in Marie's café, a middle-aged man in a dirty suede coat, with jam on his fingers – licking at them with short dabbing licks like a child or an animal; in Sainsbury's with an empty metal basket in the crook of his arm, staring up and down the tinned meat aisle. He didn't seem to have anything to do. I saw him on a day trip bus to Matlock Bath, wearing one sheepskin mitten. His trousers, which were much too large for him, so that the arse of them hung down between his legs in a gloomy flap, were sewn up at the back with bright yellow thread as coarse as string. The bus was full of old women who nodded and smiled and read all the signs out to one another as if they were constructing or rehearsing between them the landscape as they went through it.

'Oh look, there's the Jodrell Arms!'

'... the Jodrell Arms.'

'And there's the A623!'

'... A623.'

The first time we spoke Mr Ambrayses told me, 'Identity is not negotiable. An identity you have achieved by agreement is always a prison.'

The second time, I had been out buying some Vapona. The houses up here, warm and cheerful as they are in summer, become in the first week of September cold and damp. Ordinary vigorous houseflies, which have crawled all August over the unripe lupin pods beneath the window, pour in and cluster on any warm surface, but especially on the floor near the electric fire, and the dusty grid at the back of the fridge; they cling to the side of the kettle as it cools. That year you couldn't leave food out for a moment. When I sat down to read in the morning, flies ran over my outstretched legs.

'I suppose you've got the same problem,' I said to Mr Ambrayses. 'I poison them,' I said, 'but they don't seem to take much notice.' I held up the Vapona, with its picture of a huge fly. 'Might as well try again.'

Mr Ambrayses nodded. 'Two explanations are commonly offered for this,' he said: 'In the first we are asked to imagine certain sites in the world – a crack in the concrete in Chicago or New Delhi, a twist in the air in an empty suburb of Prague, a clotted milk bottle on a Bradford tip – from which all flies issue in a constant stream, a smoke exhaled from some appalling fundamental level of things. This is what people are asking – though they do not usually know it – when they say exasperatedly, "Where are all these *flies* coming from?" Such locations are like the holes in the side of a new house where insulation has been pumped in: something left over from the constructional phase of the world.

'This is an adequate, even an appealing model of the process. But it is not modern; and I prefer the alternative, in which it is assumed that as Viriconium grinds past us, dragging its enormous bulk against the bulk of the world, the energy generated is expressed in the form of these insects, which are like the sparks shooting out from between two huge flywheels that have momentarily brushed each other.'

A famous novel begins:

> I went to Viriconium in a century which could find itself only in its own symbols, at an age when one seeks to unify one's experience through the symbolic events of the past. 'I saw myself go on board an airliner, which presently rose into the air. Above the Atlantic was another sea, made of white clouds; the sun burned on it. The only thing we recognised in all that immense white space was the vapour trail of another airliner on a parallel course. It disappeared abruptly. We were encouraged to eat a meal, watch first one film and then another. The captain apologised for the adverse winds, the turbulence, of what had seemed to us to be a completely tranquil journey, as if apologising for a difficult transition from childhood to adolescence.
>
> In Viriconium the light was like the light you only see on record covers and in the colour supplements.

Photographic precision of outline under an empty blue sky is one of the most haunting features of the Viriconium landscape. Ordinary objects – a book, a bowl of anemones, someone's hand – seem to be lit in a way which makes them very distinct from their background. The identity of things under this light seems enhanced. Their visual distinctness becomes metonymic of the reality we perceive both in them and in ourselves.

I began living in one of the tall grey houses that line the heights above Mynned.

You can't just fly there, of course.

Soon after my trip to York I got a job in a tourist café in the town. It was called the Gate House, and it was attached to a bookshop. The idea was that you could go in, look round the shelves, and leaf through a book while you drank your coffee. We had five or six tables with blue cloths on them, a limited menu of homemade pastries, and pictures by local artists on the walls. Crammed in on the wooden chairs on a wet afternoon, thirteen customers seemed to fill it to capacity; damp thickened in the corner by the coats. But it was often empty.

One day a man and a woman came in and sat down near one another but at separate tables. They stared at everything as if it was new to them.

The man wore a short zip-fronted gabardine jacket over his green knitted pullover and pink shirt; a brown trilby hat made his head seem small and his chin very pointed. His face had an old but unaged quality – the skin was smooth and brown, streaked, you saw suddenly, with dirt – which gave him the look of a little boy who had grown haggard round the eyes after an illness. He might have been anywhere between thirty and sixty. He looked too old for one and too young for the other: something had gone wrong with him. His eyes moved sorely from object to object in the room, as if he had never seen a calendar with a picture of Halifax town centre on it, or a chair or a plate before; as if he was continually surprised to find himself where he was.

I imagined he had come up for the day from one of the farms south of Buxton, where the wind sweeps across the North Staffordshire Plain and they sit in their old clothes all week in front of a broken television, listening to the gates banging.

He leaned over to the other table.

'Isn't it Friday tomorrow?' he said softly.

'You what?' answered the woman. 'Oh aye, Friday defnitely. Oh aye.' And when he added something in a voice too low for me to catch: 'No, there's no fruit cake, no, they won't have that here. No fruit cake, they won't have that.'

She dabbed her finger at him. 'Oh no, not here.'

Tilting her head to one side and holding her spoon deftly at an angle so that she could see into the bottom of her coffee cup, she scooped the half-melted sugar out of it. It was done in no time, with quick little licks and laps. When she had finished she sat back. 'I'll wait while tea time for another,' she said. 'I'll wait.' She had cunningly kept on her yellow-and-black-check overcoat, her red woollen hat.

'Will you have a cup of coffee now?' she asked. And seeing that he was gazing in his sore vague way at the landscapes on the walls, 'There watercolours those, on the wall, I'd have to look to be certain: watercolours those, nice.'

'I don't want any coffee.'

'Will you have ice cream?'

'I don't want any ice cream, thank you. It cools my stomach.

'You'll be better when you get back up there, you'll get television on. Get sat down in front of that.'

'Why should I want to watch the television?' he said quietly, looking away from a picture of the town bridge in the rain. 'I don't want any tea or supper; or any breakfast in the morning.'

He put his hands together for a moment and stared into

the air with his solemn boyish eyes in his delicately boned dirty face. He fumbled suddenly in his pockets.

'You can't smoke in here,' said the woman quickly. 'I don't think you can smoke in here, I thought I saw a sign which said no smoking because there's food about, you see, oh no: they won't have that in here.'

When they got up to pay me he said, 'Nice to have a change.' His voice was intelligent, but soft and clouded, like the voice of a hospital patient who wakes up disoriented in the afternoon and asks a new nurse the time. 'It's a day out, isn't it?' They had come over by bus from a suburb the other side of Huddersfield which he called Lock Wood or Long Wood. 'Nice to have a change,' he repeated, 'while the weather's still good.' And before I could reply: 'I've got a cold you see, really it's bronchial pneumonia, more like bronchial pneumonia. I've had it for a year. A year now or more: they can't help you at these Health Centres can they? My lungs seem inside out with it on a wet day –'

'Now get on,' the woman interrupted him.

Though his voice was so low they could have heard nothing, she grinned and bobbed at the other customers as if to apologise for him.

'None of that,' she said loudly to them.

She pushed him towards the door. 'I'm not his wife you know,' she said over her shoulder to me. 'Oh no, more his nurse companion, I've managed for two years. He's got money but I don't think I could marry him.'

She was like a budgerigar bobbing and shrugging in front of the mirror in its cage.

I looked out of the window half an hour later and they were still standing at the bus stop. Nothing could ever come of them.

The meaning of what they said to one another was carefully hidden in its own broken, insinuatory rhythms. Their lives were so intricately repressed that every word was like a loose fibre woven back immediately into an old knot. Eventually a bus arrived. When it pulled away again he was in one of the front seats on the top deck, looking down vaguely into the florist's window; while she sat some rows back on the other side of the aisle, wincing if he lit a cigarette and trying to draw his attention to something on part of the pavement he couldn't possibly see from where he was.

When I told Mr Ambrayses about them he was excited.

'That man, did he have a tiny scar? Beneath the hairline on the left side? Like a crescent, just visible beneath the hair?'

'How could I know that, Mr Ambrayses?'

'Never mind,' he said. 'That man's name is Doctor Petromax, and he once had tremendous power. He used it cleverly and soon stood the thickness of a mirror from what we all seek. But his nerve failed: what you see now is a ruin. He found an entrance to Viriconium in the lavatory of a restaurant in Huddersfield. There were imitation quarry tiles on the floor, and white porcelain tiles on the walls around the mirror. The mirror itself was so clean it seemed to show the way into another, more accurate version of the world. He knew by its cleanliness he was looking into one of the lavatories of Viriconium. He stared at himself staring out; and he has been staring at himself ever since. His courage would take him no further. What you see is a shell, we can learn nothing from him now.'

He shook his head.

'Which café was that?' I asked him. 'Do you know where it is?'

'It would not work for you, any more than it did for him, though for different reasons,' Mr Ambrayses assured me. 'Anyway, it is known only by the description I have given.'

He said this as if it was remote; on no map. But a café is only a café.

'I think I recognise it,' I said. 'In the steam behind the counter is a photo of an old comedian. Two men with walking sticks and white hair smile feebly at a round-shouldered waitress!'

'It would not work for you.'

'That man's name is Dr Petromax.'

Mr Ambrayses loved to preface his statements like this. It was a grammatical device which allowed him to penetrate appearances.

'That boy,' he would say, 'knows two incontrovertible facts about the world; he will reveal them to no one.' Or: 'That woman, though she seems young, dreams at night of the wharfs of the Yser Canal. By day, she wears beneath her clothes a garment of her own design to remind her of the people there, and their yellow lamps reflected with such distinctness in the surface of the water.'

On a steep bank near my house was a domestic apple tree which had long ago peacefully reverted amid the oaks and elder. When I first drew his attention to it Mr Ambrayses said, 'That tree has no name in botany. It has not flowered for ten years.' The next autumn, when the warm light slanted down through the drifting willow-herb silk, hundreds of small hard reddish fruits fell from it into the bracken; in spring it bore so much blossom my neighbours called it 'the white tree'.

'It bears no flowers in Viriconium,' said Mr Ambrayses. 'There, it stands in a courtyard off the Plaza of Realised Time, like the perfect replica of a tree. If you look back through the archway you see clean wide pavements, little shops, white-painted tubs of geraniums in the sunlight.'

'That man's name is Dr Petromax.'

Rilke describes a man for whom, 'in a moment more, everything will have lost its meaning, and that table and the cup, and the chair to which he clings, all the near and commonplace things around him, will have become unintelligible, strange and burdensome', and who nevertheless only sits and waits passively for the disaster to be complete. To an extent, I suppose, this happens to us all. But there was about Dr Petromax that vagueness which suggested not just injury but surrender, a psychic soreness about the eyes, a whiteness about the mouth, as if he was seeing the moment over and over again and could not forget it no matter how he webbed himself in with the woman in the yellow coat. He did no work. He went constantly from café to café in Huddersfield, I had no means of knowing why, although I suspected – quite wrongly – at the time that he had forgotten which lavatory the mirror was in, and was patiently searching for it again.

I followed him when I could, despite Mr Ambrayses's veto; and this is what he told me one afternoon in the Four Cousins Grill & Coffee Lounge: 'When I was a child my grandmother often took me about with her. I was a quiet boy already in poor health, and she found me at least as easy to manage as a small dog. Her habits were fixed: each Wednesday she visited the hairdresser and then went on to Manchester by train for a day's shopping. She wore for this a hat made entirely out of pale pink, almost cream feathers, dotted among which were peacock eyes a startling brown-red. The feathers lay very dense and close, as if they were still on the breast of the bird.

'She loved cafés, I think because the life that goes on in them, though domestic and comfortable, can't claim you in any way: there is nothing for you to join in. "I like my tea in peace," she told me every week. "Once in a while I like to have my tea in peace."

'Whatever she ate she coughed and choked demurely over it, and for some time afterwards; and she always kept on her light green raincoat with its nacreous, gold-edged buttons.

'When I remember Piccadilly it isn't so much by the flocks of starlings which invaded the gardens at the end of every short winter afternoon, filling the paths with their thick mouldy smell and sending up a loud mechanical shrieking which drowned out the traffic, as by the clatter of pots, the smell of marzipan or a match just struck, wet woollen coats hung over one another in a corner, voices reduced in the damp warm air to an intimate buzz out of which you could just pick a woman at another table saying, "Anyway, as long as you can get about," to which her friend answered immediately, "Oh it's something, isn't it? Yes."

'On a rainy afternoon in November it made you feel only half awake. A waitress brought us the ashtray. She put it down in front of me. "It's always the gentleman who smokes," she said. I looked at my grandmother sulkily, wondering where we would have to go next. At Boots she had found the top floor changed round again, suddenly full of oven-gloves, clocks, infra-red grills; and a strong smell of burning plastic had upset her in the arcades between Deansgate and Market Street.

'Along the whole length of the room we were in ran a tinted window, through which you could see the gardens in the gathering twilight, paths glazed with drizzle giving back the last bit of light in the sky, the benches and empty flower beds grey and equivocal-looking, the sodium lamps coming on by the railings. Superimposed, on the inside of the glass, was the distant reflection of the café: it was as if someone had dragged all the chairs and tables out into the gardens, where the serving women waited behind a stainless steel counter, wiping their faces with a characteristic gesture in the steam from the *bain marie*, unaware of the wet grass, the puddles, the blackened but energetic pigeons bobbing round their feet.

'As soon as I had made this discovery a kind of tranquillity came over me. My grandmother seemed to recede, speaking in charged hypnotic murmurs. The rattle of cutlery and metal trays reached me only from a great distance as I watched people come into the gardens laughing. They were able to pass without difficulty through the iron railings; the wind and rain had no effect on them. They rubbed their hands and sat down to eat squares of dry Battenburg cake and exclaim "Mm" how good it was. There they sat, out in the cold, smiling at one another: they certainly were a lot more cheerful out there. A man on his own had a letter which he opened and read.

"Dear Arthur," it began.

'He chuckled and nodded, tapping a line here and there with his finger as if he were showing the letter to someone else; while the waitresses went to and fro around him, for the most part girls with white legs and flat shoes, some of whom buttoned the top of their dark blue overalls lower than others. They carried trays with a thoughtless confidence, and spoke among themselves in a language I longed to understand, full of ellipses, hints and abrupt changes of subject, in which the concrete things were items and prices. I wanted to go and join them. Their lives, I imagined, like the lives of everyone in the gardens, were identical to their way of walking between the tables – a neat, safe, confident movement without a trace of uncertainty, through a medium less restrictive than the one I was forced to inhabit.

"'Yes, love?" I would say to introduce myself. "Thank you, love. Anything else, love? Twenty pence then, thank you, love, eighty pence change, next please. Did Pam get those drop earrings in the end then? No, love, only fried."

"'I think it's just as well not to be," they might reply. Or with a wink and a shout of laughter, "Margaret's been a long time in the you-know-where. She'll be lucky!"

'At the centre or focal point of the gardens, from which the flower beds fell back modestly in arcs, a statue stood. Along its upraised arms drops of water gathered, trembled in the wind, fell. One of the girls walked up and put her tray on a bench next to it. She buried her arms brusquely in the plinth of the statue and brought out a cloth to wipe her hands. This done, she stared ahead absently, as if she had begun to suspect she was caught up in two worlds. Though she belonged to neither, her image dominated both of them, a big plain patient girl of seventeen or eighteen with chipped nail varnish and a tired back from sorting cutlery all morning. Suddenly she gave a delighted laugh.

'She looked directly out at me and waved. She beckoned. I could see her mouth open and close to make the words "Here! Over here!"

'She's alive, I thought. It was a shock. I felt that I was alive too. I got up and ran straight into the plate glass window and was concussed. Someone dropped a tray of knives. I heard a peculiar voice, going away from me very fast, say: "What's he done? Oh, what's he done now?" Then those first ten or twelve years of my life were sealed away from me neatly like the bubble in a spirit level – clearly visible but strange and inaccessible, made of nothing. I knew immediately that though what I had seen was not Viriconium, Viriconium nevertheless awaited me. I knew, too, how to find it.'

People are always pupating their own disillusion, decay, age. How is it they never suspect what they are going to become, when their faces already contain the faces they will have twenty years from now?

'You would learn nothing from Dr Petromax's mirror even if you could find it,' Mr Ambrayses said dismissively. 'First exhaust the traditional avenues of research.' And as if in support of his point he brought me a cardboard box he had found among the rubbish on a building site in Halifax, the words WORLD MOSAIC printed boldly across its lid. But my face was down to the bone with ambition.

Old people sit more or less patiently in railway carriages imagining they have bought a new bathroom suite, lavender, with a circular bath they will plumb-in themselves. April comes, the headlines read, BIBLE BOY MURDERED; KATIE IN NUDE SHOCK. The sun moves across the patterned bricks outside the bus station, where the buses are drawn up obliquely in a line: from the top deck of one you can watch in the next a girl blowing her nose. You don't think you can bear to hear one more woman in Sainsbury's saying to her son as she shifts her grip on her plastic shopping bag with its pink and grey Pierrot, 'Alec, get your foot off the biscuits. I shan't tell you again. If you don't get your foot off the biscuits Alec I shall knock it straight on the floor.'

April again. When the sun goes in, a black wind tears the crocus petals off and flings them down the ring road.

'I can't wait,' I told Mr Ambrayses.

I couldn't wait any longer. I followed Dr Petromax from the Blue Rooms ('Meals served all day') to the Alpine Coffee House, Merrie England, the Elite Café & Fish Restaurant. I let him tell me his story in each of them. Though details changed it remained much the same: but I was certain he was preparing himself to say more. One day I kept quiet until he had ended as usual, 'Viriconium nevertheless awaited me,' then I said openly to him: 'And yet you've never been there. You had the clue as a child. You found the doorway but you never went through it.'

We were in the El Greco, at the pedestrian end of New Street. While he waited for the waitress he stared across the wide flagged walk, with its beech saplings and raised flower beds, at the window of C&A's, his sore brown eyes full of patience between their bruised-looking lids. When she came she brought him plaice and chips. 'Oh, hello!' she said. 'We haven't seen you for a while! Feeling any better?' He ate the chips one by one with his fork, pouring vinegar on them between every mouthful; only afterwards scraping the white of the plaice off its slippery fragile skin until he had one in a little pile on the side of the plate and the other intact, glistening slightly, webbed with grey, in the middle. His dirty hands were as deft and delicate as a boy's at this. Once or twice he looked up at me and then down again.

'Who told you that?' he said quietly when he had finished eating. 'Ambrayses?'

He put down his knife and fork.

'Three of us set out,' he said. 'I won't say who. Two got through easily, the third tried to go back halfway. On the right day you can still catch sight of him in the mirror, spewing up endlessly. He doesn't seem to know where he is, but he's aware of you.

'We lived there for three months, in some rooms on Salt Lip Road behind the rue Serpolet. The streets stank. At six in the morning a smell so corrupt came up from the Yser Canal it seemed to blacken the iron lamp posts; we would gag in our dreams, struggle for a moment to wake up, and then realise that the only escape was to sleep again. It was winter, and everything was filthy. Inside, the houses smelled of vegetable peel, sewage, perished rubber. Everyone in them was ill. If we wanted a bath we had to go to a public washhouse on Mosaic Lane. The air was cold, echoes flew about under the roof, the water was like lead. Sometimes it was hardly like water at all. There were some famous murals there, but they were so badly kept up you could make furrows in the grease. Scrape it off and you'd see the most beautiful stuff underneath, chalky reds, pure blues, children's faces!

'We stuck it out for three months. We knew there were other quarters of the city, where things must be better, but we couldn't find our way about. At first we were so tired; later we thought we were being followed by some sort of secret police. Towards the end the man I was with was ill all the time; he started to hear the bathhouse echoes even while he was in bed; he couldn't walk. It was a hard job getting him out. The night I did it you could see the lights of the High City, sweet, magical, like paper lanterns in a garden, filling up the emptiness. If only I'd gone towards them, walked straight towards them!'

I stared at him.

'Was that all?' I said.

'That was all.'

His hands had begun to tremble, and he looked down at

them. 'Oh yes. I was there. What else could have left me like this?' He got up and went to the lavatory. When he came back he said. 'Ambrayses has a lot to learn about me.' He bent down, his eyes now looking very vague and sick, as if he were already forgetting who I was or what I wanted, and quickly whispered something in my ear: then he left.

As he walked across the street he must have disturbed the pigeons, because they all flew up at once and went wheeling violently about between the buildings. As they passed over her an Indian woman, who had been sitting in the sunshine examining a length of embroidered cloth, winced and folded it up hurriedly. Though they soon quietened down, coming to rest in a line along the top of the precast C&A façade, she continued to look frightened and resentful – biting her lips, making a face, moving her shoulders repeatedly inside her tight leather coat, from the sleeves of which emerged thin wrists and hands, powdery brown, fingernails lacquered a plum colour.

The older Asian women fiddle constantly with their veils, plucking with wrinkled fingers at the lower part of their faces. In the bus station they lift their feet – automatically looking away from him – to let the cleaner run his brush along the base of the plastic banquette. They have features as coarse and wise as an elephant's but underneath they are in a continual nervous fidget.

The furniture in Mr Ambrayses's front room, inert great drop-leaf tables and sideboards with stained, lifting veneers, was strewn with the evidence he had accumulated: curled-up grainy photographs, each a detail enlarged in black and white from some colour snap until, its outline fatally eroded and its context yawing, it reached monstrous or curious conclusions; articles cut from yellowed newsprint found lining the drawers of an empty house; cassettes furred with dust, which when you played them gave out only the pure electric silence of the machine, punctuated once or twice by feral static; his notebooks, where in a clear hand he had written;'Each event, struck lightly against its own significance, can be excited into throwing off a spark; it is this energetic mote which lies at the heart of metaphor – and of life;' or: 'The lesson we learn too late is that we cannot have only by wanting.' Then on another page, 'Nothing impedes us, we need only learn to act.'

He preserved the circulars, bills, Christmas cards, charity appeals and small parcels which came through his letterbox for the previous tenants of the house. Almost as if by accident a little of this lost or random communication was addressed to him, from Australia: he gave it pride of place. This was how I learned that his daughter had married and emigrated there several years before.

'She was ungrateful,' he would say, avoiding my eyes and staring at the television. (A car drove slowly out of some factory gates, then faster through a housing estate and on to an empty road.) 'She was an ungrateful girl.'

Two chimney sweeps called to see him the Wednesday after I had talked to Dr Petromax in the El Greco. He was out.

'Is he expecting you?' I asked them.

They didn't seem to know. They waited patiently in the garden for me to let them in – a large awkward boy in Dr Marten's boots, and a man I took to be his father, much smaller and more agile in his movements, who said: 'You've a fair view here anyhow. You can see a fair way from here.' The boy didn't answer but stood as if marooned on the concrete path which, like a mirror in the rain, reflected one or two thick yellow crocus buds. Piles of red bricks, rusty brown conifers, the conservatory with its peeling paint, the shed door held closed by a spade, everything else that afternoon was dark; it was more like October than April. 'We're used to working in town.' The boy looked warily at the rain, rubbed some of it into the stubble on his bony, vulnerable skull. He seemed to cheer up.

'You'll have a few accidents in these lanes then,' he said. 'With tractors and that.'

Later he brought the brushes in, and, glancing away from me shyly, spread two old candlewick bedspreads on the lino to protect it. He knelt with a kind of dreamy conscientiousness in Mr Ambrayses's tiled hearth, like a child fascinated by everything to do with fire: arranged the canvas bag over the fireplace; fixed it there with strips of Sellotape which he bit carefully off the roll; pushed each extension of the brush up through the bag until the smell of soot came into the room, rich and bitter, and he was forced to stop suddenly.

'There's still three exes here,' said his father. 'It'll go three more.'

'No it won't,' said the boy, stirring and pummelling away at the chimney.

'I'll go and look.'

When he came back he said, 'I can hear it rattling at the top.'

'It might be rattling but it's not going up.'

They stared at one another.

'I can hear it as plain as day, there's something at the top. I can fair hear it, plain as day, rattling against it.'

At this the boy only pummelled harder.

'Has plenty come down?' his father asked.

'Aye.'

'That's all we can do then.'

The boy pulled the brush gently back into the room, disassembling the extensions one by one while the man stood looking down at him breathing heavily, hands on hips, watching in case he had fetched the obstruction out. They ripped the bag off, revealing the fireplace choked to threequarters of its height with soot: nothing else. The boy screwed the Sellotape up contemptuously into a glittering sticky ball. He invited me to look up the chimney, but all I saw was a large dark recess, much rougher than I had imagined it would be, blackened and streaked with salts, like a cave.

'The fact is,' he said to me, 'I don't know how your friend keeps a fire there at all.'

When I told Mr Ambrayses this he said anxiously. 'Was Petromax with them?'

I laughed.

'Of course he wasn't. Is he a sweep?'

'Never let anyone in here,' he shouted. 'Describe them! That boy: were his hands big? Clumsy, and the nails all broken?'

'How else would a chimney sweep's hands be?'

He ignored this and as if preoccupied by the answer to his first question whispered to himself, 'It was only the sweeps.' Suddenly he got down on his back among the hair-clippings and screwed-up bits of paper on the floor, pulled himself into the hearth, and tried as I had done to look up the chimney. Whatever he saw or failed to see there made him jump to his feet again. He went round the room pulling cupboards open and slamming them shut; he picked up one or two of the postcards his daughter had sent him from Australia, stared in a relieved way at the strange bright stamps and unreal views, then put them back on the mantelpiece. 'Nothing touched,' he said. 'You didn't let them touch anything?' When I said that I hadn't he seemed to calm down.

'Look at these!' he said.

He had used up an entire pack of Polaroid film, he told me, photographing three pairs of women's shoes someone had thrown into a ditch at the top of Acres Lane where it bends right to join the Manchester Road. 'I noticed them on Sunday. They were still there when I went back, but by this morning they had gone. Can you imagine,' he asked me, 'who would leave them there? Or why?' I couldn't. 'Or, equally, who would come to collect them from a dry ditch among farm rubbish at the edge of the moor?'

The pictures, which had that odd greenish cast Polaroids sometimes develop a day or two after they have been exposed, showed them to be flimsy and open-toed: one pair in black suede, an evening shoe with a brown fur piece; one made of transparent plastic bound at the edges in a kind of metallic blue leather; and a pair of light tan sandals with a criss-cross arrangement of straps to hold the upper part of the foot.

'They were all size four,' said Mr Ambrayses. 'The brand name inside them was "Marquise": it was a little worn and faded but otherwise they seemed well-kept.'

All at once he dropped the photographs and went to look up the chimney again.

He whimpered.

'Never let anyone in here!' he repeated, staring helplessly up at me from where he lay. 'You have a lot to learn about Petromax.'

Two or three days later he locked up his house and went to Hull, to look, he said, for a rare book he had heard was there. The door of his garden shed banged open in the wind half an hour after he had gone, and has been banging since.

If Mr Ambrayses was, as I now believe, the other survivor of the experiment with the mirror – the one who, sickening in that slum behind the rue Serpolet, heard even in his sleep echoes of a voice in the deserted bathhouse; and who, dragged delirious and sweating with wrecked dreams through the freezing back lanes on their last night, never saw the ethereal lights of the High City – why was his memory of Viriconium the reverse of Petromax's?

It seems unlikely I will ever find out.

Petromax avoids me now he has set his poison in me. I see him around Huddersfield; but his wife keeps close to him. If they notice me they go up another street. They often have a child with them, a girl of about ten or eleven whose legs stick out of the hem of a thick grey coat however warm the weather. She dawdles behind them, or darts away suddenly into a shop doorway; or she stops in front of the Civic Centre and refuses to walk with them, making a grunting noise as if she is suppressing a bowel movement. You can see that this is only another formalised gesture: they are a family, and her effort not to belong is already her contribution.

Petromax's mirror, if anyone wants to know, is in the lavatory of the Merrie England Café, a little further down New Street than the El Greco, between the Ramsden Street junction and Imperial Arcade.

Go straight through the café itself, with all its cheap reproductions of Medieval saints and madonnas, '*Mon Seul Desir*', all those unicorns and monkeys, where the iron lamp-fittings and rough plaster bring you close to the Medieval soul in its night 'untainted by any breath of the Renaissance', and you find on the left a doorway made to look like varnished oak. The steps are painted Cardinal red; for a moment they appear wet. Go down them and the warm human buzz of traffic and conversation fades, distance dilutes the familiar scraping hiss of the espresso machine. There behind the pictogram on the neat grey door, above the sink with its flake of yellow soap and right next to the Seibel hand-dryer, is Petromax's mirror. It is smaller than you would think, perhaps eighteen inches on a side.

How did they force themselves through? The mere physical act must have been difficult. You can picture them teetering on the sink, as clumsy and fastidious as the elephant on the small circus chair. Their pockets are stuffed with whatever they think they might need: chocolate, Tekna knives, gold coins, none of which in the last analysis will prove to be any good. They have locked the door behind them (though Petromax, who goes through last, will open it again, so that things remain normal in the Merrie England up above), but every sound from the kitchen makes them pause and look at one another. They try an arm first, then a shoulder: they squirm about. At last Petromax's feet disappear, kicking and waving. The soap is stuck to the sole of his foot. The lavatory is vacant. 'Well that's it, isn't it?' says a voice from the corridor. 'It's for the kids really, isn't it?'

Mr Ambrayses was right, the mirror is of no use to me. I went down there, I stood in front of it. Except perhaps myself, I saw no one trapped and despairing in it. When Petromax whispered me its location, did he already know I would never dare go through, in case I found Viriconium as he found it?

A couple with two children live on the other side of me to Mr Ambrayses. The day he went to Hull they came out and began to dig in their garden with a kind of excited, irritable energy. A gusty wind had got up from the head of the valley, rattling the open windows, blowing the net curtains into the room. They had to shout to make themselves heard against it; while the children screamed and fell over, or killed worms and insects.

'Do you really want this dug up?'

'Well it hasn't done very well.'

'Well say if that's it. Do you want it dug up or not?'

'Well, yes.'

It didn't seem like gardening at all. The harder the wind blew the faster they worked, as if they were in some race against time to dig a shelter for themselves. 'A spider, a spider!' bellowed the two little boys, and the father humoured them with a kind of desperate calm, the way you might in the face of an air attack or a flood. He is a teacher, about thirty years old; bearded, with a blunt manner meant to conceal diffidence. 'Is it going to break, this storm?' I heard him say to his wife. It was hard to see what else he could have said, unless it was 'this stuff'. Soon after that they all went back in again. The wind buzzed and rustled for a while in my newspaper-stuffed fireplace, but it was dying down all the time.

Viriconium!

1985

Science & the Arts

MONA WAS IN HER late thirties. Two years before we met she spent some months in a psychiatric hospital. By the time it became clear that the constant pain she complained about was not imaginary but the result of a botched operation, her career was ruined and her immune system had broken down. She was anorexic, subject to panic attacks and suffering from depression.

She lived for a while in Stoke Newington, where she had a short affair with a journalist, then moved to Camden, where she took courses in pain management. She enrolled at the Slade. We were introduced about a year after that, and began seeing one another every two weeks or so. She was unhappily involved with a sculptor – a dependent, manipulative man in his fifties. I was unhappily involved with a woman who had turned to novel-writing after a career in TV drama. For a while our mutual friends tried to matchmake us, but they weren't successful.

Mona's flat was in a quiet crescent north of Camden High Street. It comprised three rooms (one of which she used as a studio), kitchen and bathroom. The kitchen was very small.

Mona didn't eat much so she lived mainly at the other end of the flat in the room which faced on to the street. There she had a computer, some bookshelves, a sofa, a television and, arranged so she could watch the television from it, her bed.

The bed was a small double, made up with a quilt and a stained white throw. There were two pillows, one old and very yellowed and without a pillowcase. When the pain was bad, or when she was cold, Mona would pull the quilt up to her chin and watch television from the bed while her visitor sat on the sofa. Or halfway through the evening she would get into bed like a child, with all her clothes on.

It was disconcerting. Even though you knew she was dressed, there was always a moment of uncertainty when she threw back the covers to get out again.

A bad day always made Mona feel as if she was on the edge of a relapse. She phoned me at seven o'clock one evening. 'I don't think I've been eating,' she said. The week before, she had finally managed to end her relationship with the sculptor, who had just had major surgery of his own. I went over to Camden to see if I could help. She was glad to have someone look after her for an hour or two, but careful to make it clear that though she was attracted to me, and knew I was attracted to her, she didn't want an affair with anybody at the moment.

I said I hadn't come for that. I didn't expect a return on helping someone.

She asked if she could hug me. I said yes. I was sitting on the sofa. She knelt on the floor in front of me and I put my arms round her. It felt awkward to me but it was what she wanted.

'I'm listening to your heart,' she said at one point. 'It's a great comfort to me.'

'You should cry as much as you want to,' I said.

She knelt on the floor like that for nearly an hour. To someone coming in we would have resembled one of Egon

Schiele's relentlessly awkward couples, but without the sex. All I could think was how much her knees must hurt. I hadn't seen her for a month and she was even thinner than I remembered. Eventually she got up and went to bed. As soon as I thought she was feeling better, I cooked her a meal which we ate in front of the television. I made her promise to eat more often and take things easy for a few days. When I stood up to go at half past eleven or a quarter to twelve, she said anxiously, 'Are you sure you can get home at this time of night? If it's difficult you're welcome to stay.'

I would be all right, I told her, home was only a few stops along the Northern line. In fact I was tired out by the effort of cooking. I wanted to go back so I could think about what any of this meant.

Two days later we were in a Pizza Express. She had asked me to explain the idea of 'quantum memory' to her so she could incorporate it into some work she was doing for the Slade foundation course. I was just saying something like, 'Light can be a wave or a particle according to what the observer expects,' when she interrupted: 'This is very phallic, isn't it? Here you are talking about very small things and look what I'm doing.' She was rubbing her fingers up and down the candle-holder on the table between us. I didn't know what to make of that so I said: 'It is, isn't it? Ha ha,' then I went back to explaining the dual nature of light.

'I've written it all down,' I said.

I walked her home. She went into the bathroom and changed into a pair of cotton pyjamas and a scruffy, homemade-looking grey pullover. 'I took what you said to heart,' she told me. 'I really did. Honestly, I've been eating much more.' She spread a portfolio of her work on the floor so that we could look at it. There were photographs of strange tall constructions she had made using bandages, wire, scraps of paper with quotations about illness on them. She had photographs of her surgery, and of the sculptor's. She was interested in text as object. She said that she used quotes from other people because she found it hard to trust her own opinions. I said that I had got round that in the 1970s by presenting my own opinions as quotations from other people, which seemed to authorise them for me until I had enough confidence to present them as my own. Then I made a cup of tea, watched part of a television programme about risk management, and got up to go at about half past eleven.

'It's quite late,' she said. 'You're welcome to stay if it's too late to get home.'

'The tubes run for another hour,' I said.

Earlier I had signed one of my books to her. Inside it I had written, 'Eat well. Get strong. Take care.' It was a novel about a woman who wanted to fly but the best she could get was a cosmetic treatment that made her look like a bird. I apologised to Mona that all my books seemed to feature women who became very ill after a series of operations.

This is what I had written down for her about quantum memory:

> Every particle that has ever been involved with another particle somehow remembers that involvement & takes it forward into the next transaction. Everything that has ever been joined remains joined in some way. This is only at the level of very small things.
>
> Quantum indeterminacy:
>
> (a) If you know where a particle is, you can't know its velocity. If you know its velocity you can't know where it is.
>
> (b) Light can be described as both a wave-form or a particle. It is not 'both at the same time': it is genuinely one or the other according to what kind of machinery you use to observe it.
>
> Quantum particles begin as a potential of the

condition we call empty space. They are then 'observed', or locked into place, by the rest of the universe: that is, one of their potential states is contexted by local conditions and 'chosen' to become real. The option the universe didn't take up, however, still continues to exist in some more informal way.

Since each of these options can be spoken of as having a 'memory' of the other, and since every mechanism for human memory proposed so far – from chemical cellular memory to a more broadly distributed holographic memory – has been discounted, some scientists have toyed with the idea that memory may be stored at the quantum level in transactions like those I've described.

As science it is speculative. As a metaphor quite nice. All the rest – quantum indeterminacy, the dual nature of light and so on – is fact, as far as fact can be ascertained using contemporary experimental tools.

It was time I learned to protect women from my enthusiasms: so the ex-scriptwriter had told me, just before she ended our relationship on the grounds that a photograph of me with an old girlfriend had appeared in the pages of *Publishing News*. Women, she believed, saw men's enthusiasm as a form of bullying. She called it 'male energy'. I wasn't protecting Mona from my enthusiasm by sending her confused ideas about quantum physics printed in 18 point Gill Sans Condensed Bold type. Perhaps Mona thought of enthusiasm as male energy too. Perhaps that was why she had found herself giving the candle a hand job in the Pizza Express.

Mona haunted her flat wearing her shabby pullovers with very short skirts and thick tights. She was part of the clutter, an uncompleted gesture, thin as a stick but always elegant. She was so composed I walked past her in the living room without seeing her. When I went back in she was standing by the table with one hand flat on the tabletop, staring down at a page of the newspaper, lifting it but not quite turning it.

'Hi,' I said.

'Oh, hello!' She spoke as if she had forgotten there was anyone else in the flat; or as if I had rung her up after a long absence.

'I thought you were in the other room,' I said.

'No,' she said. 'I was here all the time.'

That evening we went into the West End to see *The English Patient*. Mona walked very slowly along Shaftesbury Avenue to the cinema. We got seats at the end of a row and sat leaning a little away from each other. She had taken the outer seat so that she could stand up in the aisle when she needed to. Standing up was one of the techniques she had been taught to help manage her pain. In one scene in the film a man was supposed to be having his fingers cut off. Or perhaps it was his thumbs. You didn't see anything, but there was a sudden indrawn breath from the audience. All over the cinema people were wincing in case they did see something. Mona gasped and clutched my hand. She pulled me closer to her and we sat like that for a moment or two.

'I'm not sure about that film,' she said on the way out of the cinema. 'Its heart's too far in the right place.'

I asked her what she meant.

'Oh, I don't know,' she said. 'I think I need a cup of tea.'

When we got back to her flat, I went to the kitchen to make it. While I was in there putting teabags in the cups and doing a bit of washing up while I waited for the kettle to boil, I heard her go into the bathroom then come out again. 'I'm getting into bed,' she called. 'It's cold in here. Aren't you cold?' I said I was OK. When I took the tea into the front room, she had the television on. We watched that and drank our tea, and then I got up to go.

'I worry about you leaving so late,' Mona said. 'Are you

sure you can get a train this late? It would be so easy for you to stay.'

'No,' I said. 'Honestly, the trains seem to run forever.'

'You could be mugged or anything,' she said.

I laughed.

She had the bedclothes up to her chin. She was just eyes.

'I want you to stay,' she said.

'That's different,' I said.

I took the cups away and switched the TV off. She watched me undress. Then she lifted the edge of the quilt to encourage me to get in with her.

'I thought you'd still have your clothes on,' I said.

She looked up at me anxiously, holding the quilt back so I could see.

'I'm bleeding a bit,' she said. 'You won't mind, will you?'

2003

The Incalling

THE INCALLING WAS HELD somewhere in that warren of defeated streets which lies between Camden Road and St Pancras, where the old men cough and spit their way under the railway arches every evening to exercise their dogs among the discarded fish-and-chip papers. Clerk had made a great point of punctuality and then failed to give me precise directions. I don't think he expected me to turn up at all. He had reached some crux only partly visible to the outsider, and his life was terribly muddled – a book was long overdue, he had been evicted suddenly from his furnished flat in Harrow, he had a sense of impending middle age which he obviously felt he couldn't face without company of some sort; and beneath all this was something deeper which he hinted at constantly but refused to unveil. A publisher has a limited vocabulary of responses to such a situation; to show him that I knew my responsibilities I took him frequently to the pubs and restaurants of Great Portland Street – where he inevitably ate little, seemed nervous, and instead of discussing the work in progress murmured almost inaudibly of Frazer and Blavatsky, or his quarrels with G –, and where, among the turned heads and plump shoulders of lunching secretaries, his thin white acne'd face hovered like the ghost of a child starved to death. I was curious; he sensed this, and made energetic efforts to draw me in. He was lonely; I wanted to help, of course, if I could, but not from so intimate a distance; and lately our meetings had become memorable as a series of comically protracted farewells on station platforms and embarrassed, hasty protestations of friendship made through the windows of departing taxicabs.

Anyway: I went to Camden that night not because I had any interest in the proceedings, but because I felt sorry for him, because lunches aren't enough, and because he was one of those people who can't seem to enjoy their follies without a sense of complicity. I would have accompanied him with equal enthusiasm to the Soho backstreet of his choice. Thanks to an unexplained delay on the North London line I arrived shortly after the thing was due to begin, with no idea of exactly where it was to take place.

I found myself in a short empty crescent at one end of which stood a shuttered greengrocery – the pavement in front of it stacked with broken wooden boxes and some spoiled foreign fruit filling the cool air with a thick, yeasty odour while feral pigeons pecked about on the flagstones in the failing light – and at the other the second-hand clothes shop owned by Clerk's mentor, a woman of uncertain nationality who called herself Mrs Sprake. This was a dim, oppressive cubbyhole with a cracked wardrobe mirror propped up against one wall, where faded tea-gowns hung limp and vacant behind the wire-screened windows like the inmates of a political prison for women. Before the war it had been a 'corner café'; faded glass panels above the door advertised vanished soft drinks, and its atmosphere still felt etiolated as if from passage over gas burners on foggy November nights. Here I had to ask directions from the boy behind the counter, a fat-legged ten or eleven-year-old in short grey trousers who

I imagined then to be Mrs Sprake's son – although now I'm not sure if their relationship could ever have been described so simply.

He was sucking something as I entered, and stooped quickly to take it out of his mouth, as if he were afraid whoever had come in might confiscate it. Over his shoulder I could see down a narrow passage to where a small television screen flickered silently and greyly in the gloom. A dog was moving about in another room. Dusty clothing pressed in from all sides, touching my wrists. When I told him why I was there he stared into the mirror and said uninterestedly, 'It's the fourth house down.' His voice was peculiarly mature for his clothing and his prepubescent, sidling eyes. There was aniseed on his breath, and whatever he had been eating had left a brownish deposit in the downy hairs at the corner of his mouth. 'Mr Clerk invited me,' I explained, 'but I forgot the way.' He shrugged slightly, and his hand moved behind the counter, but he said nothing more, and I doubted if he had even taken any notice of the name. As I turned to go he had transferred his gaze to the distant television and, with a motion too quick to follow, had reclaimed his titbit and was chewing again.

On the way out I brushed against a stiff peach-coloured bodice covered with green sequins, to be startled by a sudden smell of the empty dance hall – some American perfume, faded and innocent; and beneath it, like a memory of the disingenuous festivals of a post-war Saturday night, the quick thin bitterness of ancient perspiration.

Much of the crescent was untenanted. In company with the surrounding streets it had been built as a genteel transit camp and matured as a ghetto. Now it was a long declining dream. I stood at the door of Mrs Sprake's house, staring at the cracked flags, the forgotten net curtains bunched and sagging like dirty ectoplasm, the tilted first-floor balconies with their strange repetitive wrought-iron figures, and wondering if it might not be better to leave now before anyone had time to answer the bell. All the other doors were boarded up. Old paint hung like shredded wallpaper from the inner curve of an arched window. Across the road one whole building was missing from the terrace – fireplaces and outlines of extinct rooms clung to the walls of the flanking houses. I could telephone Clerk in the morning and tell him I hadn't been able to find the place; but it was too late now to go in search of a cinema, and too early for anything else; besides, the boy had seen me, and if I left I should look a fool.

Clerk himself opened the door, but not before I had heard footsteps approach, pause and recede, then a woman's voice saying clearly, 'We don't normally encourage gatherings,' and, 'He must come in, of course,' on a rising, partly interrogative note.

His white face tilted out at me from the darkness of the hall, like the head of some long-necked animal thrust unexpectedly round the door. He looked tired and a little ill. Warmer air seemed to flow out past him, and for a second I was whirled along the sensory interface of outdoors and in, the one reeking of pulpy exotic fruit, the other of aniseed and dusty hessian, rushing together like incompatible ocean currents. The light of a single low-wattage lamp yellowed a passageway made narrow by piled tea-chests and bales of folded clothing, out of which the staircase, uncarpeted but thick with chocolate brown paint, ascended into a deeper gloom. It appeared to be a mere annex of the shop, and smelt so similar that I wondered if the chewing boy had somehow got ahead of me.

'Oh, hello Austin,' said Clerk. He blinked. 'For a moment I thought you were someone else.'

I was relieved to see him, but not for long. It was plain he'd made some sort of gaffe by inviting me and was regretting it. 'You're late,' he told me nervously; he said that I should 'try and fit myself in'; we had a ridiculous whispered misunderstanding over who should go first along the cramped hall. Finally he hurried me through into a small front parlour with bare white walls, where in preparation for the ceremony all the furniture had been shoved away from the centre of the room, exposing about ten square feet of freshly scrubbed unvarnished floorboards. On one side of the hall door were two ordinary wooden dining chairs, a spindly table between them draped with the same greyish imitation lace that hung before the window. Pushed up against the facing wall there was a two-seat sofa covered in fawn PVC material, marked about the arms by a cat or other small animal. A second door, opposite the window, led off into a kitchen, from which came the sound of water being run into a sink. On the sofa, still and ill-determined in the poor light, sat Alice Sprake.

Clerk introduced her proprietarily as 'the daughter of the house', becoming animated when he addressed her; she said nothing. She was eighteen or twenty years old and only her eyes, brown and unemotional, recalled her relationship to the boy in the clothes shop. She was vague. Although she looked levelly enough at me, I hardly felt the touch of her hand.

'I expect you're tired of waiting, are you?' I said brightly. Both of them ignored me, so I sat down. A small thickset woman wearing the perpetual mourning of the Greek Cypriot widow came through the scullery door. She was a little under middle age, but moved slowly as though her legs pained her; her face was thickly powdered in a strange lifeless orange colour; the sound of her breathing was quite plain in the room. She had under her arm one of those cheap religious pictures you see gathering dust in Catholic shop-windows, and this she proceeded to hang – with what seemed a great deal of effort – on a nail above the sofa. It was a Gethsemane, in the most lurid stereoscopic greys and greens. For a while I couldn't understand what was wrong with it; then I saw that it was upside down, the feeble soon-to-be-martyred face swimming out of it loose-mouthed and emotionally spent, staring into the room like a drowned man in a restaurant fish-tank.

'There,' she said thickly. 'That is that.' She slumped on the sofa beside the girl, to stare exhaustedly at a spot on the wall above my head.

The silence drew out interminably. Clerk and I sat on the hard chairs; Alice Sprake and her mother sat on the sofa; nobody spoke, nothing was done. After a few minutes of this I realised that Clerk was staring so avidly at the girl that his eyes were watering. I couldn't see what absorbed him so. She belonged in some shop window herself, her flat adolescent face prim in the confinement of a gilt frame, the whole musculature immobile and stylised, the profile very slightly concave, the mouth so small and secretive. She had a dreamy manner certainly (which appeared at times to extend into an actual vagueness of physical presence – one might come into a room, I sensed, and spend ten minutes there before realising she was in it); but it was the unattractive fake dreaminess of the convent girl and the mass production madonna, the self-contemplatory lassitude of pubertal iron deficiency. I changed my opinion of Clerk's motives; then changed it back again, out of charity. He was oblivious. I felt like a voyeur. None of us after all understand our own motives. Mrs Sprake, meanwhile, twitched her feet – she sat sprawled back, hands limp at her sides – and seemed to be perfectly occupied with the wall. I tried to see through the grey net curtains. It was dark now in the street, but no lamps had come on. Someone walked slowly and heavily under the window, dragging footsteps close enough to be in the room. Clerk adjusted his spectacles, coughed. The drowned man mouthed at us from the iridescent gloom of his fish-tank. I couldn't bear it. 'Er, why must the picture be upside down?' I said. 'I suppose there's some particular significance to that?'

Clerk stared at me like a betrayed dog. The streetlights came on, filling the place with a dull orange glare.

Both women got up at once and left, Mrs Sprake going into the scullery, where she unlatched the back door, Alice into the hall. I heard retreating footsteps on the stairs, then the sound of someone coming in from the garden. The chewing boy put his head round the scullery door and gazed at the icon. Mrs Sprake reappeared standing on tiptoe behind him, looked straight at me and said, 'You must kip silent, you understand? Kip very quiet.' She cuffed the boy's ear. 'You eat too much of that. There will be none left, and then what will you do?' And to me again, with what I thought must be pride, 'My children are very good children, Mr Austing, very, very good. They do all their poor mother can't.' The boy smiled at me with a mixture of shyness and impudence. He shifted his titbit from one side of his open mouth to the other, letting it pause for an instant on his stained tongue so I could almost see it. 'Fetch the chalk then,' he said, watching me closely. He had no vestige of her Mediterranean accent. The ghost of aniseed whispered from his mouth and reached into the corners of the room. 'It can be done, Mr Clerk,' called Mrs Sprake from the kitchen. 'It has not been done for fifteen hundreds of years, but my children are clever children.' Clerk looked dazed now that the girl had gone. He blinked at the boy. 'Shut up and give me the chalk,' said the boy.

He knelt down on the scrubbed floor and stared up at the icon, licking the half-inch or so of green chalk she had brought him. Suddenly he put it wholly in his mouth. When it came back it was pasty and covered with spittle, and the aniseed reek in the room had redoubled. He quickly used it to draw a large and irregular circle on the floor, shuffling along backwards on his haunches and dragging the hand with chalk in it along behind him. When he had completed this he sat in the middle of the circle for a second, his eyes vacant. Then he popped the chalk back into his mouth and seemed to swallow it entirely.

He got up stiffly and perched on the arm of the sofa, stretching his legs and grinning. One of his shoelaces had come undone. He caught my eye, made a little motion of the head to implicate me in some irony directed at Clerk, who had taken off his horn-rims, folded them carefully away, and was yearning toward the hall door with watery eyes. When I refused to join in, he shrugged and laughed quietly.

The door opened and back came Alice Sprake, to be trapped on Clerk's adhesive gaze like a small grey fly.

She went straight to the centre of the green chalk circle and stood there, one leg relaxed, the other stiffened to take her weight. She had dressed in some sort of complicated muslin shift, the drooping skirts of which revealed the lower part of her thighs. Her legs were short and plump, inexpertly shaved. Her feet were bare, the soles grubby. She brought with her faint odours of dust and perspiration; the decayed echo of *fin-de-siècle* water sprites and eurhythmical entertainments. She faced the boy as if waiting for a cue. The boy chewed and raised his hand. In the scullery Mrs Sprake switched on a small portable gramophone, which began to play an aimless, thready piece for violin and flute. With a shuffle and slap of bare feet on bare boards, Alice Sprake started to dance about in the chalk circle, her fixed and tranquil face now turned to Clerk, now to the reversed icon, now to the chewing boy. It was harmless at first. She waved her arms, trailing ectoplasmic fans of muslin in the peculiar light. She was a very poor dancer. Clerk had put his horn-rims back on; they followed her every movement, sodium light flashing from their lenses as he turned his head. Mrs Sprake leant on the doorframe with her arms folded, nodding to herself. The chewing boy let himself slide to the floor; back against the sofa, he drew one knee up to his chest, clasped it, and rocked himself to and fro. I coughed unhappily behind my hand, wondering how much Clerk had paid, and wishing I'd never seen him in my life.

But there was something wrong with the record player,

and the music diminished steadily into a low, distant groan; the boy grew rigid (orange twilight limned his clenched jaw), while his mother let her arms fall to her sides, allowed all interest to leave her eyes; Clerk's expression became strained with greed. And abruptly Alice Sprake had ceased to be a village hall *danseuse* from some vanished Edwardian summer-twilight rehearsal, awkwardly pirouetting, heartbreakingly inept and weary, and was fluttering in what might have been real panic round and round in a circle, impaled and fluttering there on Clerk's stare, awash in the lurid glare beneath that drowned green man. The boy coughed painfully. Through clenched teeth he said, 'Now, Mr Clerk!' His mother jerked awake and reached out her arm. Bleak white light flooded the room from an unshaded two hundred watt fitment in the ceiling. The drowned man leapt stereoscopically from his frame into the space above the sofa, caught open-mouthed in that act of unspeakable despair. The music ended, or became inaudible. Clerk scrambled to his feet and stepped into the circle. Alice Sprake made a strange writhing motion and pulled off her shift.

She began to trudge along the chalk line, round and round, compliant and bovine, Clerk not far behind, his eyes locked in that peculiar spasm of unsexual greed, fixed on her thick white back and low, pear-shaped buttocks. There was gooseflesh on her thighs, the light had bleached her pubic hair to a pathetic greyish tuft. Her degradation, it seemed to me, was complete: as was that of everybody else in the room. Her feet scraped interminably, and Clerk's scraped after. Round and round they went.

'Fucking hell, Clerk,' I said. 'You must be mad.'

I got up, meaning to wait for him outside – or perhaps not even to wait, or ever see him again. Mrs Sprake had vanished, but her son had now joined the endless shuffling procession in the centre of the room. As Clerk followed the girl, he followed Clerk. His jaws were rigid and he had forgotten his titbit. An unending trickle of brown fluid was running out of the corner of his mouth. I slammed the front door and stood on the cooling pavement. My hands were shaking, but to this day I honestly believe it was out of fury. Clerk came out after about an hour, wiping his mouth as if he'd been ill. I don't know why I waited. Neither of us apologised for our behaviour. We went in silence down the High Street, past the alcoholics muttering behind locked news-stands, past the ticket office and down the moaning escalator, to be sucked into the echoing passages, the hot zones and sudden cold winds of the Camden Underground, to breathe the thin dingy air of two separate carriages on the same train (and for all I know to read, with the same sensation of time suspended and an endless life under the earth, the same life-insurance posters and No Smoking signs). We made no plans to meet again. I thought he seemed depressed and fearful, but that may have been a moral judgement.

Why he was indulging himself in so shabby a farce I couldn't conceive: but it was plain that none of his problems would be solved by encouraging it, so I sent a letter to the agency which represented him, reminding them that his book was due (indeed, long overdue), that our contract had been, if anything, overly generous as to completion dates, that we hoped he would soon see his way clear, and so on. I had given him up, or so I told myself, but I had my assistant sign it. A couple of days later they wrote to tell me that he had changed his address and they were having trouble getting hold of him.

As for the Sprakes, I couldn't think of them as having much existence at all outside the strained and grubby events of that evening. I imagined them as spending most of their time in a sort of dull stupor – immobile on a third-floor landing, looking mechanically down into a back garden full of rusty wheels, hard-packed earth and willow herb; silent and still behind the till of the second-hand clothes shop, eyes unfocused. I knew of course that they must get around the world somehow – shop for food, hurry along under the black rains of Camden to a launderette, do the things ordinary people do – but saw them only as withdrawn and barely human, lying perpetually but indifferently in wait for the credulous.

A languorous, unthinking contract exists between charlatan and victim, an understanding of which both are deeply aware. It didn't occur to me that there might be anything more to Clerk's obsession than the occasional reaffirmation of this covenant – until, about a month after the Incalling and out of an impulse I didn't understand, I found myself spying on him down by Charing Cross Pier.

It was a squally afternoon on the Victoria Embankment, one of those afternoons that wraps you one minute in a clinging mist of rain and the next surprises you with the pale lucid airs, the clarity and the depth of vision of quite another kind of day. The long arcs of Waterloo Bridge sprang out white and tense against the heavy blues and greys of the distant City. The river was agitated, high but falling under a cloudy sky. Gulls swirled in low flat circles over something in the water. The wind blew from Parliament, smelling of rain and fried food, and I was huddled in the shadow of the Gilbert memorial, waiting for a bus. A pleasure boat docked, a crowd developed on the covered gangways of the pier behind me – camera bags swinging, flapping nylon waterproofs, American and Japanese voices – and there he was, his white face unhealthy and out of place among all the tanned ones, his thin shoulders hunched and splotched with rain. He came up the oily black duckboards tearing his ticket in half and staring anxiously about him. I suppose I should have gone up to him and said hello; instead I turned my head away and pretended to be studying the plump complacent features of Frampton's bronze Gilbert, hoping to be taken for a sightseer.

I don't know why I did it. Something stealthy in his
manner found an echo in my own. He was obviously waiting
for someone; out of the corner of my eye I saw him go up to
the confectionery kiosk by the railway bridge and stand there,
glancing frequently back at the still-emptying boat as it
wallowed at the pier.

A moment later Alice Sprake materialised at the head of
the gangway and turned right towards Cleopatra's Needle.

She passed not six inches away from me, her hair blowing
out from under a damp headscarf. She had on a dove grey
suit with a long skirt and puffed sleeves which had once
belonged to a much older woman. Hurrying along the wide
empty pavement under the lamp standards with their iron
fish and strings of fairy lights, she looked like the ghost of a
Victorian afternoon; and as she went, the band in
Embankment Gardens struck up the march from Lincke's
'Father Rhine'. Clerk, too, passed close by me, his face a
white smear between the sodden, turned-up points of his
collar and his eyes so occupied with Alice Sprake I might
have been a mile away. His trousers were soaked, his cheap
shoes waterlogged, and he seemed to be shuddering with
cold. He looked more ill than I had ever seen him. I think
she was unaware of what was going on. He kept fifteen yards
behind her, and when she showed signs of stopping or
slowing became suddenly interested in a balk of rotting
timber bobbing far out in the river. She vanished for a
second or two then reappeared on the water stair of the
Needle. Rain blew round Clerk's dark lonely figure. When
she left the stair and crossed the road, he drifted after her.
The dripping trees of the gardens shook briefly in the wind
then closed over them.

I watched all this without surprise, feeling as detached as
a man trying to follow, without benefit of commentary and
through the condensation on a television dealer's window, the
announcement of some foreign war: then, suddenly depressed,

went over to the Charing Cross underground station and bought a ticket to Camden Town.

There, the sky was high, and for a moment at least, clear. If a wind blew down from Hampstead, it was a benign one; and as the old men dragged their dogs from intersection to intersection, the pavements were drying out. The blue-painted frontage of Mrs Sprake's shop looked shabby but less malicious in the watery light. No-one moved in the street or behind the counter; the clothes were only old clothes; and the smell of spoiled fruit drifting down the crescent from the greengrocer's made me quite hungry as I loitered on a nearby corner. I had been there for perhaps three quarters of an hour when Alice Sprake came into view, walking more quickly now and carrying a plastic Marks & Spencer's bag. She closed the door of the shop firmly behind her; a face appeared briefly at an upper window; emptiness seemed to grip the place more tightly than before.

A little later, Clerk hurried up and took station in the street. He shuffled his feet; settled his raincoat closer about him; bent his long neck this way and that like a disturbed waterfowl. His gaze switched from tilted balcony to empty shop, then back again. I think he had begun to follow the girl about the real world (the world, that is, outside the strained liberty and grubby constraints of the ritual) long before this incident took place. I found myself furious with him – with his miserable damp trouser legs, cracked suede shoes all cardboard and dye, his face like melting floor-wax – and not a little disgusted with myself. The smell of spoilt fruit plugged my throat. It was coming on to rain in heavy, isolated spots. I strode off down the crescent as though my anger alone might be sufficient to end the episode – reluctant for some reason to leave even as I wondered impatiently why on earth I had wasted my time, and not caring much if he saw me.

Nothing ended, however. I simply got lost among the unfamiliar backstreets beside Regent's Canal. I could find neither the tube station nor the North London Line; not even the High Street. I blundered on to the canal towpath, and, with the dull green water full of greedy little fish on one side and the high decaying walls of a goods yard on the other, convinced myself I was walking toward Islington, not Camden at all. I had to go further out of my way to get off it again. I didn't want to get into the brick wastes east of York Way. The cloud base lowered and the wind whipped across the lock basins, picking at the tethers of the crumbling boats and the plumage of a few miserable-looking ducks. Concrete steps rescued me finally, but now it was teeming with rain. I glimpsed from a distance the curious Greek shops of Pratt Street and lost them again almost immediately. Then, wandering past the urns and stone draperies of a Victorian cemetery that had been turned into some sort of park –empty yellow swings, a child's roundabout gravely turning, sleepy alcoholics muttering the spirit's language from the benches – I caught a whiff of rotten fruit.

I was back at the end of the crescent. The light seemed to be fading already. I had lost an hour. Clerk still stood patiently at his corner, like a tethered animal with its fur plastered down by the rain. Water streamed from his uplifted face. I thought I detected movement at an upper window – but Clerk's eyes were as vacant as the shop, and he seemed preoccupied by something else. It occurred to me that he wasn't strictly 'watching' anything: rather, it was as if he had got as close to some object as he possibly could, and was content just to be bobbing about at the interface until such time as he was able to penetrate it. Whatever it was, I left him there. A couple of streets away, I knew, the evening rush hour was beginning on a main road full of illuminated shop signs, tyres hissing through the wet. I turned to it thankfully, feeling sympathetic (or so I described it to myself) and intrusive, willing to leave him to it without further comment, voiced or otherwise. I was, perhaps, simply relieved at having found someone familiar, if not comforting, among all those doomed wet streets.

I was some yards along the pavement when he said suddenly and clearly, 'Leave me alone Austin. I know what you're up to.'

When I looked back, astonished, he hadn't moved. The rain humiliated him and he stared on, that indefinable expression of need and illness pulling his face slowly out of shape, flesh into putty, into water and chaos.

A few days later September set in like an infection. The air throbbed, and in less than a day grew thick and humid; by the next morning the traffic was piling it up and pushing it down Fitzroy Street into the Square, where it died before we had a chance to breathe it. When Tottenham Court Road became sticky and intolerable after ten a.m., and my office untenable after eleven, I gave up and went to Scotland for a three-week break. I didn't expect Clerk's dreary entanglements to follow me as far as the Buchaille Etive Mor, but the day I was due to leave I got a sour letter from him, and they did.

It was a peculiar letter, complicated, full of hidden accusations and reproofs. He was muddled, spoke of an illness – although he wasn't specific – and quoted extensively, for some reason I couldn't follow, from *Gerontion*. He made no reference to the Sprakes but went into detail about the 'insulting' letter he presumed had originated in my office, going on to attack his agent quite bitterly for forwarding it; and he left me in no doubt as to where our 'late' friendship stood. At least he had done some work – his completed manuscript came under separate covers. The agency rang me up that afternoon to ask me if I'd heard from him. 'He won't answer the phone, and he's ignoring everything but cheques,' they said, and seemed a bit hurt that he'd sent the book direct. Realising that I was about to be embroiled again, this time in some silly professional squabble, I left the whole thing with my assistant. 'If they ring again, get them to try a registered letter,' I told him. 'I'm not Clerk's keeper.' But it had begun to look as if I was, and he only grinned cynically. 'There can't be much wrong with him if he's cashing his bloody cheques.'

When I got back, found Clerk's manuscript still cluttering up the office.

'You should have a look at that,' said my assistant maliciously. 'They won't typeset from that. I didn't really know what to do with it. It hasn't even got a title.'

I sighed and took it home that night and couldn't read more than a couple of pages – the typescript was scrawled all over with illegible corrections in a peculiar brownish ink, and I couldn't tell whether it was a novel disguised as a memoir or a diary disguised as a novel.

'I'll have to go and see him about it, I suppose.'

'More fool you.'

Clerk now lived somewhere in the bedsit belt of Tufnell Park. Fool or not, I caught a bus over there, the manuscript under my arm in a box meant for foolscap typing paper. It was shortly before dusk at the end of a protracted, airless day: my sinuses ached, and the evening wind curling between the rows of tall shabby houses was no relief – it stirred briefly, nuzzling at the gutters where it found only the dust and heat of a month past, then settled down like an exhausted dog. Five or six bell pushes were tacked up by the outer door. I worked them in turn but no-one answered. A few withered geraniums rustled uneasily in a second-floor window box. I pushed the door and it opened. In some places we're all ghosts. I swam aimlessly about in the heat of the hall, knocking and getting no response. Up on the first-floor landing a woman stood in a patch of yellow light and folded her arms to watch me pass; in the room behind her was a television, and a child calling out in thin excitement.

Clerk lived right at the top of the stairs where the heat was thickest, in three unconnected rooms. I tapped experimentally on each open door in turn. 'Clerk?' Empty jam jars glimmered from the kitchen shelves, the wallpaper bulged sadly in the corner above the sink, and on the table was a note saying, 'Milk, bread, cat food, bacon,' the last two items heavily underlined and the writing not Clerk's. A lavatory flushed distantly as I went into what seemed to be his study, where everything had an untouched, dusty look. 'Clerk?' Bills and letters were strewn over the cracked pink linoleum, a pathetic and personal detritus of final demands which I tried furiously to ignore; it was too intimate a perspective – all along he had forced me to see too much of himself, he had protected himself in no way. 'Clerk!' I called. From his desk – if he ever sat at it – he had a view of the walled garden far below, choked like an ancient pool with elder and *Colutea arborescens* and filling up steadily with the coming night. It was very quiet.

'Clerk?'

He had come silently up the stairs while I poked about among his things and was now standing at the window of the bedsitting room, peering round the curtain into the street. I fidgeted in the doorway, holding the manuscript in front of me like a fool. 'Clerk?' He knew perfectly well that I was there but he wanted me to see that the street was more important. Between us the room stretched dim and bleak: a bed with its top cover pulled back, some things arranged on top of a chest of drawers, books and magazines stacked haphazardly along the skirting boards. He had done nothing to make the place comfortable. A suitcase stood in the middle of the floor as if he'd simply left it there the day he moved in.

'I rang the bell,' I said, 'but nobody came.'

He stared harder into the street.

'So you made yourself at home anyway,' he said. He shivered suddenly and jerked the curtains closed. 'You've got a bloody nerve, Austin, following me around –' On the verge of developing this he shrugged and only repeated, 'A bloody nerve,' then sat down tiredly on the bed, looking at his hands, the vile cabbage-rose wallpaper, anything but me. With the curtains drawn the room became much larger and vaguer, filling up with vinegar-coloured gloom. I could hardly see him. 'What do you want, then?' he asked, apparently surprised to find me still there. 'I'm on my own all bloody day, then people come just when I don't want to be bothered with them.'

I should have left him to it, abandoned him to the cabbage roses, "Milk, bread, cat food," and the *Psychic News*, and gone home. Instead I held the manuscript up like a charm or entry permit and went into the gloom where he waited for me. He had become a spectre of himself. His miserable, aggressive face bobbed about above the bed, a tethered white balloon, what flesh remained to it clinging like lumps of yellow plasticine at cheekbone and jaw, the temples sunken, the whites of the eyes mucous and protuberant. He was wearing the bottom half of a pair of striped pyjamas, his stomach bulging out over the drawcord like some atrocious pregnancy while the rest of his body seemed reduced, temporary, all skin and bone. If the pursuit of Alice Sprake from Charing Cross to Camden had sickened him, where had he followed her since, and how far, to make him look like this? I was filled equally with repugnance and compassion, and in fighting both only made myself seem mealy-mouthed and foolish.

'Look,' I admitted, 'you're not at all well, and I realise this is inconvenient. But we really ought to discuss this book. It could be really fine, I'm sure, if we just clarify a few things, a really fine book.' This was rubbish, of course, and I could hear my assistant laughing sardonically somewhere in the more honest places of my skull. Not that I imagined Clerk would swallow it, but a publisher has his duties – and I had some idea of cheering him up, I suppose, as an easy solution to my own embarrassment. 'Why don't you get back into bed and take it easy while I make some coffee or something? Then we can thrash it out –'

He laughed quietly to himself, whether at my expense or his own I wasn't sure.

'Suit yourself Austin. Make as much coffee as you like. I'm going to sleep. You're a patronising bastard but I'm sure you know that already.'

I dropped the manuscript on the end of the bed, preparing to walk out and wash my hands of him. But it was something of a victory to have got him to talk to me at all, and somehow I found myself in the kitchen, pottering about among the dirty cups and staring out into the garden as I waited for the water to boil. I had to put money in the gas. There was an extraordinary staleness in the air, as if no-one had lived there for years, and I wondered if he'd cooked himself anything to eat that day, or even the day before. Milk, bread and cat food, but the milk was off, the cat gone, and the bread mouldy: and down in the garden twilight piling up among the elder boughs. I heard him moving about in the bedsitting room, muttering to himself. 'You don't mind black coffee?' I called. When I got back with the tray I found him sitting up in bed. He had taken the manuscript out of its box and scattered it all over the room.

'Go on Austin,' he taunted, 'be reasonable about *that*. Perhaps we could have some tea next, eh?' He had tried to tear the thing in half before throwing it about, but his only success had been to crumple a few sheets at either end. I put the tray down and went round on my knees picking pages up at random while he stared at me with dislike and misery. I had the feeling, there in the half-dark full of his desperation and my feebleness, that his head and neck had become detached somehow from his shoulders and were weaving independently about over the bed, sick and lost. 'I don't want your coffee. I don't want your advice. I won't make any changes, Austin, so forget it. Take the bloody thing as it is or leave it there on the floor. Just get out, that's all.'

'Clerk, you're ill –'

I thought he was going to hit me. The tray went over with a crash, spraying hot coffee over my legs. He struggled to his feet, and, wearing a great tangle of bed linen like a cloak, came half-running half-falling toward me, arms outstretched and fingers hooked – only to turn aside at the last instant and head for the window, where he writhed his shoulders free of the dirty top sheet and Dutch blanket, tore the curtains completely off their runners and stared into the street as if his life depended on the next thing he saw, shaking and sweating and shouting 'Fuck off!' over and over again.

'Christ, Clerk –'

'– off, fuck off, fuck off, fuck off, fuck –'

I pushed him aside. It was dark, and the sodium lamps had flared up like a forgotten war. Ten or fifteen yards away across the road, shadowy in the disastrous orange glare, his face turned up to study the window and his jaws moving firmly and rhythmically from side to side, Mrs Sprake's son sat kicking his heels on a low garden wall. Dark shrubbery moved behind him. He looked straight at me, I thought, and nodded. The room was silent. Coffee dribbled down my calf, sticky and cooling. Beside me, Clerk had closed his eyes and was resting his forehead against the windowpane. I felt his hip tremble suddenly against me, but I couldn't get my eyes off the boy in the street.

'Is this what's making you ill?' I asked. 'Being mixed up with this spiritualist stuff?' I had some mad idea that they might be drugging or blackmailing him.

Clerk groaned. 'What on earth are you talking about Austin,' he said wearily. He knelt on the floor amid the debris and, turning his head away from me, made an odd gurgling noise. At first I thought he was laughing. Then I realised he was being sick. He panted and coughed, his thin shoulders heaving.

'I've got cancer you bloody fool,' he said. 'I've had it for two years. The Sprakes are my only hope – so just go away now, will you?'

I left him there, wiping his mouth on a sheet of the manuscript and staring vacantly ahead as if he were dead already, and rushed out of the place. I was choking with nausea, self-disgust, and an anger I could barely contain. The woman on the landing was waiting for me, arms still folded.

'He's poorly is he, doctor?' she said, 'I thought so,' and shook her head slowly. 'I hope it's not catching –'

She stood in my way while, above, Clerk sobbed dryly. I knew he was staring out of the window again, eyes wide in that swollen papier-mâché puppet's face.

'Excuse me,' I said.

But when I got to the doorstep the chewing boy was nowhere to be seen. I ran across the road and looked into the bushes, which were still moving. It was the wind. I stood there for a moment. Tufnell Park was like a grave. I could hear faint, running footsteps a street away. At least I had the advantage of knowing where the child would go.

It's hard to say what made me so angry. Perhaps it was that Clerk should have to relinquish the world clutching only memories of that grubby little ceremony; that his despair should bequeath him in the end only endless puzzling images of the waste land between Camden and King's Cross, with its tottering houses and its old men spitting in corners full of ancient dust each grain of which has begun as dog-dirt or vomit or decayed food; that he could be promised only the fakery of sodium light, the deadly curve of the crescent and the far off buzz of traffic beyond Mrs Sprake's second-hand clothes shop. I couldn't quite separate compassion and personal outrage, and I don't suppose I ever shall. I went after the boy because I couldn't bear to think of a dying man made confused and hateful by charlatans – and, again, to silence a part of me which understood this: where human sympathy is absent it can't easily be replaced by lunch in Great Portland Street.

He got home before me, of course, and by the time I reached the crescent it was deserted but for the eternal reek of smashed fruit (and behind that something old, foggy, a smell which belonged to the same street, certainly, but in an unfamiliar time). I went to the house first and banged loudly on the door, but there was no reply. I shouted, but all that achieved was echoes, 'Mrs Sprake! Mrs Sprake!' racing away over acres of railway sidings, dull canal water and decaying squares, until I had a vision of my cries travelling perfect and undiminished all the way to Islington, as if the whole universe were suddenly dark, uninhabited, and sensitive to the slightest sound. After a minute or two of this I tried tapping on the front room window instead. Then I put my eye to a gap in the net curtain.

Mrs Sprake was in there, sprawled heavily on the sofa with the light turned off, arms limp at her sides. She had rolled her skirt up to her waist and her stockings down to her knees. On the wall in front of her hung the same cheap icon she had employed for the Incalling – had her eyes been open, they would have been focused on it. Perhaps they were focused on it anyway. The doomed man yearned down at her from his showcase, but her face was slack and expressionless. Beneath the horrible orange powder and soft, pitted skin lay an ignorance and indifference so intense as to seem avid, an abrogation, a vacancy, and a frightening weariness. I stared in astonishment at her exposed belly and thick white thighs; then rapped the window so hard it cracked under my knuckles. At the sound of this, she opened her eyes suddenly and peered in my direction; her lips moved exhaustedly, like those of a sick fish. I was terrified I might somehow discover exactly what I had interrupted. I shouted 'Open up!' or something equally useless, but moved off hurriedly down the street before she had a chance to comply.

In the dim grey wash of light from a forty-watt bulb inside, I fought briefly with the door of the shop; it gave only to my full weight, and then so suddenly that I went down heavily on one knee over the threshold.

Nobody was there. From the passage behind the counter, where the air was lax and hot, issued a smell of time, dust and artificial flowers (then, worked through that like a live thread, the distant familiar stink of the boy); and the television still flickered silently in its back room, as if nobody had bothered to turn it off since my last visit. 'Hello?' I went through and stood there in the fitful pewter glow, rubbing my bruised leg. If I put my ear close to the television I could hear it whisper, 'So far we have managed to avoid this.'

'I know you're here!' I called. I knew nothing. Except for Mrs Sprake at her inexplicable devotions, the universe was still uninhabited – dolorous, scoured, yet waiting to respond instantly to some crude signal I couldn't give – I felt abandoned to it, left for dead. I drifted toward the staircase in the corner, then up it, the heat pressing against my chest like a firm dry hand.

The whole top floor, knocked into one large room and all but one of its windows bricked up twenty or thirty years before, had been given over to him. The furniture was a clutter of the rickety stuff you can find any day in the junk shops toward Chalk Farm; a bed, a dresser, some bentwood chairs. On the dresser was a pile of what looked like grey feathers, and pushed away in one corner were some stuffed animals mounted on bits of wood. It all looked dreary and neglected – uninhabited, and yet at the same time as if he spent most of his life there. He was squatting on the bare floor watching me intently, his pudgy hands on his knees. 'There's nothing for you here, Mr Austin,' he said. 'Why don't you go home?'

'You don't know what I came for. Besides, I'd rather speak to whoever's responsible for you – your mother, if you can wake her up.'

He moved his jaws once, mechanically.

'You're horrified, Mr Austin, and who can blame you? It was immaterial to you what Clerk did with his life. Now you find you can't ignore him any longer, and you care what he does with his death. Good!' In front of him on a low occasional table he had arranged a fragment of mirror, two ordinary white candles, and an old bottle dug up from some Victorian towpath: all positioned so that when he looked into the glass the twin unsteady flames underlit his face without themselves being reflected. 'Good! It's never too late to find compassion –' And he smiled suddenly, rubbing his hands on his knees – 'You're safe! *You* need nothing we have here!' The bottle contained a few inches of cloudy preservative. Floating in that was something which looked like a thick, contorted black root. It was corked, but even so, every fibre of the grey floorboards and white plaster, every bit of furniture, had soaked up the reek of aniseed – now they gave it back into the air like a fog, to fill the mouth and coat every delicate membrane of the nose. 'Later you may discover your compassion is not as pure as you imagine, or your rage for justice; but for the moment... We're all revolted by illness, Mr Austin, revolted and frightened... There's no reason on Earth to feel ashamed of that!'

For a moment he gave his attention to the little altar, and when he spoke again his voice was thoughtful and cold.

'I know exactly why you're here, you see. You came for reassurance. In any case it was useless to bother. Go home now.'

I went over to the window, but it wouldn't open. Outside was that absorbent, sodium-lit vacancy, stretching all the way to Islington. If I concentrated, I could hear something that might have been traffic on Camden High Street. I tried breathing deeply to acclimatise myself to the stink, but that only made me feel worse. 'I'm not leaving here until I know what you promised him,' I said, 'and what your mother charged him for it. It's a grubby fraud and I'll have it stopped –'

'Leave the window alone!' He swivelled round irritably, his pudgy legs suddenly shooting out in front of him. He stood up and came rapidly across the room. 'My mother is shit, Mr Austin, under my feet. Why do you keep going on about her? I give her this –' And he writhed the fingers of his right hand. He stared up at me. 'Why don't you go home?' he said savagely. 'I don't want you here. Clerk? Clerk is shit too –' He shrugged. 'What do I care? We gave him nothing he didn't want. He's a tinkerer.'

Nothing moved in the street.

'Christ,' I said softly, 'you little brat, you.'

I tried to catch hold of his shoulder, but somehow my hand made no contact. He twisted from under it and ran off a few steps. When he turned back his face was as I'd first seen it, blank and uninterested, hardly even self-involved. 'Fucking cunt pig,' he said distinctly, without any human emphasis. He began chewing rapidly. 'Fucking cunt pig.' He went and sat down in front of his altar, hunching his shoulders and gazing into the mirror. The whole room forgot me and filled up with silence. He laughed, then coughed urgently. 'The window, Mr Austin!' he hissed. He seemed to be having some sort of choking fit. 'Goon!'

I stared down into that hopeless little landscape of death, at the blistered paint, the gaps between the houses and the ancient rubbish in the gutters. Nothing. Then Alice Sprake walked sedately into view on the other side of the street, with Clerk drifting along in her wake like a dead waterfowl. She was wearing the same dove grey skirt I had seen on the Embankment, and her prim adolescent features were dreamy, secretive. He had put his raincoat on but was otherwise as I had seen him an hour before – and down from its hem poked his long scrawny legs in their striped pyjama trousers. His feet were bare. I watched her draw him along behind her at a steadily increasing pace toward St Pancras. They never once looked up. He was very close to her as they were sucked out of sight, but she didn't seem to know he was there, or sense in any way his white awful face bobbing loosely about over her shoulder, his gaping pain and greed. In a moment the universe was uninhabited again and they were pulled deep into it toward some crux of railway lines and dark water.

Behind me the chewing boy stretched his arms and scuffed his feet. He yawned. 'You see?' he said. 'Go home now, Mr Austin,' he added, almost kindly. 'There's nothing you can do for him. You never could.'

I went across to him and kicked the table over. The mirror broke: the bottle fell on the floor and came uncorked: the candles tumbled end over end through the brown and stinking air. I bent down and hit him while he sat there, as hard as I could on the left cheek.

'Speak like a child,' I said.

He rolled about in the mess spilled from the bottle, making a high, thin chuckling sound, then lay there grinning up at me. His head rolled to one side, he let his mouth fall open and brown fluid gushed down his chin. He chewed and chewed.

'Yes sir?' he enquired. 'Do you want to buy something or sell something? My mother isn't available presently for buying, but I am allowed to sell. We buy and sell all kinds of garments sir —'

I ran out after Clerk and the girl but I never caught up with them.

Clerk died perhaps two months later, somewhere in the black end of a rainy November; slipping over the edge of a pulmonary complication at two in the morning, that hour which erodes all determination and wears the confused substance to a stub. The cancer had eaten his insides entirely away, but he was trying to correct the manuscript of the novel which finally appeared last week as *The World Reversed* (a title suggested by my assistant). We discovered the following pencilled against the opening sentences of Chapter Eight: 'When the dead look back, if they look back on us at all, they do so without rancour or pity, sadness or any sense of the waste of it. They crumble too soon and become too much a minute part of events to have any more involvement with us, and waste quickly away like footmarks on an oily pavement in October. This I know, though not from personal experience. Yet their evaporation is continual, they boil up continually around us, we inhale them as we go, and each resultant outward breath impregnates the soft brick of the city like smoke, dampens every blown newspaper, and as a curious acidic moisture loosens the pigeon dung on the ledges above... There is more, but the handwriting is difficult to interpret.'

On the night he died, or it may have been a couple of nights later, I had this dream –

I was walking along the grass verge of some provincial road, one of those roads which always seem empty and bleak, the hedges crusted at their roots with a thin grey mud thrown up by the wheels of passing vehicles, the fields on either side empty of livestock yet cropped short, the isolated houses unlit and shut up; a landscape apparently untenanted but showing signs of a continual invisible use. It was dark, but not night. Light had been bleached out of the still air and drained from all objects so that although there was no reversal of contrast the scene had about it the feel of a photographic negative. Walking beside me in her dove grey suit, her head bowed and prim, her expression at once placid and secretive, was Mrs Sprake's daughter, Alice. Why I should have been so close to her, whether there was any feeling between us, I can't say. It seems unlike me. Her bovine calm had repelled me – and still does – when awake; but we cannot be responsible for what we feel in dreams. What is clear is that I felt a sense of unease on her behalf, and turned continually to stare backwards at the distant figure which followed us.

'We should have a pleasant time,' she said. Awake, I cannot imagine this: but I remember it clearly.

'You had better go ahead of me,' I told her, and we walked like that for some minutes, in single file, while our pursuer remained a mote of energy in the middle distance, trotting doggedly along but seeming to make no headway. After a little while we were drawn into the outskirts of a small dull manufacturing town, along a protracted, gently curving dual carriageway, lined with the semi-detached houses and recessed shop fronts of some post-war ribbon development. Through the gaps in the houses I glimpsed the vacant cinders of a transport café car park, puddled and luminous; then a scrapyard full of bluish moonlight, and a canal, and a crematorium in a muddy park. There was no wind or noise. I imagined the road falling into darkness behind us as we went, each traffic intersection, each garage with its peculiar rusted petrol pumps and abandoned forecourt dissolving into the vacuum through which our pursuer flailed his way, panting and groaning as he fought his own dissolution. When I looked again, he was no closer. I began to drag Alice Sprake along nonetheless, urging her on with 'We must hurry,' and 'Please do hurry.'

There was no relief to be had from the vast silent space beyond the thin crust of buildings. It was uninhabited and smelt faintly of burnt rubber and ancient summer dust, it was a magnetic emptiness which had drawn us there simply for the sake of being there. Ages seemed to pass. If there were echoes of our quickening pace, they came back transmuted from that vacancy which is the source of everything, and we did not recognise them. Eventually it became plain that the curving road was merely an enormous circle, and all that part of it we had already walked only a few degrees of arc. Later still, the scrap yard passed again, the distant sports fields and crematorium, the cinders and the puddled forecourts and the hanging signs. Within the circle and without it were only acres of unemotional darkness, dragging at the footsteps of old men and invalids, sifting down to end as dust in gutters at windy corners, absorbent of all effort, all anxiety, all movement except that of the desperate creature behind us.

I glanced back to make sure that he remained in the middle distance, held there by his very effort to progress – I glanced back and he was at my heels, his face was Clerk's, looming white and pasty like melting floor wax over my shoulder an inch from my own, bobbing and weaving on the end of that pale rubbery stalk. His eyes were huge and avid, full of terror, his huge mouth vomited brown fluid, an abscess of misery and desire so close I knew it must burst and drench me. At the instant of touching, between the cup and the lip, that bleak image of the provinces flew apart and faded, as if he had brought with him landscapes of his own, a thin envelope of relics to insulate against the vacuum. Late taxicabs and mid-day restaurants formed briefly around us only to evaporate and give way to the Sprakes' front room, the watery, quivering purlieus of Embankment Gardens and finally the cracked pink linoleum, the walled garden, the cabbage roses, the milk, bread and cat food of his rented grave in Tufnell Park, the thinning atmosphere of self-disgust which had sustained him in desolation. 'I'm on my own all bloody day,' he whispered. 'My bloody day –' I winced away, afraid of some infinite prolongation of our last, hopeless meeting; yet in that moment felt whatever substance he now had left to him dissolve: and like smoke sucked from some distant corner of the room toward the hearth he was drawn through me and into Alice Sprake, who waited on the greenchalk line, bovine and compliant, all grey degraded gooseflesh and grubby feet, one ill-shaved leg stiffened to take her weight. She made no attempt to move at the moment of penetration, and he was absorbed. I woke up sweating in a pale grey dawn with a faint, remote sound of shunting engines dying in my skull, and stayed at home that day.

I give this for what it is worth: as a completion, perhaps. But if you take it as such you must remember that it is a personal one, and I draw nothing from it in the way of conclusions. I never knew what the Incalling was supposed to achieve – or even whether what I witnessed in Camden represented failure or success. Clerk had said that the Sprakes were his last hope: on the evidence, their crude urban magic doesn't seem to have done him much good. He is, after all, dead. Perhaps it would have worked better elsewhere in Europe, where they still have some small link with older traditions. My own part in it, if I can be said to have had one, I would prefer to forget.

1978

The Ice Monkey

WHEN JONES TURNED UP he was dressed to see his wife. Clothes were meaningless to him. He had no taste, and needed none until occasions became 'official'. This distinction, vestigial of a middle-class upbringing, caused him great pain. He drew the line between official and unofficial himself, by some process I have never understood; and on the far side of it, where the habitual no longer offered its comfort and common sense no alternative, lost his nerve and fell back on the usage of a redbrick university youth – that is, he tried to make himself look as much as possible like the ghost of some young Kingsley Amis. It was a dim and propitiatory instinct and today it had also advised him to shave and have his hair cut, a process which, while it threw his harsh cheekbones into prominence and emphasised the aggressive boniness of his jaw, yet made him seem young and vulnerable and silly.

I knew what he wanted but I hadn't the heart to pretend to be out.

'Look, Spider,' he said. To hide his embarrassment he fiddled with the handkerchief he had wrapped round his knuckles. 'Could you do me a favour?'

'I'd like to, Jones,' I said, 'honestly –' Then I remembered that because of his performance that afternoon he couldn't very well ask Henry. And no-one else he knew was in London, so I put on my coat and went with him to the tube station. 'It's my turn anyway, I think,' I said, trying to make light of it. He shrugged and stared at the platform. This was habitual too. 'I don't want another set-to,' I warned him as we got on a Metropolitan Line train: 'I'll have to leave if it's anything like last time.' But my voice was drowned by the hiss and thump of the doors closing behind us. At the other end the wind had dropped and a thick rain fell straight down on us, and on London E3, in rods.

'I quite liked Maureen, you know.'

They – by which I really mean Maureen and the child, since Jones rarely lived there even when she allowed him – had a small furnished flat on the second floor of a house somewhere between Bow and Mile End. For five years or more it had been scheduled for demolition, and now it stuck up with two or three others out of a contractors' waste land a mile across, the enormous floor-plan of a slum, full of lazy fires, silent bulldozers, and trees which seemed naked and doomed without the garden walls they had once overgrown. We forced a route through the rutted clay and piles of smouldering lath, and when we got there a plump West Indian girl put her head round the front door. She winked. 'He's here, Maureen love!' she called up the stairs. 'Don't you forget what I said!' She grinned defiantly at us, and stage thunder rolled over the Mile End Road, but I think the effect was wasted on Jones. It was more than a game to him and Maureen: neither of them had seen E3 until the age of thirty, and their failure to deal with it was ground into the stairwell walls along with all the other dirt.

'You aren't half going to catch it, Mr Jones,' the West Indian girl said to me.

Maureen was standing at the front window of the flat,

nervously smoking a cigarette and staring out across the waste as if measuring it against some other landscape she'd once seen. Her shoulders were at once rounded and tense. At her feet the child was playing happily with an imaginary friend. 'About time,' she said distantly to Jones. She was thinner than the last time I'd seen her, a short, harassed blonde in paint-stained jeans and an unravelling Marks & Sparks sweater, the flesh carved off her originally heart-shaped face by anxiety and loneliness, her voice dull and aggressive. 'Oh my God,' she said, 'what do you look like?' She blew smoke fiercely down her nostrils and jabbed the cigarette into the bottom of a glass ashtray. 'Just look at yourself!' Instead Jones stood in the centre of the room like a marooned sailor and let his eyes roam helplessly over the open makeshift shelves stuffed with baby clothes, the brown carpet, the yellow plastic potty. He was already desperate and puzzled.

'Twenty years on,' Maureen told the fires and silent, shrouded bulldozers. 'Christ, it's still 1958 for you, isn't it?'

'*Up* the hill and *down* the hill,' chanted the child. It had rubbed chocolate into its hair and clothing.

Jones lifted his hands slightly. 'They're all I've got,' he said. 'Have you been decorating? It's nice.'

Maureen laughed. She compressed her lips. 'Sit down,' she told me, giving up the security of the window. 'Your turn this time was it? How's trade, Spider? How's Henry? It'll have to be tea. I can't afford coffee.' She went into the kitchen, scrupulously avoiding Jones still aground there in the middle of the room, and began knocking things about in the sink. 'Which of you decided to get his hair cut?' she called. She came back with a tray. 'It's not all that bad for 1958. Have a ginger nut, Spider. Where's my maintenance, Jones? You owe me three months and I can't get by without it anymore.' She made her way quickly back to the window as she said this, and gazed out into the rain, measuring, measuring. Round her neck she was wearing a little silver monkey on a chain. The tiny hoop that attached its head to the middle link had broken, so she had wrapped the chain round its neck to hold it on. Jones cleared his throat and drank his tea. There was a silence. The child looked up at its mother. Suddenly it squatted down and made a loud farting noise. 'Up the hill and down the hill,' it said. A horrible smell filled the room. 'They knocked the pub down,' Maureen said, 'so I've got no job. This place goes next month and the council still haven't rehoused me. You've *got* to write to them about it this time.' She picked the child up and dropped it in Jones's lap. 'There's your daddy,' she told it. 'Ask him to change you.' It stared up at him for a second then set up a startlingly high-pitched whine. Jones stared back.

'Can't you see you're going to be in trouble with the maintenance? Tansy says they can easily make you pay –'

'Tansy!' yelled Jones suddenly into the child's face. 'Tansy?' he laughed wildly. 'Oh great! Who's bloody *Tansy*? That silly cow downstairs? Of course they can bloody make me, you've got your own brains to see that!'

'She's all I've got!' shouted Maureen, and burst into tears. 'Oh you rotten bastard, I've got nobody else to tell me –'

The child waved its arms and whined. Jones put it roughly on the floor and ran out of the flat calling 'Tansy says! Tansy says!' and laughing desperately. When he'd gone I took refuge in the kitchen, which was less smelly, and made some more tea. 'You don't have to stay, you know,' said Maureen. 'He'll be kicking about out there on his own.' She dabbed hopelessly at the child, found a clean nappy. ('Up the hill and down the hill,' it went, looking up over her shoulder at some invisible friend.) 'I don't know what happens when he comes here,' she said. 'I can't be any more reasonable.' And, 'Remember Swansea, Spider. It was all different then. I did Art. I loved his hands. Look at them now, they're all scabby.' She sipped her tea, staring past me out of the window, recalling perhaps the times when she'd been accustomed to wear a white two-piece and swim, while Jones made his name on the heroic Welsh sea-cliffs of a distant summer, and the water was the colour of a new blue nylon rope.

'His hands were pretty scabby then, Maureen,' I reminded her gently.

'Get stuffed, Spider. Fuck off.'

At the door I offered her a job serving in one of the shops. 'Get in touch if you need help with solicitors or anything,' I added.

She said: 'I'd believe you really wanted to help if you just made him come on his own for once.'

He was out among the smoky contractors' fires, his thin silhouette appearing and disappearing mysteriously as he moved from one to another in the rainy gloom, kicking at the embers and, I thought, trying to get up the nerve to go back inside again. It took me a while to attract his attention.

'They're the only good clothes I've got,' he kept saying as we sat miserably on opposite sides of the tube carriage. 'Why does she keep picking on them like that?'

It would have taken too long to explain it to him, so while the train roared and swayed its way back to the civilised areas west of Farringdon I let him stare dumbly at himself in its dark windows, touch curiously the sore shaved pink cheeks of his furry inaccurate reflection, and fuss (puzzled but on the edge of resentment and already taking advantage of the self-righteousness that would enable him to stay away for another month or two) with the mustard yellow knitted tie, the tobacco brown corduroy jacket and the white shirt with the thick chocolate-coloured stripes he'd had since the last proud birthday of his adolescence.

Meanwhile I imagined Maureen, in E3 where all horizons are remembered ones, dwelling on vanished freedoms: how on Monday mornings in the summer term, after two nights toothbrushless in Llanberis, in a barn or cheap cotton tent, she would hurry down the long polished corridors of the teacher training college eating burnt toast, late for History of Art, still slightly crumpled and sleepy and hungover in one of Jones's unravelling Marks pullovers and pale blue jeans, focus of all interested, jealous eyes.

'I bought her that thing round her neck,' said Jones peevishly. 'I notice she's broken it.'

'Come on, Jones,' I said.

Preoccupation is easily mistaken for helplessness. This was how Jones survived in a world which didn't understand him, although I don't think he employed it often as a conscious device. His obsession with climbing was genuine, and had begun long before Swansea or Maureen. Five weeks after the maintenance fiasco, in the middle of the coldest February since 1964, I took him up to Scotland. I was going to see my parents who have retired to Bearsden, a comfortable suburb where they own a garage. The motorways were covered in black ice: there were extensive detours, and I ended up driving all through Friday night. Jones slept in the back, and then ate three fried eggs in a café straddling the road, watching with his head tilted intelligently to one side as the sparse traffic groaned away south and a kind of mucoid greyness crept into the place through its steamed-up windows. He talked of the time he had fallen off a famous limestone route in Derbyshire and broken his nose. His chalk-bag had burst and his face had been daubed with blood and chalk. He had a photograph which someone had taken at the time. 'The worst bit was a feeling of not being able to breathe,' he said. 'I thought I was dying.' He repeated this two or three times with what seemed at the time a superstitious enjoyment.

He told me he wanted to do Point Five Gully on Ben Nevis that weekend, and asked me to go with him. 'Henry won't come,' he said. 'I suppose you know why.' He sat there pouring tomato sauce on his plate.

'I can't go, Jones,' I said. 'They're expecting me.' I hadn't been ice-climbing for years; neither of us had. After Bridge of Orchy I let him drive, hoping to get some sleep. He put us into a snowdrift in Glencoe; I watched the carnivorous bends of the A82 gape open all the way to Fort William. (Sitting on the back of his motorcycle ten years or more before, I had driven a tent-pole straight through the rear window of a Mini as he tried to overtake it on one of those bends. I can't imagine why I had it under my arm, or how he persuaded me to carry it at all.) When I next woke up he had the van in a car park somewhere and cold air was spilling into it through the back doors. He had put on a pair of filthy stretch breeches and a Javelin jacket completely threadbare in the forearms from climbing on gritstone. An ancient Whillans harness flapped between his legs like some withered orange codpiece. He was talking to somebody I couldn't see.

'Excuse me,' he said. 'Would any of you have a cigarette?'

Giggles answered him, and I went back to sleep.

We walked up to the climb early on Sunday morning. It was still dark, and the weather was appalling. 'Come on, Jones,' I said: 'Nobody bothers with it in conditions like this.' When you could see it, the Ben looked just like a mountain from a Fifties film about Alpine guides: not pointed, true: but just as cardboardy, dioramic, painted on. Powder snow blew about like fog on a bitter east wind, cutting at our faces. We set out with some other people but got separated from them as we blundered about on Tower Ridge. For a few minutes we heard their voices thin and urgent-sounding against the boom of the wind; then nothing.

Jones made me lead the first pitch.

With front-point crampons on your feet and one of the new short axes – their acutely-angled picks like the beaks of pterodactyls – in each hand, even overhanging ice can be climbed. Waterfalls are the most fun: suspended up among the huge icicles which have grown together until they look like a sheaf of organ pipes, balancing on half an inch of steel two hundred feet up on a sunny morning, you can quite enjoy it all. *Chunk!* go the axes, as you drive them into the ice. I couldn't hear myself think on the Ben that day. Eddies of wind exploded continually into the gully. In places there was hardly enough ice to take an axe – it starred and flaked away under the pick; while elsewhere the route was choked with powder snow like a laundry chute full of Persil. After a bit I couldn't see Jones below me anymore (or hear him singing), just a greyish space boiling with ice particles, the two nine-millimetre ropes vanishing into it. I could only go up – chopping, floundering, front-pointing delicately on black verglas while the wind first pushed me into the gully-bed then sucked me out again, forcing spindrift down my neck, under my helmet and into my eyes… Eventually bulges of good ice appeared. I got up on to one of them, smashed in a couple of ice screws for a belay, and gave Jones a tug on the rope to indicate he should climb.

By the time he joined me on my little melted ledge, conditions had improved. The wind had dropped; we could see each other, and hear each other talk. The next pitch turned out to be a fifty-foot bulge, curving out above us fringed with short twisted icicles and showing up a greenish colour in the growing daylight. It looked like good firm ice. Jones lit a cigarette, rubbed his hands together and moved off up it at a terrific rate, showering me with chunks of ice. He quickly got up to the difficult overhanging section, beneath which he put in a tubular screw and had a rest. I could just see him if I craned my neck, a dark figure dangling from a bright orange sling, turning gently from side to side like a chrysalis in a hedge. The sound of singing drifted down. 'Come on Jones, we haven't got all day.'

'Bugger off.' We had begun to enjoy ourselves. I flexed my fingers inside my fibre pile mitts; checked the belays; whistled. When my neck got stiff from looking up at him I rested it by peering out of the gully. No view. 'I'm moving off again,' called Jones. 'This is easy.' Rope ran out through my hands. He stuck both axes in the ice above the overhang, jabbed his front points in. The whole bulge exploded like a bomb and he tumbled backwards into space above me.

He'd been catapulted right out of the gully. His protection screw failed the moment his weight came on it and he hurtled down past me screaming. Thirty feet of rope slid through my hands before I braked his fall; even then the impact pulled my belays like rotten teeth. I fell, mostly through clear air, turning over and over. I was thinking 'Christ, Christ, Christ,' in a sort of mental monotone. Part the way down I landed feet first on something solid, tearing the ligaments in my legs. For an instant or two I was sliding down a slope: I tried to use the one axe remaining to me as a brake, rolling over and digging the pick into the ice: it ripped out. I fetched up at the bottom of the gully in a foetal position, gasping and groaning and choking on the powder snow which had saved me. My legs hurt so much I thought I'd broken both of them. I could see Jones a few feet away. He was kneeling there in a fog of spindrift making a queer coughing noise. I lay there thinking about being crippled. This gave me enough strength to get up and help him.

The ropes had wound themselves round him as he fell. One turn had gone round his neck and was supporting his whole weight. I couldn't get it off him. The rope was snagged on something further up. His tongue was still moving but he was black in the face and he was dead. He would have died anyway in the time it took me to crawl down the hill.

The funeral was awful. It was held a few days later in one of those places trapped between Manchester and the gritstone moors (Mottram, perhaps, or Stalybridge, where nothing is clear cut and there is neither town nor country, just a grim industrial muddle of the two), in a huge bleak cemetery on the side of a hill. Jones's open coffin was displayed in the front room of the terrace in which his brother lived. When it was my turn to file past I couldn't look at him. His relatives sat dumbly drinking tea; each time one of them caught my eye, my legs hurt. We always blame the survivor, I suppose. The funeral cars took what seemed like hours to crawl through the grimy wet streets behind the town: and at the burial plot some old aunt of his teetered on the edge of the hole in the wind, so that I had to drop my stick and grab her upper arm to stop her falling in. Under my hand her bones felt as fragile as a bird's. We tried to talk to one another but the wind whipped the words away.

Afterwards there was a dismal meal in an assembly room above a baker's. It had wooden panelling, and the lukewarm roast lamb was served by local women wearing black dresses and white aprons. I was alone there. (Some of his other climbing friends had turned up earlier, but left after the ceremony in a group. In any case I didn't know any of them very well.) When they served him, Jones's brother jumped to his feet suddenly and said: "No meat! I told them, no meat!" All the old women looked at him. He was much older than Jones, a tall thin man with lines of tension round his mouth that might have been vegetarianism or pain; he died himself a few months later, of cancer of the bowel, which just left the women. After they had persuaded him to sit down again he burst into tears. The place catered for functions of all sorts. Someone had left a crude little monkey, a tourist souvenir with limbs plaited from jute and a wooden head, hanging above the serving hatch; and there were faded Christmas decorations up in the ceiling.

I stayed the weekend in a hotel and before I left on the Sunday afternoon went over to the cemetery on my own. I don't know what I expected to find. The road outside it was littered with satin ribbons and florist's cellophane which had blown off the graves during the night. When I wound down the window of the van there was a smell of wet moorland, and

I thought of how Jones had begun to climb here as a child, coming home ravenous and sore late at night from the outcrops near Sheffield. In the summer, as he inched out across the big steep gritstone faces, there would have been the sudden dry odour of chalk-dust; the warm rock under the fingertips; a laugh. The grave looked unfinished, and his brother was standing over it with his head bowed. He had heard me limping along the gravel path so I couldn't very well leave. I stood there and bowed my head too, feeling at once intrusive and intruded upon. After a few minutes he blew his nose loudly.

'She didn't come, then. The wife. You'd have thought she'd make the effort.'

I pictured Maureen, staring out of the window at the ruins of east London, the falling rain.

'I think there was some sort of strain,' I said.

'Strain?'

'Between them.'

He obviously didn't understand me, and I didn't want to explain. I tried to change the subject. 'He'll be missed,' I said. 'He was one of the best rock climbers in the country.'

He looked at me.

'You'll all miss him, will you?' he asked bitterly. 'You should have had more sense than to encourage him.'

Maureen remained at the back of my mind but events kept me away from E3. The shops were doing well: in anticipation of a good summer season I went to New York and California on buying trips, coming away with a line of lightweight artificial fibre sleeping bags and the English agency for a new kind of climbing harness which I thought might compete with the Whillans. When I got back the weather in London was raw and damp, and it was late March. My legs ached intermittently, like a psychic signal. It was quite a sunny afternoon when I got off the eastbound train at Bow.

The mud of the contractors' battlefield had frozen into hard ruts, and only two houses were still standing, saved – if that is the word – by a temporary withdrawal of labour in the building trades. I couldn't remember which one it was. I chose the one without the corrugated iron nailed across its ground floor windows; I waited for someone to come and answer the door. Bulldozers lay all around me hull-down into the earth as if exhausted by a lengthy campaign, a hard winter. Grey smoke drifted between the little beleaguered aluminium huts which dotted the waste. Some attempts had been made to begin building. I could see trenches full of cement, piles of earthenware pipes, and here and there a course of new brick waist high above the ruts. They were fortifications already doomed: a kind of reversed archaeological excavation was taking place here, revealing the floor plan of the slums to come. 'Oh, hello Spider. It's a bit inconvenient just now,' said Maureen.

'I'd ask you in,' she said, 'but I'm waiting for someone.'

She'd had her hair cut short and was wearing clothes I'd never seen her in before. Her fingernails were varnished a curious plum colour, the varnish chipped where she had bitten them. She saw that I didn't quite know how to react. 'I'm a bit smarter than usual!' she said with a nervous laugh. 'Oh, come on up.' Upstairs she lit a cigarette. 'Coffee, Spider?' There was some new furniture in the kitchen – cupboards and a table with clean Formica surfaces, little stools with metal legs; while in the front room the makeshift shelves full of baby clothes had been replaced. In a bookcase with a smoked glass front were a few paperbacks and a dictionary. The flat was somehow unchanged by all this, resisting, like her fingernails, all her attempts to normalise her life. It still smelt of the child, which was squatting on its yellow potty looking vacantly up into the opposite corner of the room and whispering to itself. 'You must have finished now,' Maureen told it.

She looked at me anxiously. 'I would have come to the funeral but I just didn't have any money. They wouldn't give me social security that week.' She stubbed out the cigarette. 'I got a letter from his brother,' she said.

'You can always go up there later. I don't think they understood the situation, that's all.'

'I don't know when I'll have time now,' she said. 'I've got a job.'

It turned out she was the secretary of a local businessman. I asked her how she managed with the child. 'It goes to a creche,' she said vaguely. She was looking out of the window at a car making its way round the perimeter of the battlefield, a big European model rolling on its suspension as its front wheels dipped into the holes left by the contractors' plant. As if the arrival of this thing, with its overtones of comfort and prosperity, were a signal, a reminder, she turned round suddenly and said: 'Spider, I expected that police car day and night for bloody years. They came in the middle of the night and they weren't sure which of you was dead. They got the names all wrong.' I tried to say something but she rushed on. 'I cried all night, what was left of it. For him, for you, for me, for all of us. What we were at Swansea. Oh, if only he'd just once earned some bloody money!' She started to cry and dab at her eyes. The car outside came to a halt under the window. A man in a leather coat got out and locked it carefully. He looked up, smiling and waving. Maureen went down to let him in.

His name was Bernard. He had a dark suit on, blue or brown, I forget; and neat, longish hair. He used some sort of aftershave, and seemed ill at ease. He was decent enough but I gave him no help. 'How's the little chap, then?' he said, picking up the child. 'Oh Christ.' Maureen went to make him some coffee. 'Bernard's a computer programmer,' she called through, as if this might encourage us to talk. 'It's systems analysis, Maureen,' he corrected: 'systems analysis.' They held a whispered conversation in the kitchen and I thought I heard him say, 'But we were going to the *film* theatre. It's *The Exterminating Angel*. You said you'd love to see *The Exterminating Angel*.' When he came back it was to excuse himself and take the potty to empty in the lavatory. While he was out Maureen said defensively, 'We're getting married, Spider.'

After that we talked about Jones's climbing gear, which I had held on to in case she wanted it.

'I don't think it would be good for her to have all that brought back, do you Spider?' Bernard appealed (certain perhaps that it never could be). He sipped his coffee which he took without milk. 'While she's still on her own, anyway.' He looked at his watch. 'Is it about time we were moving, Maureen love?' Maureen, though, sat forward and rummaged through the bag I'd brought the stuff in. 'There's a pair of double Alpine boots here,' she said: 'Quite new. Could you sell them in one of the shops, Spider?' Bernard looked irritated. 'I don't think we're that badly off, Maureen,' he said. He laughed. 'Could you, Spider?' Maureen said. I told her that I'd try. (I sent her the money for them a couple of months later, but it can't have been forwarded from Bow because I've never had an answer.) There was an awkward pause. They invited me to the wedding, which was to be in May. 'I don't think I can make that,' I said. 'I have to go to America on a buying trip. A range of sleeping bags I'm interested in.' The child crawled round the floor breathing heavily. 'Up the hill and down the hill.' As I got up to go it was trying to climb the side of the bookcase, its little feet slipping off the shiny new melamine.

Bernard saw me to the door of the flat. 'I hope I can make her happy,' he said, and thanked me for coming. Maureen, I realised, had already said goodbye.

It was getting dark as I went down the stairs. The landing windows showed a waste land; fires. Further down I met the West Indian girl, Tansy. She was wearing Maureen's little silver monkey and chain. They glittered against her skin in the brownish gloom. Maureen must have given them to her, I suppose. 'Cheerio,' she said; and smiled.

1980

The East

I LIVED FOR SOME time in central London. My work kept me busy in the evenings. But during the day, especially the early afternoon, I had nothing better to do than sit in Soho cafés. I liked Soho. I can't remember now if the Bar Italia was open in those days. I know the Living Room wasn't. Anyway, I tended to frequent old-fashioned places with a mixed clientele. Places like Presto's where you could still meet someone over thirty, someone who wasn't in films, advertising or comics: someone with – or more likely without – a real job.

In late 1989, at about the time of the opening-up of East Berlin, I used to see around the streets and parks an old man, a bit frail, strangely dressed, clearly a foreigner in a world where there are few clear foreigners anymore. He was reluctant to talk. Sometimes he seemed reluctant even to stop walking. After some effort I cornered him one day in Soho Square. He was sitting on a bench with some pigeons round his feet. He wasn't feeding them. They seemed agitated with pleasure anyway, bobbing and dipping and walking up and down in the sunshine.

'You're reluctant to talk,' I said.

He smiled.

'You would be too,' he said. 'If you were me.'

When I say that he was old I am using the word in a special sense. At first I put his age at sixty or seventy. Later I realised that time had less to do with it than use. I began to think of him not so much as an old man as a young one who had been used up or tired out by some enormous effort of will.

The way he dressed was in itself odd. He always wore a long, very dark gaberdine, unbelted and buttoned from the neck right down to his knees with large buttons of the same colour. It was tight at the shoulders and loose at the hem. The cloth was dusty and had faded unevenly – as if at some time in his life he had stood still for very long periods in strong sunlight – so that it looked grey in one light, purple in another. He also wore a stiff black hat with a round crown and a wide round brim. Both of these items had a strikingly foreign, old-fashioned air.

All the time I knew him he never seemed to shave. Despite that his beard was rarely more than a white stubble. Strong curly white hairs sprouted out of his nose, from deep in his nostrils. Also from the edges of his ears. His eyes, pink-rimmed, with irises of a very pale blue, were always watering. One day they gave him a look of intelligence, and you thought he might be an academic of some kind; the next, a look of cheerful cunning and you didn't know what to think. Every so often he would take out an enormous cotton handkerchief – white with a border of blue and brown lines of different thicknesses – and blow his nose loudly on it. This never failed to attract attention, especially in the crowded Patisserie Valerie.

He reminded me of someone but I could never think who. He claimed to have come from the East.

'So. What do you do?' he said.

'I'm an entertainer,' I said. 'Conjuror. Look.'

'Very impressive,' he said.

'What do you do?'

He indicated Soho Square, the pigeons, the young women in the windy sunshine.

'I do nothing, as you see.'

Drawn to one another the way a young man and an old man often are, we began to meet frequently. It was always in Soho. I introduced him to caffe latte and zabaglione. I found, too, that he would eat anything baked with crushed almonds. Confectionery like that reminded him of something eaten daily in the East. He couldn't successfully explain what, and I was left feeling that if I didn't understand him the fault was mine. It was a small thing.

After a while, he began to tell me the story of his escape. He always began the same way, by giving me this advice:

'Michael, never be a refugee.'

'Will I have a choice?'

'A clever answer. Someone as clever as you doesn't need to hear my story.'

'I'm sorry. Go on.'

'I mean this: never try to shove your life into a cheap suitcase at the last moment. Never try to save your books. Never wear your best overcoat. Have a light rucksack ready-packed. Take it with you to the office. Take it to the homes of your lovers. Always wear tough outdoor clothes and boots. Never try to save your family –'

There he broke off, breathing hard and staring at me intently. One side of his lower lip trembled.

'Promise me that, Michael.'

And before he would carry on I had to promise.

'Your English is good,' I said one day.

He smiled.

'Why shouldn't it be?'

'You're a linguist then,' I said.

'We're all linguists in the heart,' said the old man. And his blue eyes glittered like water seen from far off on a good day.

His English was very good indeed. There was never any doubt about his English. But the story he told had such a skewed feel it was like a bad translation, full of innuendos just where you wanted clarity. The language he couched it in was good, it was more than good. The story itself was what needed translating. This he failed to do.

'Every spring, the thaw leaves black mud eighteen inches deep on top of the permanent ice. The day we came west from Zoostry, we were up to our knees in it. People from further back kept catching us. We stumbled along as best we could. They drove past in everything from post vans to horse-drawn sleds. Then, on the outskirts of Avigdor: a child run down ten minutes before we arrived! Stolen military vehicle. Her little white leg was like a stick someone had driven into the mud until it broke. She looked up at us with such dumb surprise.'

He put his face in his hands.

'What could we do? Menkorad, Zentny Norosh, the Triangle: we'd come three hundred miles. We had no morphine, no blankets. No supplies of any kind. The Vorslatt people hadn't eaten for days. You could see them in the evening, trying to cook their shoes.'

We were conscious of our roles. I was young, he was old. I would listen while he spoke. Each time we met the old man had a new story for the young one. But he was careful not to monopolise our conversations. He drew a history from me, too. Who was I? How had I come to be what I was? He listened to my drab little tales – Northern colleges, Northern towns, Hell, Hull and Halifax – with as much interest as I had in his exotic ones.

'What I hate is the women with faces like buns,' I tried to explain. 'Every one of them carrying this plastic bag with a Pierrot printed on it. Do you know what I mean?' Or: 'Up there it still smells of the coking plant. The buses are always late. And there's always this kicking sign on the baker's van:

"REAL" BREAD. I mean,' I asked the old man, 'what's that? Inverted fucking commas! Even the fucking bread calls its own existence into question?'

I don't know what he made of Britain through my eyes. But each of his stories further wrenched my idea of Eastern Europe. It dawned on me one day that he wasn't describing any Europe, any East, I knew. Was he using some abandoned nomenclature? For instance, when he spoke of 'Autotelia' perhaps he only meant Bulgaria. Just as when you say 'Bohemia' you are essentially talking about the place we know today – well anyway, the place we used to know – as Czechoslovakia. Encyclopaedias and atlases could tell me nothing. The tiny nation-states he described had gone unrecorded. They lay curled up inside his memory, but nowhere else: bereft of landscape or tradition, cultural heritage or political and economic history.

'The Triangle,' I tried one day: 'I'm not sure I understand you when you say that.'

We were upstairs at Maison Bertaux. Despite that, the old man looked off into the distance, as if the walls were no impediment.

'You said,' he reminded me, 'that my English was perfect.'

'Oh it is. It is.'

His escape, the old man often said, had exhausted his reserves not just of physical but psychic energy: imagination, hope, his whole sense of himself. But in the end I had to ask myself this. If he had come from the East, why should he have had to escape? Wasn't that the whole point? No one had to escape from there any more. I stopped believing him. Slowly he assumed a new definition. Just another old man, I told my friends, who had gone mad in a bedsit in North London. This didn't make his stories any less entertaining (if entertaining is the proper word to use here). Neither did it prevent me from following him around London to see if I could discover more.

At the British Museum he studied trays of broken artefacts

from vanished Polynesian cultures. At the Science Museum he was afforded some amusement by an exhibit meant to deconstruct the phlogiston theory of burning. At the Imperial War Museum he stood for almost an hour in front of a diorama of Mons. His face was illuminated by nostalgia. I kept a list. I still have it, though it grows more meaningless to me every year. He visited more than forty sites of this type, including the incomplete buildings of the new British Library. He attended an opera scored by Philip Glass, during which he slept; and the Man Ray exhibition at the Serpentine Gallery. There he smiled sadly over an amazing photograph entitled Rrose Selavy, 1924, as if he had once known its subject.

(Was 'Rrose' the proper spelling here, or a mistake of the Serpentine's? Was the whole name perhaps only an alias or Surrealist nom de guerre, 'Selavy' code for 'C'est la vie'? How would one ever find out? I still puzzle over this. Had Man Ray somehow managed to reach out over the years and counter the old man's mystery with a mystery of his own?)

Museums, art galleries, exhibitions.

These are not inexplicable locations. But how to describe the others? Abandoned cinemas in Haringey and East Finchley. The filled-in dock network between Surrey Quays and the river. Railway arches in Forest Hill and Putney. He visited them all. Even less explicable were the deserted intersections of arterial roads, viewed at midnight; the rainswept forecourts of Ikea, Wickes, Do It All, entered after closing time. At these venues he met other displaced people. They were men or women with white faces, often well dressed but bothered by two or three winter flies. I never heard them speak. They stood in groups of two or three, apparently studying the entrance arch of the Blackwall Tunnel or the north-west corner of the Tottenham Hale one-way system.

I don't know why I say 'apparently' here. But it seems apt enough. I shadowed him for a month. Nothing was revealed.

Did he know I was there? Was the very meaninglessness of his itinerary a way of telling me how little I could learn?

Eventually, irritable and determined, I followed him all the way home.

Well, in fact I didn't.

He lived on Anson Road, one of the wide, endless, tree-lined streets that connect Tufnell Park and Holloway. An entire generation disappeared into those streets and never came out again. They came to attend the polytechnic and ended up staring at the peeling wallpaper above the Ascot. They put money in the gas meters and payphones. They paid or were unable to pay the rent. Answering the doorbell, they left a trail of wet footprints on the stairs from the bathroom – it was for someone else. They arrived young and quickly became middle-aged – in the end they owned a shell of outdated sociology texts and some albums on the verge of collectibility. They had become bald men in black leather jackets, women like fat pigeons with woollen coats and very red lipstick.

Motionless in the pouring rain, I watched him move to and fro behind an uncurtained third-floor window. It was three o'clock in the afternoon. Light from the bare bulb above his head gleamed dully on the yellowed wallpaper. He still had his hat on. If you had asked me then, I would have identified him as the perfect inhabitant of the vanished '60s bedsitland I have just described. It was the last time I could have claimed that. I was wrong about the old man. Perhaps I was wrong about Tufnell Park, too.

About an hour later he left the house and went off towards Holloway. I watched him out of sight then hurried up the cracked stone steps and rang doorbells until someone buzzed me in. The lino on the stairs was grey-green, the fire-retardant door of each bedsit a starved matt white. I let myself into the old man's room – Hey Presto! – and looked around.

It was one of three single rooms partitioned out of the original double, with about twelve feet by seven of floor space.

The stuff crowded in there fell into two broad categories, that which had been provided by the landlord and that which belonged to the old man himself. Into the former category fell the single bed (but not its yellow coverlet); the Baby Belling stove (but not the coffee-maker on its blackened front ring); the wardrobe with its peeling veneers, but not the short feathered stick propped up in one corner of it. Into the latter, a random collection of small objects (but not the chipped green chest of drawers he had arranged them on); an oval mirror (but not the stained sink he had positioned it above); and two or three items of clothing hanging on a hook on the back of the door.

I sat on the bed for some time studying these things. I felt only faintly guilty for being in there with them, perhaps because I could make nothing of them or the life they represented. The coffeemaker seemed bulbous and misproportioned. The mirror frame featured in bas-relief what appeared to be a fight between mink. The feathers were dyed fluorescent greens and reds; or were they? One moment the items on the chest of drawers looked like the residue of a hundred days out – trips to the seaside, trips to the country, river trips in hired boats – the next they seemed otherwordly, unreadable, impassive. A brass lizard, part of a triangular candle, a few polished stones, a tiny red tin of ointment, two or three ornamental boxes – all placed carefully around a framed photograph and smelling faintly of incense. As the light went out of the air outside, they seemed to shift a little, to settle towards one another. There was a faint, objective sigh in the air – the sound that inanimate things might make if they relaxed – a smell of dust.

Suddenly I realised what the design on the yellow bedcover was intended to represent. I got to my feet quickly and, blundering out of the room, slammed the door behind me, breathing as if I had run halfway down the Strand after a bus. I was desperate to get out of there. Then something compelled me to go back in and break everything I could find. In the end, I was breaking perfectly ordinary things. They seemed wrong to me. I broke a Birds of the World tea tray; a mug with Ronald McDonald's face.

The old man vanished from Soho. Within a week I missed him. I missed the challenge of him. Also, I remembered his watery blue eyes and his trembling lip, and wondered if I had gone too far. About a month later he walked into Presto's and sat down opposite me. His coat was glazed with dirt, as if he had been living in the street. He looked ill. His face was emaciated, his movements stiff; his hands had a continual slight tremor. When he spoke, I could hear his breath going effortfully in and out in the pauses between sentences.

'You don't look too well,' I said. 'Can I get you something?'

When the waitress came he ordered zabaglione but had trouble with the spoon. 'I can't eat this,' he said helplessly. To start with it was hard to get him to say anything else. He kept looking at me out of the side of his eye, like a nervous horse. If he wasn't watching me, he was watching the pedestrians entering Old Compton Street.

'No different here,' he said.

Suddenly, he laid his hand over mine.

'Michael, these people are animals! You must be so careful with them!' He stared hard at me. 'Michael, promise me you'll be careful!'

'I promise,' I said.

This seemed to relax him. He began spooning up the zabaglione very fast and noisily.

'I haven't eaten!' he said. 'I haven't dared eat!' He said: 'Someone broke into my room. My things. I −'

He looked out of the window.

'Look, that man!'

'It's just a man,' I said.

'No. He −'

He stopped.

'I haven't been back there,' he said.

'You feel violated,' I said.

'It's not that,' he said. He took his hat off and looked inside it. 'It's the terror of the return journey. You know?'

I didn't know.

'Despite that,' he told me, 'I'm determined to go back.'

'Do you mean the bedsit?' I asked.

He stared at me.

'Home,' he said. 'The terror of the journey home.'

'Ah.'

He said that he could no longer get on with the Western life. That was what he called it: the Western life. He shrugged, wiped around the inside of the hat with his handkerchief.

'I'm going back to the East.'

By then, I suppose, every journey had become a terror for him. As soon as he finished eating, I offered to help him along Charing Cross Road to the tube station and put him on a train. He eyed me uncertainly. I saw that he was frightened of me now, whatever he might say. Not because I had wrecked his room. He couldn't know I had done that. It was because I was human.

He thought. Then he said:

'Very well. Thank you. At least someone has been kind to me.'

It was the early evening rush hour. We walked slowly. He leaned on my arm. Despite it all, he was still interested in the West. The newest Japanese sports car or motorcycle, parked at the kerb like a halogen-lit sculpture, would stop him dead. A bookshop window would draw him across the pavement against the grain of the crowds. Paperbacks and maps, cheap souvenir T-shirts: he winced away from secretaries, but he wouldn't be put off the things that attracted him.

Leicester Square station was a nightmare. Tourists and schoolchildren marbled a solid pack of commuters like the fat in beef. He clung to the escalator rail. When he found his platform at last, he wavered near the edge of it, nodding morosely as the older kids kicked the younger ones and tried to push them on to the rails. 'I suppose the train will be crowded,' he said. It was. 'I don't think I can get on,' he said; but he did. Before it pulled away, there was one of those empty moments typical to the Underground. (The carriage doors remain open. Apart from some faint ticking noises the train is silent and goes nowhere. People begin to look at one another.) For perhaps a minute the old man stared out at me from between two women in business suits and heavy eye make-up, terror in his eyes. I stared back uncomfortably, aware that everyone was watching us. He fumbled suddenly in his coat.

'Take this, Michael. Please take it.'

He pressed into my hand something small and angular, folding my fingers round it gently with his own.

At that the doors banged shut and the train drew away from the platform.

That was the last I saw of him.

When I looked down I saw that he had given me the little framed photograph which had stood on the chest of drawers in his room, surrounded like an icon by the votive objects of his exile. Something I had failed to break.

I found it difficult to pick up my existence where it had left off.

At night I worked, drawing dyed feathers out of a top hat. Hey Presto. By day I could not get the old man out of my head. I was bitterly sorry to have been the cause of his despair. But how could I help that now? In addition, Soho seemed empty to me without his ironies. I missed the sound of him snorting into his large handkerchief. I was bored.

To get away – and perhaps as a kind of penance too – I revisited many of the sites I had followed him to, haunting a street of deserted factories here, the strip of derelict land behind a Sainsbury's there. I was attracted to Hackney and

Wanstead, the bleak parks, the chains of reservoirs which lay like mirrors discarded northward along the Lea Valley. Winter turned to Spring. In Clissold Park the wind tore the petals off the crocuses and blew them about. Male pigeons fluttered down to the paths, inflating themselves to bob and dip. The females looked up in faux surprise and walked in rather aimless arcs. It was Spring, and suddenly the streets were full of haggard young men and women from Stoke Newington, made tired and anxious by their success at marriage, culture journalism and modern parenting. They looked so awkward somehow, so uncomfortable with their lot. I stared at them puzzledly all one afternoon. They gave me an idea. I went back to the old man's bedsit.

It was empty.

Even the carpet had gone. All I could find of him was a diagram drawn on the floor in chalk; a permanent sense that the room had only just been vacated.

I sat there in the silence.

I thought to myself:

So. The world is now full of people like him. People who have taken advantage of political change to infiltrate a society in which they would otherwise be easily discovered. They are all less from the East than the 'East'.

Is it possible to believe that?

The photograph he had given me was no help.

It had been taken in a garden darkened with laurel and close-set silver birch – a family picture centred on a very attractive black-haired woman in her mid-thirties. She wore a long jumper over jeans. Her brown eyes had the round, frank, slightly protrusive look and nervous vivacity associated with thyroid disorder. Her smile was delighted and ironic at once – the smile of a lively art student rather surprised to find herself a matron. In front of her stood two boys five and ten years old, resembling her closely about the mouth and eyes. And there, behind the three of them, with his hand on her shoulder and his face slightly out of focus, stood the old man: younger-looking but clearly himself. Was he her father? Or were they a marriage? It was hard to say. I inclined to the former. I found myself staring as deeply into the photograph as he had stared into my face when he said:

'Michael, never become a refugee!'

I placed it on the floor in front of me.

Towards dark, the world spun briefly. Vertigo! I thought. I thought I heard a bird call sweetly from one of the laurel bushes in the picture. I felt myself falling in towards it. I thought I heard a woman's voice exclaim –

'Aren't we lucky to have this? Aren't we?'

I stopped myself in time.

Those were the words I used to myself, 'in time'; although what I meant by them I wasn't then entirely sure. I went out of the bedsit and locked the door behind me. I went down into the quiet street.

The room is mine now. I don't live in it. I keep it locked when I'm not there. I bought a small chest of drawers and painted it green. On it I put a few of the things that have had meaning in my life so far. A ceramic rose brooch bought from a stall in Camden in 1986. A box of Norwegian matches. Some shells which, if you put your nose close to them, still give off the faint smell of the East Anglian coast. One or two things like that, set in front of the old man's photograph. Once a week I go there and stare into his daughter's eyes until I begin to feel myself falling. 'In time,' I tell myself. 'In time.'

1996

'Doe Lea'

The Magus Zoroaster, my dead child,
Met his own image walking in the garden

MY FATHER AND I had our ups and downs but in the end we were good for each other. His name was Alan. After he died, which was on a Wednesday, I wasn't sure what to do. In the end I left the hospital and went and sat on the steps of the nearby tube station, which, though busy, didn't seem as crowded as the waiting areas. It was quiet, too. Out of the warm wind and noise I felt more able to think. I sat a few minutes, smiling up at the people who picked their way down past me. I thought that sitting there like that might help me acclimatise to the experience, and all the other experiences I would now have to become used to. Then I walked down the road and took the 10.40 from St Pancras home.

On its way to Dover, the high-speed line passes smoothly across the grain of shallow wooded valleys south of the Medway. What you see on that route is a toy-town landscape, new cuttings, slopes at precise angles, grass with a look of astroturf, stiff model trees in a fringe. Occasionally the view opens up to reveal a motorway running alongside; or the land drops away startlingly to the left or right and a narrow ride swings away at the speed of the train through the softwood plantations. But you never seem to see a house. Everything is new but already lost.

After half an hour the train stopped for a few minutes. It lurched suddenly, started up again; then stopped for a longer period. Everyone expected an announcement, but none came. Out of the window could be seen a town, a lot of blackened churches close together; and at its edge, vague with heat haze, a stretch of suburb. I thought there must be a breakdown somewhere, along the line, or in the train.

People were leaning forward in their seats to look out of the windows. I heard someone say:

'Over there, behind the screen of trees.'

'Oh God, are they still standing?' a second voice said. 'Even now.'

'Wonderful.' Laughter.

Eventually the train began to move. The suburbs drew close and pulled in around the line. They were as tidy as the new cuttings, but at least they were houses. Among them I caught sight of a steep pile of sand – or perhaps less a pile than a bank: a bank of sand baked and eroded concave until it resembled a wave glimpsed at a distance at the end of a toy-town street, the foam on its top represented by a scruff of vegetation faded to dusty green. It was a curious, threatening feature for a contemporary housing estate. A few minutes later, very slowly, the train pulled into a station. The first thing I heard there was a recorded voice advising passengers to stand back from the edge of the platform. 'Trains passing through this station can cause turbulence.' The name on the station signboard was Doe Lea, and later I would come to believe this was the name of the place itself.

Hospital corridors always seem to be patrolled by middle-aged men with flimsy plastic carrier bags. As people, they're well turned out but lonely-looking; perhaps a little irritable. Shaven-headed. A Ben Sherman style short-sleeved shirt, worn loose with cargo shorts. That generation. If they don't take care of their appearance, their selves, they seem to be saying, who will? Who'll remain true to the assumptions of their youth?

'But you don't have to constantly *declare*,' my father would say of them.

By then he was quite frail. If you asked him how he felt, he would consider, then conclude, 'Frightened, of course.' The last thing he asked me was, could I remember what the acronym DBX stood for. I had no idea, nor any idea why he thought I would know. Morphine had caused him to confuse me with someone else. I said I thought it sounded more like a protocol than a system or a thing, and that seemed to satisfy him, because he made a slight movement of the head and closed his eyes. I went home expecting to see him again, but as I've said, he was dead the Wednesday morning.

The passengers weren't sure what to do. Some opened their laptops and resumed work; some continued talking on their phones. We would all be at a loose end until a relief train arrived. Two or three of us got down from the carriage and walked about on the platform reading the advisories – 'Please take care around the station, as some surfaces may have become slippery' – while we waited for something to happen.

I was the only one who went out into Doe Lea, where the streets seemed pleasantly deserted. Afternoon had come early. The air was hot and silent. The shops were closed and peaceful. You were soon through the centre and out at the other side, surveying the turn of a river, a field with a horse in it or a roundabout and a big box store beyond which you glimpsed an empty cattle yard with metal dividers; then railway lines curving away towards the coast.

After that the only thing left to look at was the little suburb, which was, if anything, quieter than the town. It had absorbed more of the morning's warmth. The new houses, laid out in cloverleaf curves and clusters, were small enough that, for a moment, you couldn't quite trust your sense of scale. It's easy – and tempting – to dismiss a sensation like that. With little else to do, I got the idea of looking for the sandy bank I had noticed from the train. Everything was easy to see in toytown but harder to reach. You would get an angle on it, but then something intervened and you were unsighted again. When I found what I was looking for, it proved taller than I expected, south facing, and made of sandstone, not sand. Its base was hidden beneath nettle and ragwort, brambles through which I had to force my way. Heat radiated from the stone.

Twenty or thirty feet up, towards the top of the curve, I could see a thick tangle of rose briars and dozens of shallow niches containing pots and jars, which I thought must be earthenware beehives, rather crudely made, with the bees flying in and out. They were painted, although the colours had faded to chalky pastels; beneath them, worn into the cliff, stretched a line of sloping, smoothly-eroded footholds, set at awkward angles and irregular intervals. These I began to ascend without thinking, surrounded by a calm, musty smell of nettles, late elder and dog rose – then something I couldn't name – until I was about halfway up. Anxiety overcame me at that point, although I can't explain why. I saw the hives above and heard the comfortable sound of the bees. I could see that I wasn't high up. But the steps were dusty and sloping, and suddenly I slithered back to the ground and stood among the nettles feeling disappointed in myself, as if I had let someone down; and after that turned away.

The town streets were as quiet and empty as streets from sixty years before, when everyone was in work during the day. You might see a figure emerge from a garden door and make off along the pavement between baking brick walls. You might see a dog in the distance, or hear a metal gate clanging shut, down where the hot wind blew across the cattle market; but that was the end of it. I wandered about between rows of terraced townhouses with red brick facades and shiny front doors. I felt as if I wanted to go into one of those high, comfortable-looking places, though I couldn't make up my mind which one. Later, as I stood in the street looking upwards, a couple came out of one of them to ask me in.

'We wondered,' the woman said, 'if you needed help.'

Early on, the hospital kept my father in a bed by a window on the third floor, out of which he could see, past the tops of the plane trees, the back of a different hospital. At that time he was still generally cheerful, could dress himself and walk; we would take the lift down to the ground floor and drink tea in the waiting area.

There he crumbled his favourite cake on to a plate but never ate much of it. He was already suffering the attacks that would characterise the later stages of the illness, during which lights seemed to dance on the surface of everything. They were blue, lilac, pink and green, he said. They danced on the coffee in his cup and meant as much to him as if someone had spoken. During these episodes everything else would remove itself. Voices receded, the sound of activity in the cafeteria drew away, as if the world was already out of earshot. He would feel as if everything was operating like that, not just sound. Even the information the conversations were carrying would cool down and contract and move into the middle distance, taking up some distant position in terms of its import to him. It wasn't that my father felt remote from things, he said: it was that things felt remote from him. As if to make up for this, every colour, every sound had what he described as 'a halo' of extra meaning.

Later, under a care regime that featured increasing doses of diamorphine, he stayed on the third floor and at the same time drifted slowly away. 'Funny, isn't it?' he would say, in the voice of a teenager. 'I've walked over this bridge a million times and I don't remember those lamps.' Then: 'Is there someone else here? Is someone with us?' He was fully aware of them, he said, but he couldn't see who they were.

My father loved a wet afternoon in summer; he loved to hear rain. One of the things he said most often after the condition took hold was, 'I keep thinking it's going to rain, can you look out of the window for me and see?'

'We wondered if you needed help,' the woman said.

They stood smiling at the top of the townhouse steps, quite thin and tall – in their sixties, I thought, but still calmly attractive – dressed very simply – and I went up into their house, which didn't have as many rooms as you might expect for a place that size. It was tall and deep, but it was thin – a slice through a terrace, among other tall, thin elegant slices. 'Let's have tea inside,' the woman said. 'It's so much cooler in here.'

'Let's have it in cups!' the man said, as if this was a new idea. 'Give me your coat and I'll put it on the back of this chair.'

So I gave him my coat and had a cup of tea, and they asked me how I had got to Doe Lea. They smiled when I told them about the broken train and the way I had wandered around the town; but when I described the little cliff with its wavelike architecture and its colonies of bees, they looked at one another puzzledly.

'Bees?' the man said, and shook his head. The woman shook her head too and said:

'We've never heard of anything like that.'

Then they showed me over their house – although I didn't get much more than a look into the rooms, because their habit was to stand in the doorways and draw my attention to an interesting picture, a favourite item of furniture. My main impression was of well-proportioned flights of stairs lighted by tall windows from which you could see down into a garden. They were proud of the garden, much of which was taken up by a pond and an area full of brambles and rose suckers they called 'the wilderness section'. Between the wilderness section and the back of the house lay a lawn the size of a pocket-handkerchief, rather rubbed down, as if dogs were often over it.

When we had looked round the house, and they had offered me another cup of tea, which I declined, and the woman had said, 'If you're sure,' they asked if I would do them a favour. They were going out – but they wouldn't be gone for long and they wondered would I wait in for the old man who mowed their lawn? 'He isn't really a gardener, although that's what he prefers to be called.' It was charity to give him work, she said. And then, a moment later: 'But you will do that, won't you? If it isn't much to ask? When the old man comes, you will let him in? He's very independent of mind and wants to mow the lawn this afternoon.' It wasn't convenient for him to mow any other day. 'If you will, we'll get ready now. We need to bathe and change and get ready to leave.'

Of course I would, I said. After all they had been kind enough to invite me in. I thought I owed them that. Before they left I heard them arguing in another room. 'Well, I've never heard anyone mention anything about bees,' the woman said, quite sharply. When they came out, their clothes didn't look any different.

After they had gone, I wasn't sure what to do, so I wandered about the house, in and out of the rooms I hadn't been invited into before. Out of a top floor window I could see that a man in the street below had lost control of his child. I heard his footsteps thumping along the pavement and his voice bellowing – really bellowing – until it echoed through the baking, silent streets: 'Zoe! Zoe!' Zoe was a long way ahead by then. 'They're not going that way,' he shouted after her. 'They're going this way, Zoe!' The street still seemed completely empty, except for the delighted toddler, her father's voice, and the panic it sent ringing back off the pavement, up to the window where I stood. Not long after that, the gardener arrived.

My father would often wake with the words, 'The one thing I remember –' While he slept, shifting neurological states had shaken loose glimpses of his past, which turned out to be less memories in themselves than scenery, the backdrop to recollected anxieties of forty years ago.

Some of his earliest memories included:

Black sticks of reeds where a towpath had collapsed into the canal. The movement of people through streetlight, projected faintly on to the ceilings and upper walls of a bedroom; the bang and squeal of old-fashioned trains coupling and decoupling in the night; the dry cold winds of the early part of the year, on building sites, on the corners of the streets down by the railway, under bridges, across pond-ice, over the vast empty expanse of the cattle market with its moveable metal dividers. Like any child he had wanted security, in a place convinced of its own feelings. Instead, his parents, young, tentative, full of post-war disquiets, were moved from rental to rental on half-constructed company estates with confusingly similar street names. They lacked agency; when he was young, everything communicated itself to him – so he felt – through their unconscious acknowledgement of that. He remembered a dead cat in a gutter in melting snow. A new kettle. 'The original one we had never worked properly, especially on cold mornings. It sparked and buzzed and blew the fuses. It came with the house.'

By the end he was attributing the whole of his illness to the uncertainties he had inherited then: his mother's fear that 'there was no government in the country'; his father's obsession with the electrical wiring. He was determined to remember what he could, and if not come to terms with it, then offer it to me like a half-finished crossword in case I could help. But how do you begin to retrieve a landscape you clearly spent so much of your life trying to forget?

'Not by using satellite maps,' he would warn me with a laugh and a cough. Because at that distance all they could record was its disappearance. And then: 'The earth in those back gardens was always cloddy and dry, with a strong smell of chamomile and quicklime.'

The couple had been quick to assure me that their gardener wouldn't need supervision. I let him in and he was soon at work. He started a petrol driven lawnmower, bending over it stiffly and doing something that produced large volumes of white smoke, which drifted across the surrounding gardens and between the houses themselves in a thick, obscuring cloud. Then he walked around the lawn, stared into the wild section of the garden as if he had seen something among the brambles, and entered the kitchen via the back door.

For ten minutes the lawnmower sat unattended. Its engine ran up and down the power curve in a slow, queasy cycle, continuing to emit white smoke and making the noise you hear when a helicopter hovers close above. Then the old man emerged from the kitchen and, holding out at arm's length in front of him a square of old towel, began to dodge in and out of the smoke. He dabbed at the mower. Nothing changed. The engine continued to run up and down its power curve. The amount of smoke generated, its chemical edge in the nose and on the palate, had a real power to astonish. The old man dodged into it and out again.

A decade before, this might have resembled in the eye of a viewer – a viewer like me, pressed up against the glass, distanced by the height and angle of an upstairs window--a kind of dance: bend down, dart in and out, dart in and out, round and round, round again, dab from a distance, dab from close up. But now the gardener was too stiff and too slow and too bow-legged for it to seem like that. After a further five minutes, he sneezed and his nose and eyes began to run copiously. He used the towel to wipe strings of mucus from his cheeks and chin. He bent over and vomited suddenly. Then he began to mow the lawn with the smoking lawnmower, the blades of which churned up what little grass remained, wrenching it out of the ground in tufts, leaving a tormented, scraped-looking surface.

Once the job was finished, he switched off the mower and left it where it stood, at an angle beneath the rotary clothes dryer. The smoke began to thin and drift away. The old man stopped shaking. He blew his nose. He went back into the house, through the house, down the hall, out of the front door and along the street outside, in a single fluid, swooping movement as if his trajectory of intention had begun at the back door with utter confidence and energy and would end only at the pub in which he spent most of his day, and where he and his friends would soon be chuckling about some prank of his when he was young.

The afternoon wore on. Down in the town, the shops were waking up; a breeze came up from the direction of the suburb, moving at random from street to street, bringing smells of honey and chamomile. I could hear the fast trains coming and going along the high-speed line through Doe Lea station.

I waited as long as I could, but in the end I was forced to admit that the gardener wasn't going to return. Obviously I had no idea where his employers might be. He had pocketed his money, which they had left in an envelope on the kitchen table. I put on my coat to go; took it off again.

While I stood by the window wondering what to do, three men walked past in silhouette against the brightly lit buildings across the road – one of them pointing at something in the sky and the others following his gaze. This provoked the memory of a baking summer evening in my childhood, shadows slowly filling the spaces between the houses, the smell of hot brick, dull voices; my father calling me inside. After they had gone I looked up. A single cloud was drifting slowly past the window high up, north to south in the otherwise empty blue. That was when I knew things would change forever but I didn't know if it would be for everybody or only for me.

The relief train had already left. I sat in the buffet to wait for the next one. I drank a cup of coffee, examining its surface for lights and listening to the women at the table next to mine.

'Every time I glimpse it out of the corner of my eye,' one of them said, 'I mistake it for a cat I used to have. It's too big to be a cat, but I never owned a dog so I don't see it as one;' and the other replied, 'There's no government in the country at the moment.' Outside, a man had parked a low-loader in such a way as to block the little roundabout outside the station and left it there with its engine idling. Every so often he returned and moved it ten or twelve yards back or forward, always keeping it on the curve of the roundabout, after which he would sit in it for five minutes with his thick hands on the steering wheel, looking straight ahead.

Later, as the train was pulling slowly away from Doe Lea, I found in my coat pocket a note from the couple in the townhouse.

'Dear Alan,' it began.

'Dear Alan, we were delighted by your visit. We're sorry to have to leave, but this is an important afternoon for us.' They didn't say why, but after more of the same kind of apologies, went on to ask: 'We wondered if you might like to take over the job of mowing the lawn? We're always looking for someone younger.'

I read this suggestion twice, then a third time. I turned the paper over and looked at the other side. Then I folded the letter carefully along its original creases and returned it to my pocket. When I looked up again, I could see the town, with its sleepy little red cliff, falling away behind; and I wondered what might have happened to me if I had kept my courage and climbed all the way up to the beehives. Soon the train was racing to meet the sea. Everything – fields, hills, buildings, hedges, trees, warehouses and distribution centres – was palely-lit by that strange coastal light you often see in paintings but so rarely in the world. Gulls were blown across the sky.

2019

Cicisbeo

SUMMER WAS HALF OVER before it had even begun. With a sense that my life was in the same state, I phoned Lizzie Shaw. She hadn't changed.

They lived in East Dulwich now, she told me, her and Tim, in a little house 'practically given' them by a friend. She had worked for a while as a buyer for John Lewis. 'You'd have been proud of me,' she said. 'I was properly industrious.' She had bought a Mercedes. Enjoyed the money. Missed her kids. 'I wasn't getting home 'til eight. I had a seventeen year old Polish girl looking after my family, I mean can you believe it?' Jobs pall, she said, as soon as you start thinking like that. She said she couldn't wait to see me. 'People count more as you get older.' She was thirty seven now. Then she said: 'I'm pregnant again,' and burst into tears.

That house was always full of sex.

'You will come and see us?' Lizzie said.

'I'm not sure,' I said. 'Would that be a good idea?'

'Please,' she said.

I thought about it. I drove across London, intending to go

there, but lost motivation somehow and fetched up in Brixton or Blackheath instead. Lizzie kept phoning. Would I go and see them again, or not?

'Why don't we meet where we used to?' I suggested. 'Just the two of us?'

'It can't be like that again,' she warned me.

'I know,' I said.

I wanted to put the phone down and not speak to her for another three years.

'All right then,' she said. 'When?'

We had lunch at Angels & Gypsies on Camberwell Church Street. She was late, a little nervous. 'I can't get over you,' I said. The pregnancy threw her off-balance a little, but it suited her. 'You look so well.'

We talked about her boys for a bit. She had got them into a good school. They were so grown up, she said. So emotionally intelligent. 'I don't know what I'd do without them, especially Ben.' Of the buyer's job she would only say: 'I felt it was right at the time. But now I feel it's right to be pregnant again.'

'And how is Tim?'

'Just the same,' she said 'You know Tim.'

I smiled. 'I do,' I said.

'He's converting the loft.'

'Is he now?' I said.

'It's such a little house,' she said off-handedly. 'He thought it would be a good idea. He thought it could be a studio.' She ate some olives and then some bread. She sat back. 'This is nice,' she said vaguely. 'I always loved this place.'

I knew that tone of voice.

'What's the matter?' I said.

'Oh, you know.' She looked away suddenly. 'It's all he ever does now, really. The loft.'

I reached across the table and tried to take her hand.

'No,' she said, 'I don't want that.'

She told me about Tim. Something happened to him, she

said, the day he was forty. He went up into the loft. He liked it there, the very first time he stuck his head and shoulders up through the trapdoor. He called down from the top of the ladder, something like, 'Hey!' or, 'Wow!' and that was it. Something clicked for him. Soon he was up there every available day, working, but not at his job. He had started out to store things up there. Then he was going to convert it. Then he was moving himself into it, bit by bit. He even had his own TV up there.

'He was forty,' she said. Looking back, you could see that's when it began. 'His life was so good,' she said. 'But something went wrong with his view of it.'

After a pause she said, 'He misses you.'

I couldn't take that seriously.

'I bet he does,' I said.

'We both miss you.'

'I've missed *you*,' I said.

'I know. I know,' she said. 'So you will come over? To supper?'

I began to say, 'I'm not sure that's such a good idea,' but she was already adding:

'Perhaps you can even talk some sense into him.'

'I'm not the best person to do that.'

'At least come to supper,' she said. She put her hand over mine. 'It's so good to see you again,' she said.

I shouldn't have gone, but in the end I couldn't see any reason not to. I was bored. I thought she might light my life up again.

Their street was like all the others packed between the railway and the hospital. Tubs of geraniums outside narrow-fronted terraces. Roadsters parked two wheels up on the pavement. The house was nice but far too small for them. By the time you had a family you were supposed to have moved down the road to the Village, or out of London altogether. East Dulwich — or Dull Eastwich, as Tim called it — was for younger people. They would have done better, he said, in Herne Hill: but you didn't get the resale value.

He hadn't changed much since I last saw him. You found people like Tim all over London. They had rowed a little at school. At the weekend they wore chinos and a good quality sailing fleece. Boat shoes with no socks. They all had the same tall, polite good looks. They never seemed to age: instead, their self-deprecation matured into puzzlement. They began to look tired. Tim liked to cook. He had his treasured cast iron saucepans from the 80s, his five-hob Lacanche range. I watched him, and drank a beer, and asked him how things were.

'Oh, you know,' he said vaguely. 'Could you pass me that? No, the little one.'

Once we sat down to eat it became harder to sustain a conversation. 'I wish I'd learned to cook,' I said, as if I'd lived the kind of life which makes a thing like that impossible. He didn't know what to say to that. Who would? This left things to Lizzie, who grew impatient. 'It's a chicken,' she explained to me. 'A child could cook it.' He was quick to agree. 'You could soon learn, you could soon learn.' He slotted the plates into the dishwasher while she banged pudding down on the table.

'Well that was good,' I said when we'd eaten it.

'I'm glad,' Lizzie said. 'The kitchen cost him twenty thousand pounds.' When he only smiled at this, she added: 'No one puts a twenty thousand pound kitchen in a house in East Dulwich. In the Village, yes. In East Dulwich, no.' Tim shrugged a little. He looked away. Twenty thousand pounds was an exaggeration, the shrug said. It said that if you were going to cook you should have the right things.

While Lizzie made coffee in the kitchen, he gave me the tour. 'We'd gone as far as we could without opening the loft,' he said. You could see they had. 'It was a bit of a push to find somewhere for the boys.' Tim, you sensed, had turned his talents as easily to family life as to sport: but now he wasn't quite sure how he came to have a family in the first place. I poked my head into the little room he used as a study.

'No computer?' I said.

He'd moved it up there already, he said. There had never been enough room down here. 'Lizzie told me you were up to your neck in it,' I said. The study was a mess. He laughed and looked rather tiredly at the heaps of stuff. 'Eventually all this will go up there.' I asked him if I could see the loft. 'It's a bit dusty at the moment,' he said. 'Probably better to wait.' I didn't press him, even though I knew Lizzie would have wanted me to; and I left not long later. Tim had his problems, I had mine. One of mine was that I didn't really care one way or another about him. It's hard to hide that. He knew it as well as I did, and she was the only one pretending not to know. I kept in touch. I went over there once or twice, for a meal, then let it lapse again. I was working anyway.

Three months later the phone rang.

I answered it. I said, 'Hello?'

'Hi. It's Lizzie.'

I caught my breath.

'Hi,' I said, 'I –'

'There's someone on the other line, hang on,' she said. Then, 'Hi. How are you, I'm sorry about that.'

'No, it's OK.'

After a pause she said: 'It's a girl.'

'I can't believe it,' I said.

'I know,' she said. 'A girl!'

I sent flowers. I sent a card. I telephoned my friends as if I was the father. In two days Lizzie was on the phone again.

'The baby's home,' she said, 'but he won't see it.'

'That's ridiculous.'

'We're both back from the hospital, but he won't see either of us.'

'He won't see his own baby?'

He wouldn't see his own baby. He sent notes down from the loft.

'I don't know where to turn,' Lizzie said.

'Come on,' I tried to encourage her, 'he was a bit like this with the boys.'

'Well now he's got a girl and he won't come down out of the loft to even look at her. What am I going to do?'

So I found myself in East Dulwich again, hoping to get a word alone with her. The house was full of wellwishers. Her women friends had long backs and sexy voices. The men were packed with the aimless brutal confidence of people barely thirty years old earning large sums of money at banking. Even their children were successful at something. I felt old and immature at the same time. Tim was nowhere to be seen, but no one mentioned that. He was in the loft of course, but no one mentioned that either. They had called the baby Emma. I held her while Lizzie had a proper drink. I couldn't believe her fingernails.

'Look,' I told anyone who would listen, 'they come with a manicure!'

The boys stared at me as if I was simple, and Emma started crying. I took her outside. I brought her back in. It was no good. She looked up at me angrily and flexed her spine. Her face went bright red.

'Give her to me,' said Lizzie. 'She wants something you haven't got.'

This drew laughs all round.

I was there a lot the first few weeks. I helped with this and that. I learned to change a nappy. Lizzie sat up in bed, looking exhausted but pleased. 'They've taken it well,' she said of the boys. She was proud of them. After a few days, though, they grew thoughtful, painted their faces, spent money on slime. They ran in and out of the small garden whooping and shouting: but magical thinking would not save them. Change was inevitable. The tribe was doomed.

Tim watched it all from a distance. His idea, you could see, was to ride it out. Six months after his daughter arrived, the loft was his home. He cooked up there, he slept up there. 'He's living on baked beans,' Lizzie said. She looked down at the baby. 'Essentially,' she said in a tragic voice, 'he's left us.' No one had any idea what he was doing. He hauled stuff up in a plastic dustbin. Whatever it was began coming down again within a few hours. There was a lot of bumping and banging which sometimes went on all night. She asked me, 'What's he doing up there, with all those power tools?'

I said it could be anything.

'Is this something that happens to men?' she said viciously, as if I was doing it too. Shortly afterwards he installed a good-quality pull-down ladder, but he rarely used it himself and the boys were forbidden to go near it. He was a man living away from his family.

'He might as well have gone to Blackpool,' Lizzie said. 'You've got to talk to him.'

I tried. If nothing else, I thought, it would give me a glimpse of the loft. I went up the ladder. I stuck my head through the trap door. I got a confused idea of a much smaller space than I had expected, most of it curtained off by heavy tarpaulins which sagged from the roofbeams. He had put a floor in. Piles of eurothane insulation lay about under an unshaded low-wattage bulb, everything thick with damp-looking dust. It all seemed thoroughly miserable. Tim sat at an old school desk, his legs sticking out awkwardly at the sides, writing something on a sheet of ruled A4. The computer components stacked on the floor beside him were still done up in bubble-wrap. He hadn't even bothered to unpack them.

'Hi Tim,' I said. 'When do you think you might be finished?'

He got up quickly.

'Probably better if we talk downstairs,' he said.

He looked embarrassed. You don't want your wife's best friend to see you living in your attic. You don't want him to think about what that means. I'd hoped I might shock him into talking about things. But in the end we just stood there awkwardly on the landing looking past one another, and all he would say was:

'You have to get away somehow. You have to get away from it all.'

'I don't think Lizzie sees it that way,' I said. 'You know?'

This sounded futile, even to me.

After a moment I added: 'I think she'd like to see more of you. The kids would too.'

He studied the floor and shook his head.

But Lizzie did want to see more of him. She wanted to see more of someone, anyway. She called me.

'Come and meet me for a drink,' she said. 'I'm in need of, oh, something.' She laughed. 'I don't know what I'm in need of.' She left a pause and then said: 'We could meet somewhere in town.' I didn't ask who would look after the baby.

All afternoon she seemed nervous. She kept taking her phone out of her bag, studying it with a faintly irritable expression, then putting it back again. She swirled her drink around her glass. She looked up at me once or twice, began to say something, decided not to. She was wearing skinny, low-cut velvet jeans. When she saw me looking at them she said, 'Do you think they're too young for me?' They were a champagne colour, and they fastened at the back with a lace, like a shoe. She touched my arm.

'It's odd, isn't it,' she said, 'how things happen? I always loved this suit of yours. Your only suit.'

She said, 'I've never seen your house, have I?'

She drove us over to Walthamstow in the Mercedes. They always called it that, her and Tim: the Mercedes. As if they had other cars, two or three of them. When I showed her into the house she said, 'It's bigger than I thought it would be.' She stared into the kitchen for a moment, then out into the garden. We went upstairs. She looked at the bicycle in the bedroom and said, 'It's so like you, all this. Really it is.' She got her phone out again. She put it next to her ear and shook it. When nothing happened her expression hardened. Then she laughed. 'It's just what I expected, all of it.'

I don't know what I expected. I'd been waiting for her for three years; longer. After about ten minutes I said, 'I love your neck. The nape of it, here.' Then I said: 'I can't believe this is happening.' She twisted away immediately and we lay like that for a minute or two, awkward and embarrassed. My hand was still on her hip.

'This is stupid,' she said.

'Why?'

'Because it just isn't grown up.'

I got off the bed angrily. When I looked back she had covered herself up with the sheet.

'What *do* you want then?' I said.

She shivered.

'Can't you get it any warmer in here?'

'No.'

'I just want him the way he was. I'll have to leave him, if not. I don't even know what's going on in my own loft,' she told me, with a false laugh. 'Can't you at least try and find that out from him?'

I shrugged. 'Why should I do that?'

'Don't sulk,' she warned.

The second time I went up into the loft, I heard a regular metallic scraping noise, more distant than you'd expect in a space that size. The light was off and something was happening behind the tarpaulins. 'Tim?' I said. But I said it cautiously, to myself, as if I didn't want him to hear. I was curious. As much as anything else, I wanted to poke around. The tarpaulins were new, but they looked old. They sagged under their own weight, stiff to the touch, with fixed folds as if the dust had already worked its way into them. Perhaps it had. Around their edges I glimpsed the eerie white flicker of a butane lamp, or perhaps one of those portable fluorescent tubes.

I examined the desk, the abandoned computer, the piles of other stuff. Why would you keep a garden spade in a loft?

'Tim?'

This time the noises stopped immediately. For a moment we were silent, each listening for the other. Then a draught seemed to go through the loft, along with a smell which reminded me of old-fashioned house gas. I saw the tarpaulins billow, hang, resettle; and he called from just behind them, 'Hang on. I'll be with you in a second.' I backed away until I bumped into the desk, then descended the ladder. He followed me down and stood there rubbing his hands on an old towel as if he didn't know what to do next. He was covered in white dust. His hands were scraped and banged, the knuckles enlarged as if he'd been doing manual work, outside work. His fingernails were broken.

'I wasn't expecting you,' he said. 'Lizzie shouldn't really have encouraged you to come up.'

I couldn't let him get away with that.

'Tim,' I said, 'for God's sake. What are you doing?'

'I'm converting the loft,' he explained patiently. 'I'm converting the loft to give us more room.' He didn't want to be understood. He was exhausted, and that made me feel exhausted too. In the end I said:

'You hire people to do the work. You don't do that yourself.'

He shook his head.

'It's my loft,' he said, with a certainty I admired.

While we were talking Lizzie came up the stairs carrying the baby. 'Do either of you want coffee?' she asked. Then she said to Tim: 'I heard all that. What rubbish you talk.' She began to cry. 'You know it's rubbish.' Tim pulled himself to his feet and looked as if he might try to comfort her. She backed away. 'No,' she said. 'It's just an excuse. It's just another excuse.'

'Lizzie's frantic, Tim,' I told him. 'You've hardly said hello to your own daughter.'

'Don't talk about me as if I'm not here!' she said. She stood in front of me and wouldn't let me turn away. 'Can you see me?' she demanded.

'Lizzie —'

'Well I'm real,' she said. 'You always pretend I'm not.' Her voice went from contempt to puzzlement. 'You're as bad as he is.' The baby wailed and waved its arms. 'Now look what you've done, both of you.'

'You asked me to come here,' I reminded her.

I left them to it and went downstairs.

'That's right,' she called after me. 'Walk away. Walk away from everything, like you always do.'

After I left, I drove about in the dark, through Balham and Brixton, jumping traffic lights to the accompaniment of a Sonny Rollins CD. By the time I got home it was three o'clock in the morning, and she had left messages with my answering service. They were a mixed bunch. One said: 'I'm sorry. I'm really sorry.' Another said: 'Is it any wonder no one will have you? It's just so easy for you to leave people behind, isn't it? Just so *fucking* easy.' A third said, 'Please don't do this. Please answer, oh please, please.' I could hear the baby crying in the background. 'Please answer.' But I didn't; and I didn't hear from her again for two or three months.

June.

The evening air was hammered like gold on to the rubbish in my front garden. I had been thinking about her all day.

Early summer had always been a dangerous time for us. Tim would be at work, we would go to the park. I would put my arm round her while we sat on a bench and watched the boys running about in the distance and she told me, at length but without ever saying it outright or irreversibly, why nothing could happen between us. 'I'm making such a fool of myself!' she would decide at last; then appeal, 'But you do see some of what I mean, don't you?'

'Lizzie, I haven't got the slightest idea what you're talking about.'

I knew she would call, because in early summer, desperate with the smell of her, I had always been ready to give her the reassurance she needed.

'Hello?' I said.

'Hi,' she said. 'It's me.'

'Hang on,' I said. 'There's someone on the other line.'

'Don't do this,' she begged.

'Can I ring you back?'

She said: 'You've got to come. It's Tim.'

There was a confused scraping noise as if she had dropped the phone, and then all I could hear was her breathing, and a shout in the distance which might have been one of the boys.

'Something awful's happening,' she said. 'In the loft.'

She dropped the phone again.

By the time I got to Dulwich it was dark. The front door of their house was open on the empty street. Lizzie stood in the hall at the bottom of the stairs with the baby held along the crook of one arm. She was wearing a white bathrobe and she had her phone up to her ear. The hall seemed too hot, even for a night like that. It seemed packed with heat. Why would they have the heating on in June?

'He's up there now,' she said.

I wondered if I should take the baby off her.

'Lizzie? What's wrong? What's the matter?'

'I thought I could get him to answer his phone. Get him to answer his bloody fucking phone for once,' she said.

'I'll fetch him down.'

She stared at me. 'That's not it,' she said.

'I'll just go up.'

There was fine white dust all over the stairs. I could hear the boys in their room, quarrelling over the PlayStation. The house seemed to get hotter from floor to floor, a dry heat which caught at your throat. 'Tim?' I called. Then louder: 'Tim!' No answer. I had caught Lizzie's mood. I felt nervous, jumpy, angry with both of them. Why did I always have to be involved? Why couldn't they put on their futile theatre without me? 'Tim?' Dust had silted down all over the upper landing. I stood at the foot of the pull-down ladder and listened. I went up far enough to poke my head into the loft. The air was full of a grey light which, dim and distributed at the same time, seemed to come from everywhere at once. I could hear a distant, measured chunking noise. It sounded like someone using an old-fashioned pickaxe to break concrete.

'Tim!' I called.

Almost immediately there was a loud crash. The house lurched, a powerful draught parted the tarpaulins. That was enough for me. As I went down the ladder I heard him tottering about up there, coughing in the dust. He seemed to be trying to drag some item of equipment across the floor. 'Tim! For God's sake!' I called up from the landing. His face appeared briefly, framed by the trap.

'The whole lot's coming down,' he said. 'Tell her to get the kids out. See if you can persuade her to care about someone else for once.'

Lizzie, halfway up the stairs, heard this.

'You sod,' she said. 'I'd do anything for those children.'

Everything seemed to lurch again. I got her by the arm and pulled her down the stairs and into the street. The boys, sensing the future like dogs before an earthquake, had already saved themselves. They couldn't believe their luck. Their house was falling down. The hall was full of plaster. Cracks had opened up in the exterior walls. From above came the shrieking sounds of joists giving way under huge loads. It was *so cool*. They stood in the quiet street in the hot night air, staring up at the line of the roof where it had sagged into the void of the loft. Their father came running out, then stopped and turned as if he had forgotten something.

His house was done for. Window frames popped. The facade deformed and began to slip. Just before the roof fell in and it became obvious that the whole thing would come down on us if we didn't move, I saw the tunnel he had been digging out of the loft. It hung in the air, transparent but luminous, perhaps three feet in diameter. Travelling north towards the river, it rose steeply until, at perhaps a thousand feet, it linked up with a complex of similar tunnels all across London. Hundreds of them, thousands, more than you could ever count, they rose up from the houses. A 787 Dreamliner was making its way down between them towards Heathrow, engines grinding, landing lights ablaze. When it had gone, the tunnels hung there for a moment like a great shining computer-generated diagram in the night sky, then began to fade.

'See?' Tim said. 'What would you have done?'

'We'll come back,' I promised him. 'We'll come back and find another way in –'

Lizzie didn't seem to hear this. 'Twenty thousand pounds on a kitchen,' she said. She laughed.

Later, she sat on the kerb a little way down the street, with the boys on either side of her and the baby in her lap, thoughtfully watching the fire engines and drinking tea. Someone had given her a man's woollen shirt to wear, wrapped a foil blanket loosely round her shoulders. The street was full of hoses and cables, generators, powerful lights. Firemen were picking over the rubble, and a television crew had arrived.

2003

The Crisis

YOU SIT OVER A one-bar electric fire in a rented room. As soon as you feel recovered from the commute you'll boil some potatoes on the gas ring, then, three minutes before they're done, drop an egg into the same water. You can hear the family downstairs laughing at something, some dressed-up cats or something, on the internet. After people have cooked, they can often get use out of their gadgets – join a world-building game, preorder the gadget they want next – although the load soon precipitates a brownout. During the day you work in a fourteenth floor office in the stub of the Shard. Publicity for a fuel corporate. It's nice. All very heads-down but worth it to have the security. A few years ago you got involved with an East Midlands junkie who claimed to have a telepathic link to another world and to be able to control a 3D printer with his mind alone.

This was how he told it: he came down from the North and to begin with lived on the street. He was young for his age. He started at Euston where the train emptied him out, then moved into a doorway near a bus stop. It was all right for a while. Then he met a boy called Alan and they went up to the centre together. Alan wasn't that much older than Balker.

They were about the same height, but Alan knew more. He was a London boy, he had always lived there. He had bright red hair, an alcohol tan and a personalised way of walking. He could get a laugh out of anything. For a while Balker and Alan did well out of the Central London tourists. But Alan's lifestyle-choices moved him along quickly and he started to limp up and down Oxford Street at lunchtime saying, 'I'm in bits, me!' and showing people the big krokodil sore on his neck.

'Hey, look mate, I'm in bits!'

After Alan died, Balker stayed away from the other street people. They had a language all their own he never learned to speak, but he knew the same thing was happening to them as to him. He knew about the crisis, and the iGhetti. He knew the same thing was happening to everyone. There were new needs, there were new rules in. New rules had come in, and everyone in London was in the same position: if you couldn't look after yourself there was a new way to pay.

Sleeping on the street is hard. All the reasons for this are obvious. It's never quiet. The police move you about, the social services and NGOs won't leave you alone: everyone thinks the boroughs belong to them. You're hungry, you've got a cough, there's other stuff, it's an endless list. No one sleeps well in a doorway. You get fragments of sleep, you get the little enticing flakes of it that fall off the big warm central mass. Wake up, and everything seems to have fallen sideways. You guess it's four in the morning in November, somewhere along Bloomsbury Street; but you could be wrong. Are you awake? Are you asleep? Rain swirls in the doorway. You've got a bit of fever and you can't quite remember who you are. It's your own fault of course. You wake up and he's there in front of you, with his nice overcoat, or sometimes a nice leather jacket, to protect him from the weather. You never really hear his name, though he tells you more than once. He seems to know yours from the beginning. 'Your health's going,' he says. 'You want to start now, before it goes too far.'

So he leaned into Balker's doorway – maybe it was the night, maybe it wasn't – and took Balker's chin in his hand. He turned Balker's face one way then the other. He was gentle, he even looked a bit puzzled, as if he was wondering why anyone would choose to live that way, what bad choices they must have made to find themselves sleeping in a doorway behind the British Museum.

'You want to start now,' he repeated.

Later, when Balker told you all this, you weren't sure you believed any of it. It was difficult to believe anything then. The most difficult thing to believe was the crisis itself. No one was certain whether the arrival of the iGhetti was an invasion or a natural catastrophe.

They resembled stalks of fleshy, weak rhubarb, which appeared and evolved very quickly from nothing, like the tentacles which seem to bulge out of nowhere when you burn a piece of mercuric sulphocyanate. You would see them for a fraction of a second just at the city skyline behind the buildings, just under the cloudbase, evolving very fast like stopframe film of something organic growing, then running out of energy, then growing again. They seemed like neither a thing nor a picture of a thing: they seemed to be extruded from a space that wasn't quite in the world. The sirens would go off, all across the city from Borough to Camden. The artillery would fire and recoil, fire and recoil. The iGhetti would pulse and grow against the lighted clouds. Then they were gone again for another day.

Various simple beliefs surrounded the invasion. Some people associated the iGhetti with Dark Matter; some with the banking crisis of the late Noughties. Others believed that they 'came out of the internet'. (Indeed, this was the favoured theory of the internet itself: the medium still firmly – if a little desperately – casting itself as the message.) While none of these theories could be described as true, they did, perhaps, mirror the type and scale of the anxieties that led the iGhetti to us.

The truth was simpler. Originally they had leaked into our world from the astral plane. Most of them were found dead. At first they could manifest only as a kind of transparent jelly. This was spread on grass and the trunks of trees. In this form, for hundreds of years, they were known as 'astromyxin' or 'astral jelly'. Then, quite suddenly, at the turn of the 1980s, their efforts became both more determined and more successful. The new form appeared only in West London and only near water. Lakes and reservoirs were their preferred location, but they were also found on the banks of streams, and on one occasion at the edge of the carp pool in the Temperate House at Kew Gardens. Soon they had rolled down the River from Chiswick to Chelsea, and thence to the Square Mile, although no one could say by what means, or what that meant.

Balker started, anyway. For the preliminary tests they took him to a place in Aldgate. It was full of hospital beds. You'd get a meal afterwards, they said. They warned him that you could expect your head to swim a bit, but come on: somebody in Balker's condition was going to notice that? In the end it was easy and it was a bit of money in your hand. It was a way of being responsible for yourself. Balker passed well, they said. He showed real ability. That could be a beginning, they told him; or he could just leave it at that. But what Balker liked most was the clean bed, the warmth and the calm. It was worth it just to lie down and not think about what to do next. He looked around and fell asleep. When he woke up again, he said he wanted to go on with it.

'You want to go all the way?' they asked him.

'Yes,' Balker said. 'I want to go all the way.'

That was where it started for him, really. Aldgate, on the edge of the Square Mile, was where his whole life started, and where it finished, too, although he lived on afterwards.

All those streets – residential now, along with everything around Liverpool Street station – were in perfect condition despite the constant bombardment of the City from positions in Camden, Peckham and Borough Market. Restaurants remained open and ready to serve, in a wide arc from the Duck & Waffle round to St John. It was as if nothing had changed, as if the City fringe, like West London, still believed itself to be intact, functioning, the heart of what we used to call, before money lost its confidence, an 'economy'. Brokers were commuting into Liverpool Street every morning, where, puzzled by the disorder, they attempted to do handshake business with one another in the cafés and bars. Others, unable to place themselves, feeling that the Square Mile was still in front of them yet somehow no longer visible – like some location beyond the reach of SatNav – had chosen to become lodgers in the fringe, renting the Barbican one-bedroom of some old friend from St Paul's and on Friday evenings making the short but by now increasingly confusing train journey back to Sussex. They wouldn't give up the working week.

After he passed the preliminaries, Balker was placed with a family – Jack and Jane, erstwhile investment bankers who, though they now ran a business organising outdoor activity challenges for young adults, still hoped to return one day to the abandoned financial settlements between the river and the London Wall. Jack collected first editions of children's books from the 1950s. Jane did triathalon. Their Georgian terrace had a garden, Fired Earth on the walls, the remains of quite a nice old staircase. They thought a lot of Balker.

During the day he took the more advanced tests. The point of these wasn't clear, but they fell into two types.

The first type was held, like the preliminaries, in a dormitory furnished with hospital beds. It was a big room, Balker said: in the late afternoons, when the majority of the tests took place, the rows of beds would seem to stretch away forever into the shadows. They were firm, cool, always freshly made and clean. Balker was given pills to take, then connected up to a drip. The big idea, he told you later, was that the chemicals sent you somewhere: in reality or only in your head, he didn't know. The medium was viscous and dark. Sometimes he seemed to be in the past. Sometimes he seemed to be thrown forward into futures even more confused than the present. They called it travel. The same word could be used, by extension, as a noun for the breadth or quality of the experience. Sometimes he heard a calm, insistent voice repeating, 'Are you getting good travel?' If he agreed that he was, it told him to stay calm and look for astral jelly, or any other sign of the iGhetti; if he said no, they increased the dose. What he brought back from the journey, Balker had no idea. They debriefed him while he was still off his face and thinking was difficult. Meanwhile the chemicals made him increasingly ill. In the end the only images he remembered were meaningless in the context: a half-timbered village, thatched roofs, long rosy winter dawns and sunsets. Gorse, mud, sheep. 'It was the olden times,' he told you later, trying to describe this Victorian idyll.

*

Adolescence. West London. You always believed a hidden war was being fought, a war nobody would ever admit to. You lay awake at night, listening to bursts of corporate fireworks that seemed too aggressive to be anything other than a small arms exchange; while by day, ground-attack helicopters clattered suddenly and purposively along the curve of the Thames towards Heathrow. You held your breath in moments of prolonged suspense, imagining the smoke trails of rockets launched from the bed of a builder's pickup in Richmond or Kingston. These fantasy-engagements, asymmetric and furtive, a kind of secret, personalised Middle

East, left you as exhausted as masturbation. There was something narcissistic about them. A decade later, everyone was able to feel a similar confused excitement. With the coming of the iGhetti, everyone had a story to tell but no one could be sure what it was. Information was so hard to come by. Between anecdotal evidence and the spectacular misdirections of the news cycle lay gulfs of supposition, fear, and denial. People didn't know how to act. One minute they heard the guns, the next they were assured that nothing was happening. One day they were panicking and leaving the city in numbers, the next they were returning but rumour had convinced them to throw their tablet computers in the river. The thing they feared most was contagion. They locked their doors. They severed their broadband connections and tanked their cellars. They avoided a growing list of foods. They clustered round a smartphone every summer evening after dark, eavesdropping on the comings and goings of the local militias as they scoured the railway banks and canalsides for telltale astral jelly. Were the iGhetti here or not? It was a difficult time for everyone.

When he wasn't taking the tests Balker hung around in the coffee shops and cafés and, at night, ate with the family at a table in the garden. Jane and Jack talked about the art events they'd seen in galleries in Paris and Tokyo, while Balker entertained them by catching moths unharmed from around the table lights. They taught him to play chess. 'Now he can beat us easily,' Jane often said with a laugh, 'he wants to play all the time!' On Saturdays he learned to make breakfast for everyone, poached egg on rye with salmon, roast pepper and faux hollandaise. He loved that. It was the secure point of his week. He'd never known anything like it, just calm and middle-class comfort, life lived simply for being life. That was where the two of you met, at a dinner party of Jane and Jack's. He was standing in the garden with everyone else, staring out towards the shadowy zone beyond the Minories where something could be seen moving above the roofline and between the taller buildings. They had cornered one of the larger ones somewhere in the warren around Threadneedle Street and were pounding it with 155mm smart artillery. Airbursts lit it up in syncopated, carefully-judged sequences, but you couldn't tell any more than usual what it was. You watched Balker, and you could feel Jane watching you.

'Don't you ever wonder what's in there?' she said, and you said you didn't. You shivered. You didn't want to know, you said.

The pull of the Square Mile was still strong for people like Jane and Jack. Everyone knew someone who, unable to bear it any longer, had found their way in, to re-emerge weeks or even months later after wandering puzzledly about the empty towers, lost souls eyeing other lost souls in the deserted corridors and partner washrooms. With a good pair of binoculars you could see them, staring out of the Lloyds lifts – which still travelled in their stately way up and down the outside of the structure – in despair. In a way, the Lloyds building, designed to question the relationship between the inside and the outside, remained the great metaphor of the disaster. It was the centre of the zone in that sense, even though geographically it lay towards the western edge.

'And this is only the beginning,' Jack said. 'They've been here less than a decade.' He stared at the towers for a moment longer, then added, 'If 'here' means anything at all.'

'*I* wonder,' Balker said, emphasising the pronoun to get Jane's attention. '*I* want to know.'

His voice already seemed rueful.

Eventually, when he became too ill to continue with the first type of test, they moved him on to the second, which took place under different protocols. The test-site itself could only be reached by use of a modified GABAA agonist, a fungal preparation rubbed into the skin between the shoulder blades. It smelt, he said, a bit like Germolene.

After a few hallucinations of flying you arrived in what looked like the boxroom of a provincial house at night. Out of the window you could see the slope of a hill. Fireworks flickered intermittently across the darkness. The walls of the room were papered, in a faded primordial pattern of cabbage roses. Above the tiled fireplace a brown print of 'The Light of the World'; on the mantelpiece a tin alarm clock, the nauseous, literalistic tick of which seemed to control rather than register the passing of time. There was always a thick warm smell of talcum powder as if some old aunt had just crossed the landing from the bathroom looking for a towel. Obsolete CRT monitors were set up on every flat surface, ten or twelve of them linked through a rat's nest of cable. Everything was thick with dust.

When you arrived, Balker said, and sat in front of the keyboard, you could bet that four of the screens would be full of interference. Three would be blank. Until you looked at them closely, the rest seemed to be showing a blurry grayscale image of the room itself, from the point of view of a cheap webcam mounted high up in one corner. But things weren't entirely right with the wallpaper; and the person sitting there wasn't you. After a moment or two, someone else seemed to come into the room. Then everything vanished and those screens showed interference too. For a moment the air smelt only of dust recirculated by the system's cooling fans, as if the drive towers had briefly cooked. In all the time he spent there, Balker found only one interesting item. This was a loose-leaf journal in a black leather cover – squared paper, handwritten in coloured inks, each entry carefully timed and dated – which always lay open in a different position in the dust and tangled wires between the monitors. He would leaf through it while he waited for the drug to wear off and snap his connection to that world.

'The future doesn't make sense,' it began. 'I know that because I've seen it. In some way, to some extent, I've seen the things that happen. They make no sense.' Then, a few evenings later: 'The original figure always turns its head slowly and begins to stand up, perhaps in some kind of clumsy welcoming gesture.' Among these observations, queerly personal statements were interspersed. 'I moved back into this house twenty years ago. By then both my parents were dead.' And: 'When the work isn't going well, sleep becomes tiring and I dream I am dead.' Balker could make nothing of this. When he reported it no one seemed interested. It was the screens that interested them, they said: he should concentrate on the screens.

He often thought of adding something to the journal himself, to see what would happen; but though he found fresh entries whenever he went there, he never found a pen.

In the end, it didn't work out for him. He didn't have quite the talent they were looking for. Sometimes, as the high came groaning and roaring along his upper spine and into the amygdala, he looked along the darkening rows of beds and counted fifty or a hundred people dreaming at the top of their game in the motionless gloom. They were arriving at the house, flowing through it like a gusty breath, a flock of bats: they were making sense of the things they saw, taking notes on what they found. Balker didn't have that kind of travel. He knew he wasn't up with the best. He suspected his friend Alan would have done better. By then he had understood that the test-destinations weren't the issue anyway. All those travellers were being prepared to enter the Square Mile – not physically, but on the astral plane, the way the iGhetti themselves occupied it.

As far as you and Balker were concerned, that didn't last either. You made a stab at it, moved into a flat in Shepherds Bush together, but he turned out to be seventeen not twenty seven as he said, and after his staffie/mastiff cross, which he was looking after for a friend, bit two fingers off your ex's left hand when he came back from an oil-exploration contract in one of the 'stans – you forget which one – he fitted all the lights in the house with blue bulbs while you were out then tried to commit suicide in your bath in an excess of adolescent self-disgust. It was a cry for help. That had to be the end of that. Balker went back to the street. Jane and Jack searched for him for a month or two, Jane especially has been cold towards you since. Later you heard he was with a grindcore musician in Peckham. You were glad, although you missed his smell, which was instantly exciting; and his dysfunctionality, which you remembered as 'character'. And the sex was tremendous, if a little full on and tiring.

That was it for perhaps two years, perhaps three. Although their influence spread from primary nodes in New York, Dubai and especially the great Chinese banking cities, in London the iGhetti seemed content to be contained by the Square Mile. You had the sense they were focussed on other projects. New buildings began to appear, for instance – vast, not entirely stable parodies of Noughties vanity architecture which lasted a week or a month before toppling slowly away into a kind of dark blue air. For Londoners, things went downhill during that time. It was a different world. Life was patchy. Whether people could rescue anything from their individual circumstances depended very much on how determined they could be. It was a different kind of existence. You welcomed the challenge; it was the arrival, finally, of your teenage fantasy. Then one day you took two steps into a house by the river in Barnes, and there was a face, white, with skin like a layer of enamel paint, thrust in close to yours. It was breaking up with some emotion you didn't recognise. A voice was saying, with a kind of meaningless urgency:

'It's me! It's me!'

He was shaking, whoever he was. You couldn't process it:

you had come expecting a party. You were thinking, 'I must have had a stroke on the way here and not noticed, and this is what the world's going to be like for me now.' Then the face was just a boy you once knew, wearing a cheap Paul Smith summer suit looted from some outlet in Twickenham.

'Jesus, Balker,' you said, shoving him away.

You didn't want to be important to him any more. You didn't want him in this part of your life. You wanted him tidily in the part labelled 'the past', where he had never had much time to be a player anyway. He bumped into a wall and slid down it slowly. No one was eating much, that summer. They all had estuary fever, but Balker felt like a bag of sticks. His condition was further along than yours, and that should have been a warning in itself. You pushed him out of the hallway and watched him stumble off along the street.

Music came from somewhere at the back of the house, dance hits from the mid 90s. It seemed distant, then someone opened a door on to the terrace. A hot evening, a wedding party. The river stank. Bright flashes in the sky, heavy, muted thuds off in the north around Camden Town. You leaned on the balustrade and stared down into into the space between the house and the river, a dark strip of trampled turf – littered with discarded paper plates, beer cans and discarded condoms – where the bride, oblivious to everything but her own happiness, was dancing alone, skipping and spinning, dipping and bending, trailing her arms. It was, depending where you stood, a simple expression of joy or a complex expression of nostalgia for a time when all such moments were fuelled by money, aspiration, and a true, fully functional narcissism, a performative sense of self only hinted-at by the Twentieth Century – days when it was still possible to see yourself as a great silent beautiful blossom opening up to the economic light.

An hour after you sat down, Balker came in again, wiping his mouth as if he'd only recently thrown up. By then the party had retreated indoors, folded itself into the warm reek of beer and smoke. Shadows, beats, weird coloured light. Everyone's hyperactive kids like a billowing curtain around the dance floor. You could see what was going to happen. You made sure the two of you stayed at tables on opposite sides of the room. You kept the dancers between you. You made sure you were always talking to someone. But finally he came over anyway and tried to speak.

'For fuck's sake not here,' you said. 'On the terrace.'

'I only came to talk —' he said.

'Talk? Jesus, Balker. You should have stayed where you were.' You meant, 'in the past.' You meant, 'forgotten'. You didn't really mean anything else, but there was always more to Balker than that.

You took him by the elbow and half-led, half-pulled him out there. 'Before you know it,' people used to say, 'the worst has already happened.' We think of extreme events as abrupt in that way, but they're always the result of more than one border being crossed. An action that feels instant and seamlessly impulsive is actually very graded. By the time you got Balker out on to the terrace you knew you were going to hurt him. In the end you didn't need to square it with yourself: you were pushing him about, whispering, 'For God's sake, what do you think you're doing here?' or something like that, when his coat fell open and you saw what had happened to him.

'What's this?' you said. 'What's this?' You were frightened, but not, it turned out, for yourself.

'I don't know,' he said. 'I'm not in any pain.'

'There's something coming out of your chest.'

He looked hard away from himself. The tendons in his neck stood out. He moaned. 'Don't tell me any more. I'm not in any pain.'

'It's like a cauliflower, but bigger.'

He made pushing motions with his hands. 'Please don't tell me any more,' he said.

'I'm just trying to tell you how it looks. It's like a wart.'

Whatever it was, it was grey and pink colours, very muted and toned. 'A wart,' you said. 'Or broccoli. Like pink brocolli.' Balker thrashed around for a moment then passed out. You dragged him first into one corner, then another. You didn't know what to do. He woke up and screamed, 'Pull it out!' You got a good grip of it in both hands and pulled. It seemed to come out easily, as if it was coming out of not muscle and bone but something soft and unstructured, but then stopped. There was no blood. You could see tight red runners, like wires, attached to it, radiating out into Balker's chest. It was made out of damp, slick fibres. You wouldn't say 'woven'. It looked fibrous but not woven: it was nothing so organised as that. You were afraid if you pulled any harder, they might rip something else out of him, something he couldn't do without.

'I'm sorry,' you said, 'It won't come any further.'

Balker shrieked. 'Why is this happening to me?' he called. Then he whispered:

'I went in there. They sent me in on foot.'

You let his head fall back. 'Oh god, you idiot, you idiot,' you said.

'They were losing all their good people,' Balker said. 'In the end they were sending anyone who'd taken the tests.'

'Balker —'

He looked confused, he wasn't sure what was happening to him. Neither were you. You noticed a kind of shadow around him, cobalt blue, blue almost to black. Out of that, small white feathers seemed to be spilling, as if someone had burst a pillowcase.

'Nothing's changed in there! Inside it's still perfect. It's only from our side of things that it's a war. The iGhetti don't see it like that. They just don't notice. Inside, it might be six o'clock on a Sunday morning in summer. I could hear the artillery and the bombers outside the zone, but nothing disturbs them in there. I never saw one. Only the 'blue effects' that told me one of them was near.' He groaned. 'I'm still there,' he said, clutching at you. 'In some way I'm still in there.' The air around him became syrupy and glutinous. That panicked you and you began to ask him questions, but it was too late. 'Everything's just such a nuisance,' he said conversationally. 'You know? When all you want to do is go to sleep?' By then he was sitting on the floor with his legs out straight and his hands between them; his voice seemed both thick and distant. 'I feel odd to be honest,' he said. My eyes feel odd. My face feels odd. I feel odd.' He thought for a moment. 'I feel tired.' After a pause he added: 'I'm sorry, Alan.' A minute or two later you saw he was dead.

'Jesus,' you said.

So that was it as far as Balker went, and now you sit over the one-bar electric fire in your rented room. Perhaps you think about him, perhaps you don't. As soon as you feel recovered from the commute you'll boil some potatoes on the gas ring, then, three minutes before they're done, drop an egg into the same water. You can hear the family downstairs laughing at something, some dressed-up cats or something, on the internet. It's minus ten outside tonight and you have no idea what's happening on the old housing estates by the river. 'Welcome to London,' someone in the office said today. That got a laugh. 'Welcome to the managerial classes.' All he really meant was that like everyone else he would do anything to look after himself, stay this side of the line and not have to make the kinds of choices Balker made.

2017

ALSO AVAILABLE FROM COMMA PRESS

You Should Come With Me Now
Stories of Ghosts

M. John Harrison

M. John Harrison is a cartographer of the liminal. His work sits at the boundaries between genres – horror and science fiction, fantasy and travel writing – just as his characters occupy the no man's land between the spatial and the spiritual. Here, in his first collection of short fiction for over 15 years, we see the master of the New Wave present unsettling visions of contemporary urban Britain, as well as supernatural parodies of the wider, political landscape. From gelatinous aliens taking over the world's financial capitals, to the middle-aged man escaping the pressures of fatherhood by going missing in his own house… these are weird stories for weird times.

'The exactness, acute self-consciousness and vigilant self-restraint of Harrison's writing give it piercing authenticity.' – Ursula K. Le Guin, *The Guardian*

'M. John Harrison's sentences have the power to leave the world about you unsteadied; glowing and perforated in strange ways.' – Robert Macfarlane

'Slippery, subversive, these stories mix the eerie and familiar into beguiling, alarming marvels.' – Olivia Laing

ISBN: 978-1-91097-434-6
£9.99